Her hand was suddenly in his hand. He held her fingers in his tight, full grip.

This was nothing like his handshake. This was the hold of a man who felt her pain and wanted to bring her through it. "I'll do it," he said, his voice raw. "I'll help. Just—just don't beg me. I don't want you thinking that I'm anybody other than a guy with a hammer."

What a strange thing to say. Anybody could see he was more than that. He cleared his throat. "Besides which, Matt's a good kid. You don't have anything to give me, but Matt—well, you're the only one who can give him what he needs."

For a solid year, she'd had to prove that to teachers, adoption caseworkers, neighbors, the police. And on the worst nights, she'd lain curled on her side of the bed, knees to chin, with only the light from the phone, wondering if maybe she was wrong. To hear it now from a man who hardly spoke and when he did, it wasn't ever complimentary... She squeezed his hand back.

"Thanks," she whispered

He nodded once, rele
to the stairs. "Hey," he
show you how to mak

D1407637

Dear Reader,

Thirteen years ago, my family moved to the house in the town where we still live and which has become the focus of my fictional town, Spirit Lake. Since moving here, the town has stretched, popped up a Walmart, Canadian Tire, Sobeys and—oh, the golden standard of an Albertan town having made it big!—a Tim Horton's.

Tim Horton's is wholly Canadian, our blue-collar alternative to Starbucks. Actually, that partly describes this story: a blue-collar Canadian romance about finding family. It stars a woman struggling to hold her family together and a man struggling to not surrender to yet another lost cause. The glue that sticks them together is a boy who longs for a father and for his grieving heart to heal.

Serious stuff, but everyone who's read it so far has had plenty of LOL moments. Because that's life, right? In telling this story, I had the pleasure of introducing the hero's siblings, whose stories will appear later this year.

To peek at what's happening with them, you are welcome to come to my website, mkstelmackauthor.com. You can also find me on Facebook at M. K. Stelmack.

M. K. Stelmack

HEARTWARMING

A Roof Over Their Heads

—

M. K. Stelmack

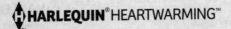

Recycling programs
for this product may
not exist in your area.

ISBN-13: 978-1-335-63352-1

A Roof Over Their Heads

Printed in U.S.A.

M. K. Stelmack writes contemporary romances set in Spirit Lake, which is closely based on the small town in Alberta, Canada, where she lives with pets who outnumber the humans two to one and with dust bunnies the size of rodents—because that's what happens when everyone in the household prefers to live in their imagination or outdoors—but she can also be found on social media, where you can share your comments on her stories or her breathless one-sentence bio on Facebook or at mkstelmackauthor.com.

In Memoriam

To Sheila.

I wish you were here to read your sister's story of love and hope—your favorite kind.

Acknowledgments

Thank you to Angela Spiller, who drew from her own experiences to share the emotional and bureaucratic journey of adoption, of cobbling together strangers, needing and worthy, into a family. Thanks also to Mark Matheson at the Red Deer office of community corrections for providing insight into how community service would look like for my hero.

Thanks to my editor, Victoria Curran, who gave my life a Point of No Return, and to Astrid Theilgaard, my tried-and-true critique partner.

With this book, I've gained a tribe in the form of the Heartwarming Sisters, who have filled me with the conviction that our stories matter. May I dwell long among them.

And to the Holy Spirit, who daily drags me through my character arc, abiding and chiding through my every kick and complaint. I am blessed.

CHAPTER ONE

Sweat was a thin glue coated on Alexi Docker, sticking her T-shirt to the driver's seat and her hot jeans to her legs, the slimy by-product of four hours on the road with no air-conditioning and a tire change in a highway ditch.

She crawled the van with the U-Haul trailer to a stop in front of the new home, and turned to her four kids in the back seats. "So, what do you think?"

Please, please like it. Or, at least, don't hate it.

While three-year-old Callie, behind the front passenger seat, kept her brown eyes fixed on Alexi, the other three kids regarded the white split-level and attached garage with a kind of hopeful hesitancy, as if waiting for someone to throw open the front door and boom out a welcome.

When, not surprisingly, that didn't happen, Matt said, "Cool."

"Where's the backyard?" asked eight-year-old Bryn from the bench seat he shared with six-year-old Amy. The big backyard was the prime selling feature for the kids.

"Duh. Behind the house. In the back," Amy said.

Bryn unbuckled himself. "Okay, I'm going there."

"How about I get a picture with—" Alexi began, but Bryn had already activated the side door and hopped out. Two more buckles unclicked, and Matt and Amy cleared the van with Bryn and were racing past the house, straight for the promised land of the back-yard.

"Matt," she called, as she rounded the hood. "Stay together, okay?"

Matt, her eldest at eleven, was the family border collie, patrolling boundaries and herding the strays. He nodded once and disappeared.

That had gone rather well. No outright mutiny, at any rate. Alexi stretched, a breeze wicking away her sweat and fanning her warm face. If a bit of fresh air could do this, imagine the powers of a dip in the lake.

"How about," she said to Callie, unclicking her car seat straps, "we all walk down to the lake this evening? Play in the water. Watch the sunset. That would make a pretty picture, wouldn't it? Whaddaya say?"

Callie stretched out her dark arms.

"I'll take that as a 'yes.' Now, let's check out our new home."

With Callie tucked against her left hip, Alexi opened the passenger door and leaned across for her water bottle. She took a pull from it and drew in warm air. Empty. As it had been for the last sixty miles. As were all the kids'. She needed to refill their bottles fast because a run in the backyard was going to dry out the kids even more.

She pressed to her other hip the box of essentials—toilet paper, phone charger, soap—with the water bottles piled on top. Making for the door, she looked around as she matched reality with the emailed pictures from Connie, her landlady. She didn't remember the lawn grass rising above her ankles and the front garden a solid green rectangle of weeds. Never mind, she could mow while the kids weeded. A family activity.

Inside an old work boot by the door she found the house key as planned and, juggling it, the box and Callie, Alexi opened the door.

Fresh paint fumes gagged her and Callie

buried her face against Alexi's neck. Alexi breathed shallowly as she lowered the box to the floor. If plywood counted as a floor. The stairs, the hallway and the living room were completely stripped. Alexi stepped across protruding nail heads and wet, coppery paint splotches to the kitchen. Or where it should've been. There weren't any cupboards or appliances, not even a kitchen sink. Just a space with pipes, hoses, outlets hooked up to nothing.

Was she in the right house? The address and the pics of the outside matched. The key was in the right place. She hadn't got the dates confused. She'd talked to Connie last week, and all was a go.

Was there even water?

She hurried to the hallway bathroom, which actually had a sink and a toilet, if not a tub. She turned on the faucet and heard sputtering and a great wheezing of air in the pipes. That was it.

Seriously?

"Right. Okay," she explained to Callie, who still had her face rooted in Alexi's neck. "All I have to do is go to the basement, find the main water valve and turn it on."

But first—she looked out the kitchen window into the backyard. All three were there, though Bryn was fiddling with the latch on the fence gate. She started toward the back door but then heard Matt call from the fire pit, "Hey, Bryn. Look!"

It was a stick. Bryn loved sticks. Had invented a million uses for them, and sure enough he changed course for Matt, who'd always known not to run after someone ready to bolt.

Callie pointed to them.

"Do you want to go play?" Fixing the water would go a lot easier without Callie.

Callie squirmed to get down.

"Okay, hold on. Let me carry you across this yucky floor first." The second Alexi opened the back door, Callie shot outside. The paint fumes must be near lethal for her to leave Alexi. A good thing for once that Callie wasn't able to tell stories. Alexi didn't want the kids, namely Bryn, alerted to the state of the house until she got the water running.

Alexi called to Matt to watch Callie, who was already toddling toward the others. Bryn was now holding the stick, an unusual one, smooth and tapered like a baseball bat. Bryn examined it, and then squatted to rummage through the pile of firewood. Good, that should buy her time. She headed for the basement stairs, placing a call that switched to voice mail as she started down the stairs.

"Connie, this is Alexi Docker. Your tenant. I just arrived at the house, and it's—it's unacceptable." She resisted saying more. The situation demanded a face-to-face meeting. "Please call me. Immediately."

In the split second she glanced from the steps to the phone to end the call, she slipped and stumbled down the last steps onto the concrete floor, the phone skittering across the cement, screen down.

No, no, no. Not the phone, not the phone. It held *everything*.

She scrambled after it on hands and knees, turned it over and—yes! A smooth screen wallpapered with a shot of the kids on monkey bars. She kissed it in relief.

She stood and nearly screamed from the sudden pain in her left ankle. Great, a sprain. All she needed. She limped around the basement until she found the furnace room with the copper water pipes.

Now, which valve and where? She tapped her phone against her chin and then realized a better use for it. After a quick internet search, she reached over and twisted a likely valve. There was a sucking pull and then—water.

She'd done it. Only when she stepped out of the furnace room did she hear exactly what she'd done. Water gushed and slapped against the upstairs floor. The other valves were already open. Alexi rushed back into the furnace room and cranked the main valve shut again.

She leaned her sweat-damp back against the concrete wall. This. Was. Insane. She'd moved to a place with a lake and didn't have a drop to drink. She ran her tongue inside her dry mouth. *Okay. Think. Figure out which pipe went where.* She traced the looping paths of the hoses and pipes. Right. Another internet search.

First, time to check on the kids.

She hopped upstairs into the kitchen in time to see Bryn climb the deck stairs to the back door, stick in hand. He would flip out if he saw the inside of the house. She needed to prepare him.

Alexi intercepted him on the back deck.

"That's a great stick."

"Yes, I'm going to put it in my room." He stepped to get around her.

Who knew what shape the bedrooms were in? She stepped with him. "How about I do that for you and you can look for more sticks?"

He shook his head. "I'm thirsty." He shifted the other way. She followed.

"How about I bring out a pitcher of water while you get more sticks?" An offer she had no idea how to fulfill.

He frowned and ducked, caught her wide-open on her weak side and darted inside. When she joined him, he was standing stock-still, his feet glued to the floor...and perhaps, considering the condition of the plywood, that was actually true. He was doing a slow scan of the place, eyes wide, jaw dropped.

Alexi held her breath. It was a disaster for Bryn if the toaster was not square to the coffeemaker. She'd spent the past week showing him pics of the place (before it was gutted), explaining over and over how it would be the same. "We have a kitchen sink. The new place has a kitchen sink. We have a fridge. It has a fridge. You have a bedroom. It has a bedroom."

Behind her, she heard the thumping of the other kids' footsteps on the wooden deck stairs, and then they, too, were inside.

There was a collective, shocked silence. Callie clutched Alexi's jeans, and Alexi automatically picked her up.

"What happened?" said Matt.

"I don't know," Alexi said. "I've left a message with the landlady."

"The place stinks," Amy commented. "It's giving me a headache."

"What are we going to do?" So like Matt to quickly move to solving the problem. Except she didn't have an answer.

What *was* she going to do? She couldn't cook, couldn't keep food cold. Could hardly breathe. She couldn't return to Calgary. New tenants were moving into their old place even as she stood in this disaster. What had she done?

At that moment, Bryn broke free of his trance and screamed, "I want to go home!" He shot out the back door, stick raised.

"Bryn! Stop feet!" she called after him and moved to follow, Callie's legs banded tight around Alexi's waist. Pain tore through her ankle. "Matt! Get the back gate."

Matt was already on it. Bryn dropped his stick and stripped off his shirt. Matt darted past him to get to the gate first, flattening himself against it. Bryn registered that, grabbed his stick and swerved in the opposite direction to the front of the house.

"I'll open the van for you," Alexi called to Bryn from the back door. "Then we'll go home." If she could get him in the van, lock the doors, then she could talk him down.

If she could open the van before he got there.

She set down Callie and did a limping run to the front door, opening it, just as Bryn, now completely nude, stick in hand, reached the van. Where were her keys? There, in the box. She double clicked on the remote and threw open the front door. Too late. She watched Bryn reach the corner of the block, turn a sharp left and disappear from sight.

"Matt!"

He was there.

"My ankle is twisted. You go. Stay with him. I'll get Amy and Callie, and follow in the van." A real nuisance with the U-Haul still attached and a bum tire to boot. She was snapping Callie into her car seat when Matt came tearing back, fear stark on his face.

"Mom! A man stopped his truck and Bryn got in. Then he drove off!"

SETH GREENE HADN'T lived his entire life in a lakeside tourist town not to have seen his share of young sidewalk streakers with mortified mothers in pursuit. Usually it was closer to the lake, or right on the beach. This was the first time one veered across the street in front of his truck. He slammed on his brakes, and the kid took advantage of the stoppage to dive into the cab.

"Drive! Let's go for a drive!" the boy ordered, waving about a long stick that Seth snagged inches before it hit the windshield. It looked familiar, and then he remembered. It was his, a baseball bat he and his dad had chiseled from an old fencepost when he'd been about the size of this kid. Which meant this boy lived in his old childhood house not three blocks away.

His sister had said she was going to rent it out, her second plan after first deciding she was going to move in.

His foot hard on the brake, Seth angled the stick toward the truck floor, the boy gripping the other end. "Here. Keep it down. How about I drive you home?"

The boy squirmed, easing his butt cheeks off the hot leather seat. Seth looked fully away, because he didn't want the kid worrying that—

Crap. There, standing frozen on the sidewalk, was another boy, taller and older, staring wide-eyed at them.

Without looking at his naked passenger, Seth pointed. "Hey, that your brother?"

"Where?"

"There on—" But the boy was gone. Probably tore back to tell his mom about the abduction of his brother. Seth edged his truck to the curb and threw it into Park, before he reached into the back of the crew cab for the only piece of extra clothing he had.

"Look at this." He held it up for the boy. "My team jersey. Brand-new."

The boy's brown eyes locked on to the bright blue-and-white jersey, emblazoned with the Lakers name, the bottom stroke of the *L* in a sweeping Nike-like check. "Put it on," Seth said. "You can't be naked in my truck."

"Is that the way it works?"

"Yep."

The boy took the jersey and examined the back of it. "Fifty-three. Why fifty-three?"

Not getting into that. "It's my age," Seth said, seventeen years off the mark.

That seemed reasonable to the boy, who nodded and wiggled into the jersey, tucking it under his butt. "To the lake!"

Seth saw an opening. "Good idea. We can get your brother and you two can play together."

"Okay! But we have to include my sisters, too. And Mom. We can't go to the playground without her. That's the rule."

Fine by him. The boy glanced from one side of the street to the other. "Wait! Where are they?"

Probably calling the police. "I know where they are."

Seth pressed the child lock button—a feature he'd never used before—then lost no time turning the corners to pull up behind a U-Haul trailer. On the paved driveway were clustered the kids, and the mom on the phone. He could only hope she was talking to the dad who was looking for the boy.

The second Seth hit the release on the lock, the boy hopped out, and for a wild moment Seth considered driving off. He'd brought back her kid, nothing wrong had happened, case closed.

But if the mom had involved the police,

Seth was known to them and doing a kind of drop-and-run wouldn't look good.

This was his one chance to clear himself. He picked up the old bat the boy had abandoned and prepared himself for whatever might come out of left field.

CHAPTER TWO

As Seth walked toward the family, the boy announced, "Come on, guys. We're going to the lake!"

None of them moved. Then the boy who had been on the sidewalk earlier strode over and slapped his brother upside the head.

"Ow! What was that for?"

"For running off. Go tell Mom you're sorry." Attaboy. Any brother worth his salt kept his siblings in line.

A little girl with Asian features was the next to break from the bunch, doing a kind of hop-run with her right leg in a brace. She was hands-on with her runaway brother, too, except with a hug so hard it nearly knocked them both to the cement. The mom was close behind, a black girl with thick glasses riding on her hip, the phone still at her ear. "It's okay, it's okay, it's okay…"

She slipped the girl down and reached for her lost boy, gathering him to her, his face mashed against her flat stomach. "It's okay, it's okay."

Seth couldn't tell if she was talking to the person on the phone or the boy. Or, from the way her voice shook, herself.

She lowered the phone and bent her head, her hair—a big, dark, squiggly tangle—tumbling onto her runaway's head. She kissed his spiky hair long and hard.

"Bryn," she said, her voice steady now, "glad you're back home."

He mumbled something and she pressed him tighter against her. "It's okay." This time it sounded as if she believed it. "We'll work something out. How about you go with Matt and Amy to the garden right there? While I finish up with this call? Matt has your shorts."

Bryn followed the other kids, while the smallest stayed glued to the mom's leg, her brown eyes behind the smudged lens monitoring Seth's every move. The mom brought her phone back to her ear to resume her conversation.

No way. His turn. He stepped forward. "Hello there. Bryn's your boy, I take it."

She held up one long finger as if he were a number at a bureaucracy and spoke into the phone. "We found him. A…man brought him back." She paused, and her eyes lifted to his. Her deep blue eyes. The color of the lake at the far shore. "The police want to know your name."

Just what he didn't want. "Seth Greene."

Those blue eyes pinned him as she silently mouthed his name, the tip of her tongue flicking against her front teeth to form the *th*, her full lips puckering on the opening of his last name.

She repeated his name aloud into the phone. She listened, frowned and passed him the phone. "The officer wants a word with you." She drew the girl against her leg even closer. This was rich. He'd brought back the kid she'd lost, and she doubted his integrity.

"Careful," she said, "with my phone."

And his ability to hold her phone. Seth switched hands with the bat to take it, and walked over to the semiprivacy of his truck before identifying himself.

"Hello there. This is Corporal Paul Grayson. I have a few questions." Suppressed laughter made the words come out choked.

Seth blew out his breath in relief. And then, because it was Paul, again in annoyance. "I've got to get to a store before it closes in twenty minutes and then I've got to get back up on a roof and finish there so I can make it to the game. You remember the game, right? Do we really need to do this?"

Seth watched the mom edge to the front garden with a limp-swing to accommodate the child still stuck to her leg. Her very long leg. The other three kids were pulling out weeds up to their chests—couldn't Connie pick up a hoe for once?—and whipping each other with them. The youngest broke free of her mom to pull up her own weapon.

Paul cleared his throat. "I have to confirm your identity. Not like you to offer rides to boys."

Kid-free, the mom banded one of her arms across her middle and tapped her fingers against her mouth. Long fingers. Long legs. Long hair. And from the looks of it, having a long day.

"I didn't," Seth told Paul. "He crossed in front of my truck. I hit the brakes and he got in. Wanted me to take him to the lake." Seth left out the part about the boy being naked. It would bring up a whole bunch of questions he didn't have time for. He checked his own phone. Twenty-three minutes before Tim-Br-Mart closed.

"You were hijacked?" Again the choked-back laughter.

Seth clamped down on his back teeth. "Am I free to go, Officer?"

"How does the mother know Connie?"

"How should I know?" Seth knew what Paul was getting at, and made a decision. "She looks legit to me. She has four kids and—" he dropped his voice and turned his back to the mom, even though she was probably out of earshot "—all of them except for the oldest have one sort of disability or another. I think she's flat-out busy with them."

"Is a dad there?"

Something he'd like to know, too. The woman clearly needed help. "Don't see one."

Paul made a noncommittal sound, one that had gotten him through a few tense situations with Seth's sister.

"Okay, then. Could you put the mom back on, please?"

Seth walked over and passed her the phone, trying to check for a wedding ring but she took it with her right hand, her left slotted into the front pocket of her jeans. As if it was any of his business, anyway. If he hurried, he might yet make it to the store. He turned to go.

Then, on his bare arm, the feather touch of her fingertips. Her left hand. No ring.

"Don't leave, Seth."

WHAT HAD SHE DONE? She'd reached for this near stranger as if she'd done it a hundred million times, as if he were— She snatched her hand away, snapped her attention back to the cop.

"…number of resources available to new-comers such as yourself. Are you aware…?"

As the officer's advice rolled on, Alexi's attention drifted as always to the kids. Just in time to see Callie whack Bryn square in the back with a weed taller than her, roots first. A splotch of dirt appeared on the 53 of Seth Greene's bright blue jersey.

"Hey!" he called and strode toward them, his big stick in hand.

No. Callie.

"…the town office is probably the best place to start—"

Callie took one look at the big man with the stick and screamed as if on fire. She shot past him to collide against Alexi's leg with enough force to throw her off balance.

Alexi hopped about on her sore ankle, sucking in the pain, and pulled the phone away from her ear. "Bryn, you need to give the shirt back to this man."

Bryn crossed his arms and gripped the jersey sleeves. "But he gave it to me."

Steady again on her feet, Alexi fought for a way to get through to Bryn. Seth beat her to it.

"I gave it to you to wear home," he said to Bryn.

"You said the deal was I had to wear it. And I am."

"Only while you were in my truck, bud."

"But then I'll be naked again."

Alexi heard the cop. "Hello? Is everything okay, Ms. Docker?"

"Yes, yes, everything's just fine. Mr. Greene is meeting the kids, is all."

Seth closed the distance between them and motioned for the phone. From the downturn of his mouth, she wasn't sure if she should. Then again, if he was talking to the officer, he wasn't with the kids. She handed it over.

"Listen, Paul," Seth said, "You need to let the mom get back to being a mom before the kid bolts again."

There was a pause.

"No, she doesn't need assistance. I'm here."

He listened a few more seconds before rolling his eyes. "Later," he said and ended the call. Clearly, Seth Greene and the cop were bros.

Bryn pointed at Seth. "You want my shirt *and* my stick."

Seth stared at the odd-shaped stick in his hand as if he'd forgotten he was holding it. "Tell you what," he said, "you give me my shirt and I'll give you back your bat."

"A bat?" Bryn asked, echoing Alexi's thought.

Seth put a choke hold on the thinner end of the bat and swung it, only a little, but Callie suctioned even tighter on her leg. Seth stilled his swing and eased his grip into a limp hold. He looked at Bryn. "We got a deal?"

Bryn hesitated and then said, "Okay, but first I'm going to get water. I'm thirsty." He headed to the house.

No, not a repeat of the last time he went inside. Alexi jumped—sore ankle, Callie and all—in front of Bryn. "How about I take you all for slushies?" She looked over to Amy and Matt. "All of you." She switched back to Bryn. "But first you have to take off the shirt."

Bryn gripped the back of the jersey to do

just that, but Matt and Amy yelled the naked consequences of that move.

Alexi could feel Seth Greene taking all this in, drawing his conclusions, passing them on to his cop-buddy tonight.

"Bryn. Look at me." She waited until his gaze connected with her collarbone. "Go to the backyard. Get on your clothes. Okay? Backyard. Clothes on. Bring me back the blue shirt. What are you going to do?"

"Backyard. Clothes on. Bring you the blue shirt." He headed off and Amy followed. She'd make sure it happened. Matt lingered. A double helix of pride—that Matt would protect her and sadness that he felt he had to—twisted inside her. She depended on him far more than was healthy for a boy his age and with his background.

She extended her hand to Seth. "I'm sorry," she said. "I haven't thanked you for bringing back Bryn. Thank you. I—well—it's been a day. There have been…a few problems."

He looked at his truck, looked at her hand. The instant he took it, she wished he hadn't. Her sweaty palm slimed his dry, muscled grip. Hot embarrassment flooded her already overheated body, cresting when he quickly released her hand. "How so?"

How so? She aimed for a light remark. Instead out poured, "The place reeks of paint. There're no floors. No floors, no fridge, no stove. No kitchen sink. It's what made Bryn run off." She licked her lips. "Worse, no water."

He straightened. "No water?" He was tall; she barely reached his shoulder. "You might need to just turn the valve. It's by— it should be downstairs in the furnace room right against the far wall. Usually about a foot or two off the ground."

"Did that. Only the valves to the taps weren't shut off and water sprayed everywhere, so I have to figure out what goes where."

"You called the owner?"

"Yes, but she's not picking up."

He hefted the stick in his hand and his thick arm muscles corded. Callie whimpered and Alexi lifted her into her arms. Seth glanced at the stick, walked to the garden, set it down and returned without a word. Alexi felt Callie's body sag with relief against hers.

"Until you sort it out with her," he said, as if there'd been no interruption to their conversation, "the outside tap runs—usually runs—through a separate pipe. You could try it."

She'd never thought of that. "Of course." She leaned to check the side of the house, Matt leaning with her. She couldn't see anything.

"Might be on the other side," Seth contributed.

Matt moved to check but halted at the man's next words. "You on your own?"

Alexi stiffened. One act of kindness didn't give him access to her life file. Besides, she wasn't about to admit to a stranger that she and the kids were alone.

Before she could answer, Matt spoke. "Daddy-R died a year ago." He swallowed. "A year ago today."

He'd remembered. Alexi had hoped that the excitement of today would make the kids forget the anniversary. Matt lifted his eyes to her, deep brown eyes Richard had described as rock and wood and land, all things solid. Right now, they'd gone soft with unshed tears.

"I'm sorry," Seth said. The standard words of condolence were low and distinct as if the man well and truly was sorry.

Matt squared his shoulders and gave a short nod. Putting on a brave face as usual.

"Thanks again for all your help," she said to Seth. "Matt, could you check—"

Bryn came up the side of the house, twirling Seth's jersey about his head like a lasso. Seth made a low grumbling noise, and Matt jumped to sort out the mess.

The jersey-for-bat exchange was made with few words and fewer movements. Alexi and the kids watched as the first person they'd met at Spirit Lake strode off and pulled away in a truck with the lettering Greene-on-Top Roofing on the doors.

Alexi turned to Matt, his face pale as he tracked the progress of the white Ford down the street. "You okay?"

Matt wiped his forehead, leaving behind a streak of dirt. "Yeah, I'm okay."

His voice was sad and shaky. When Alexi leaned to kiss him, he tilted his head away and quickly said, "Hey, I was thinking that we could set up the tent in the backyard. Be just as comfortable as sleeping inside and it wouldn't stink, either."

Alexi let him have his evasion. The whole point of coming here was to start over. Time to get on with it.

"Why not? We deserve a little fun."

UNBELIEVABLE. THERE WERE no baseball bats. Seth had reserved the diamond, answered obvious questions, posted all week to the Facebook group with reminders about the switch in dates from their regular Thursday meetup to today, Friday, *and* to bring bats and balls because he had neither. The result was thirty-three people, sixteen balls and no bats. And to think he had one in his hand not two hours earlier. Homemade, but enough to get the game underway.

Everybody arranged themselves on lawn chairs or bleachers, or leaned on trucks, content to have him deal with the consequences of their forgetfulness. Fair enough. He was responsible for—how did the legal wording go?—"generating, overseeing, implementing and attending all events associated with the recreational club, Lakers-on-the-Go."

He was about to haul his own butt off a bleacher and shoot over to Canadian Tire for a couple of bats, when Ben texted to say he'd bring over his two.

Seth wondered if one of them was a girl's bat.

Back when he and Ben were thirteen, they'd hiked across town to this same ball diamond with a bat and ball. Mel, when he wasn't roofing with their dad, came along, but Connie, four years younger, had been too much of a pain. She'd pestered him to come, and so he told her that there was only one bat, it was his, and he didn't want to share it with her. The next time they'd played, Ben had showed up with a pink-and-purple bat he said he'd share.

Seth learned then that Ben was a loyal friend unless Connie was involved.

That summer it had turned into the four of them. They'd start off taking turns pitching, hitting and fielding, but soon enough it would fall into the pattern of Connie pitching, him hitting and Mel fielding, with Ben rotating among the positions. When it had been Ben's turn to hit, Seth always moved to the field with Mel. No need for a back catcher because Ben could hit whatever Connie threw at him.

Heavy footsteps sent quivers through the stretch of metal bleacher under Seth's butt. He glanced up to see Mel plunk himself down beside him, deadening the vibrations. He carried the same box of Timbit donuts he'd had up on a roof this afternoon.

Seth jutted his jaw at the yellow box. "Aren't those hard and dry by now?"

Mel looked offended. "These are good a week later."

Mel opened the box for Seth. Seth took a plain bite-size donut ball. "How would you know? They don't last the day around you."

Mel took two sugared ones. "Sometimes they get away on me, and I don't find them till later."

Seth opened his mouth, then shut it. The less he knew, the better.

"Forty percent chance of severe thunderstorms tonight," Mel reported. "Good thing Ben and me finished off the roof."

"Yep."

Like with little kids, Mel didn't always need a lot of feedback to hold a conversation.

"Hot enough for it, humid enough, too. And it's July. Anything can happen in July."

"You bet."

"You called Connie yet?" Mel said.

"Why should I?" Seth opened his phone to check his weather app. Maybe there was something nasty coming. Hot and humid, yeah, but electrical, too. Made people lazy and twitchy at the same time.

"Maybe she didn't get the widow's message. Maybe she doesn't realize how much of a not-good situation she's in, legal-wise."

Seth's thumb paused over the phone screen. He'd told Mel about the renovation disaster over at the house but he'd never considered that the mom might call a lawyer. She struck him as more of a problem-solver than a troublemaker. Then again, hauling his sister's butt into court was one way of solving the problem.

He hit Connie's number. He didn't get through and he didn't leave a message. Seth called again. And again and again.

Mel tipped the box toward Seth, and Seth shook his head. It was part of their ritual. Seth would take one, maybe two, of whatever Mel had on hand and no more, even though Mel would continue to offer.

Connie had her own ritual around not answering her phone. She seemed to think he really had to mean it. Or, as he suspected, she liked to have him riled right from the get-go.

After what seemed like the ninety-seventh try, she answered with, "What? What!"

"Your tenants moved in today."

"They did? Today?"

"Yes. She said she left you a message."

Connie's tone switched from surprise to accusatory. "You talked to her."

"Not by choice. I don't even know her

name." He meant that last bit to prove how little he knew this woman, but to his ears it came out peeved, as if he'd missed out. Not that he was going to ask Connie because she would love to know he wanted something from her. Lord it over him, angle for something in exchange. He didn't want her to know it mattered when it was already absurd that it did.

"For your information," Connie said, "I called her, like, days and days, weeks ago to tell her not to come, but her line was disconnected."

"It was working today."

"I called her landline and I don't have her cell number."

"She called yours, so you do now." Seth heard her draw breath, no doubt for another excuse, so he got to the point. "You better do something before you've got a tenant sic'ing lawyers on you. You're in the wrong here, Connie."

"Oh, when am I not?" she snarked. "Leave it to me, will you?"

Resentment rushed through Seth but he bit it back. "I want to leave it to you. That's why I didn't tell your tenant that you were my sister, because then she would start leaning on me to fix your problems. And I think both of us can agree that I'm through doing that."

"And I think both of us can agree you have no business interfering. In case you've forgotten, it's my house now."

As if he ever could. "Then start acting like it is."

Mel nudged Seth. "Tell her we're having a pickup ball game. Tell her to come."

"Tell her yourself," Seth said and switched to speakerphone.

But Connie had overheard. "Tell him I'm busy tonight."

Mel jabbed a finger at the phone. "No, you're not. Ben ate at Smooth Sailing earlier and told me you weren't working tonight."

There was a hiss and splutter from Connie's end. "What? Did he say— Never mind. I'm busy doing something else. Thanks for the invite, Mel."

She ended the call before Seth had a chance to speak.

"I thought that went pretty well," Mel said and popped another Timbit.

"Next time you call her," Seth said.

"I can't. I don't have a cell phone," Mel explained. "Oh, look. Ben's here." And in a clear-cut case of ducking the issue, Mel was off, abandoning his box. Seth peeked inside. Empty. Of course.

He picked up Mel's garbage and carried it to the trash can at the edge of the field. He should be sorting everyone into teams but he needed a moment to calm down. He always had to after dealing with Connie. Tonight's call had left him more than normally irritated. Thirty-two years old, and still acting like a teenager. Worse than a teenager, because at least then all her rebellions had been about making something of herself. Now she was messing around and messing up, creating havoc wherever she went.

The widow and her kids were only Connie's latest victims.

Hard to think of the mom as a widow. She was too young—he doubted she was as old as him. And too beautiful. Too beautiful to have her face twist in sorrow when her boy let drop about his dead dad. Seth understood why the kid had said it. His own dad had passed twenty years ago, and he'd never forget the day it happened.

Seth cut over toward Ben's truck to thank him for the bats. Sure enough, he'd brought the pink-and-purple one. Paul was using it to lob a long one into the outfield. Mel went tearing after it, like a dog playing fetch. But it was only when Seth was up close that he saw the second bat. It was the big old wooden one. Seth should've known.

There was a time when Ben might've gone from friend to brother. About two years ago when Ben loved Connie, and Connie had loved him right back. When she'd bought him the heaviest slugger she could source, Ben converted her pitches into home runs, and she watched with a silly grin as he circled the bases, circled her—just like they were kids again.

But then she'd cheated on him in plain sight, and Ben had been forced to see her for what she was. Seth avoided talking about her as much as possible in front of Ben.

Mel had no such discretion, it turned out. On their way to the diamond, Ben said to Seth, "Mel told me you called Connie. She tell you she's in Las Vegas?"

Seth stopped cold. How was Connie going to help the widow from there? Answer: she wasn't going to.

Next question: Who would help the widow?

Ben stopped, too. "She left Monday with that guy she's with now." He put a choke hold on Connie's bat.

Trevor. A real piece of work. Of all the morons Connie had hooked up with since Ben, this one scared Seth with his level of pigheaded stupidity.

"She needs to come home," Ben declared.

"You know what she's like," Seth said.

Ben stepped back and swung the bat so hard, it whistled. "No. *You* know what she's like. I know what she *can* be like."

Ben continued on to the diamond, putting distance between them. In another country and Connie could still screw up their lives.

CHAPTER THREE

ALEXI WOKE TO wind attacking the tent. The wall beside her buckled inward, and the nylon formed a cold suction over her face, then released as it was sucked outward. Thunder rumbled on and on, low and disgruntled like how she felt.

As if her day hadn't been bad enough, now there was a night storm to endure. She hadn't thought to check the weather since the evening had been so calm and cloudless.

Payback for making assumptions about how things ought to be. She fumbled for her cell phone. It was 1:17 a.m. And 2 percent battery. More payback for waiting on a call from the landlady that never came. She would've given up a lot sooner if she'd known the charger was missing. Payback again for not thinking ahead. After patting down the van seats and floor where it ought to be, she'd crawled into the tent, ankle and head throbbing, drawn a bath towel over herself as a blanket and passed out.

She shut off her cell just as the wind threw itself against the adjacent wall where the four cocooned kids slept, Matt on the far side. The wall pulled straight but the wind hit again, and this time tore out a tent peg, that part of the wall collapsing on the smallest cocoon. Callie.

Her small daughter thrashed about, her body caught inside her sleeping bag, ramping up her panic into train-whistle screams.

That snapped Bryn upright. "Bears! Bears!"

Alexi's half hour of cuddling and low-talking at bedtime to convince Bryn that Spirit Lake was a bear-free zone was blown to pieces because she'd used a rock instead of a hammer, packed who knows where, to drive in the tent peg. Payback.

"It's okay, it's okay," Alexi slurred. She flipped back the towel and tugged Callie away from the slumped tent wall. Another part of the tent dropped onto Alexi's back like a predator. Great, the six-man tent was now four-and-falling.

"S'okay, Callie. Mommy's here." She held out her hands in the dark until Callie's arms whacked them. She snapped her fingers around them and pulled Callie's warm, vibrating body against her. "It's okay. No bears. Part of the tent just came down." She half dragged, half lifted Callie and her bag closer to Matt's side of the tent.

The news was not comforting to Bryn. "We'll all suffocate and die!"

"No, we won't—"

A vicious shriek of wind smacked the tent, and a section slumped onto Bryn's head. Now all four kids, Matt included, were screaming.

The dark form of Bryn bowled his way past Alexi to the zippered opening. "I'm dying! I'm dying! We're all going to die!"

With Callie clamped to her, Alexi caught the back of Bryn's pajama top, which threw him into more of a frenzy. She felt the cloth twist, Bryn stripping out of it. "No, Bryn, wait!" And he broke out of the tent.

"No!" Her cry was shredded in the wind, weak and useless. Cold air circled them. Icy air not right for a hot summer night.

The first hailstone bonked off the main pole.

The second, third, fourth thudded and rolled along the part of the tent still erect.

And then the number was no longer distinguishable as hail descended in a hard torrent.

They needed to get to the house fast.

She reached for Matt, banded her fingers around his upper arm. "Take Amy. Run into the house. Stay there." She groped for Amy who, good girl that she was, had already shimmied out of her sleeping bag. Alexi hauled a sleeping bag up and over their heads. "Okay. Hold it up. Keep together." She widened the tent flap for them. "Go. Don't stop."

She didn't wait to see if they made it. She needed to get Callie inside and then twice in one day, call the police for the exact same reason. A runaway. There would be a report this time. Payback, payback, payback.

At least she had enough charge to call. She tucked her phone down inside her bra, and using both hands, since there was no way on God's green earth Callie would let go anyway, she settled her bath towel above their heads.

"Okay, Callie, on the count of three, I will run to the house and you just hold on tight to me with your arms and legs, okay?" Callie flattened herself even more against Alexi, the sides of her knees like hammerheads against Alexi's ribs. "One, two, three!"

And they were off. The wind immediately snatched the towel from her hands, and hailstones pummeled her. She shaped one arm into an umbrella over Callie and hobbled double-quick. On the back stairs, her bare feet skidded on hailstones and she flung out her arms to grab hold of the railing.

Exposed to the ice chunks, Callie howled. Alexi hauled herself and Callie up the last remaining steps and to the door illuminated by the outdoor light.

It was flung open as she approached, but not by Matt.

"Bryn! You're here!"

He hadn't run off. Common sense or Matt had prevailed. Either way, it was a gift, a break, a win. She fell back against the door.

"Yep," he said to the obvious.

The inside lights were turned on, so she could see that they were all safe and sound. And wet, their pajamas stuck darkly to their upper bodies. She'd left the windows open so it was every bit as cold as outside, but it no longer stunk as much. Not that they had a choice of accommodation.

She knelt, taking care with her hurt ankle.

"Okay, guys, wait here. I'll run out and get the sleeping bags and we'll sleep here for the rest of the night. It's dry here, there's a roof over our heads. And in the morning—" she looked at Bryn "—we'll figure out the rest."

Callie stuck to her, a damp, flesh-and-bone magnet. "I want to go home."

Alexi said what she'd been repeating all through the packing. "Home is where we're all together, sweetie."

Only the promise of a warm, cozy sleeping bag and the wheedling of the other kids persuaded Callie to loosen her grip on Alexi. Once free, she lost no time plunging back outside. The fall of hailstones had thinned but they were up to her ankles. The tent roof was so weighted down that she had to hunch as she wadded all the sleeping bags into hers.

She drew a deep breath, gave herself a one-two-three count and dashed back as fast as her hurt, numbed body would allow. She dumped the bags on the kitchen floor with quick instructions to Matt, and then plunged outside again to retrieve the pillows. When she got back, Matt was sitting cross-legged on the floor with Callie curled in his lap while the other two were laying the bags out.

This time, she arranged herself like a

mother cat, the kids stretched out perpendicular to her, their heads against her belly side, all easy to reach in the night if she needed to. And like tired kittens they all fell asleep almost instantly, even Bryn.

Of course, now she was overtired and couldn't sleep. She knew why. She hadn't said good-night to Richard. Talking to him would completely drain the battery, leaving her unable to make even an emergency call. And hadn't she moved, put herself and the kids through this whole ordeal, in order for them to start to construct a new life without him? Hadn't she promised herself that to recognize the necessity of moving on she'd stop this self-destructive habit on the one-year anniversary of his death?

Except who could've predicted a day like today? God knows what she would've done if Seth Greene hadn't come to the rescue. Tall and contained and so serious. Normal people greeted other people with a smile. He watched and, she was pretty sure, judged. Whatever. She had no reason to see him again.

Or anyone, for that matter.

Alexi felt a sudden fluttering in her chest

that rose to a wild battering, like she'd swallowed a bit of the storm.

If she were to get through the night, and the next morning, she needed something—someone—to bring her a thin sliver of peace.

She slid open the phone and tapped to full screen Richard's picture. Not the one she'd wallpapered with him at the playground rope hive with the kids hanging around him. This was the one she'd taken the morning after their wedding, fifteen years ago. She'd called to get his attention and he'd looked over his shoulder at her, a smile already in place. He'd smiled all the time.

What else is a man to do, he said, *when he's looking at you?*

Seth Greene could've told him.

The battery icon slipped to 1 percent.

"Hi, Richard," she whispered. "I tried not to do this but I can't. Today has been…too much. I tried to do alone what we'd always done together. You and I moved to Calgary to make a home because we never had a real one. We'd made a family because we never had one. And it all made sense when you were alive. Now it's me. Alone. With the kids, and Matt not yet ours. Or, I guess, mine. And today was rotten. The house is not a home. It's not even a house. Tonight was worse. There was a hailstorm and—and—I think I made a mistake. I shouldn't have moved the kids from our home in Calgary. I thought I could move on. But look at me. It's been a year and I still don't know how to get through without you. There's going to be so many bad—"

The screen went black and the battery icon flashed on. Gone. "I don't know how I'm going to get through this, Richard," she whispered into the dark. "I really don't."

MATT WASN'T ASLEEP. He'd almost been there, warm and limp in the sleeping bag like a wiener in a hotdog, rain drumming his brain to mush, but then Mom's whispers set up a steady drip on his senses, until all else sank away except for her voice.

She talked to Daddy-R every night. When he was working up north, her voice, low and breathy and inaudible, would drift down the hallway and put him to sleep. After Daddy-R died, she carried right on talking to him. Matt hadn't known she was talking to a phone pic of him or exactly what she said.

Until tonight. Tonight he heard how sad

and lonely Mom was. That all her smiles and peanut butter cookies were fake.

It was all his fault.

Before living with Mom and Daddy-R, he'd run away twice. Not the way Bryn ran, a sudden bolting and a quick corralling. No, he planned his escapes. The first time it was to get away from his mom and to his dad. The second time it was to get away from his dad to his grandfather. Then when his grandfather died and he was stuck in a foster home, it was to his new dad. He hadn't known who his new dad was, only that his gut said he was at Walmart, so every day Matt walked along streets, across a field and a parking lot to the store and, while families shopped for cereal and lightbulbs, he shopped for a dad.

His gut was right. He found Daddy-R in the shoe aisle, buying running shoes for three kids, and Matt, spying through the racks in another aisle, watched him get his kids exactly what they wanted. With each kid holding their shoe box, he had said, *Now. How about we find the most beautiful woman in the store and take her home with us?*

The kids knew it was their mom, and Matt had trailed after them to where she was in the fruit section loading an already heaping cart with apples, oranges, strawberries, everything.

Matt had seen how Daddy-R kept his eye on her as soon as she was spotted, and he never stopped until he kissed her right there in the store. That's when Matt's gut had spoken. *This one. Take this one.*

When the other kids got into the van, he did, too. And once Daddy-R and the mom with the blue eyes understood he wasn't getting out, he became part of their family.

Then Daddy-R had died, and he didn't know what to do. Until two months ago his gut had spoken again as he'd stared at a map of Alberta one afternoon. *There. Go there.* His finger was on Spirit Lake. His head had argued with his gut. It was just a place where he'd built forts from sand and sticks on the beach. His gut kept right on sparking and glowing like a stirred fire no matter what he told it, so he gave in and prepared to go.

Except Mom had found his maps, his Greyhound bus ticket, his half-written letter to her. She'd hugged him, tears filling her eyes like bright pools, and asked him why. Because there was a sneaky little part of him happy she'd caught him and because it wasn't the caseworker taking notes, he told her that even after all this time, more than ten whole months, it was so hard without Daddy-R. That there were bits of Daddy-R all over the place.

She'd looked over her shoulder toward her bedroom and he quickly said no, it wasn't the urn. That would've been okay if all of Daddy-R had been poured in there. But he kept showing up everywhere—his snow boots in the storage tub, his *Canadian Geographic* magazines in the mailbox, his allergy medication in the cabinet.

Mom had said that it was the same for her, but he thought she was saying that to make him feel better. She told him, as she had told him a million times, that nothing had changed. She was going to make him theirs, hers and Daddy-R's, just as it was planned. She would do whatever it took. If that was what he still wanted.

And he did still want that, he really did, only it was getting so hard.

She'd asked him where he was planning on going. And he'd told her about Spirit Lake, how it didn't make any sense given that he was pretty sure he didn't know anyone there. But that his gut wanted him to go there the same way it had pushed him to go to Walmart where he'd found them all.

Something sparked in her eyes and for once it wasn't tears. Right then and there she made him a deal. If she and Bryn and Amy and Callie all ran away with him to Spirit Lake, would he stay? As soon as she said it, his gut felt warm and skippy. This was it. This was right for him…and his family.

Two months later, and exactly one year after Daddy-R was killed in a head-on crash, they were here in Spirit Lake. And his gut was flip-flopping like crazy.

He'd really thought the tent idea would work and he'd tried to help Alexi. But she'd had to find the tent and bend the poles into place and pound in the pegs. She'd done everything. He wasn't Richard, wasn't even a close substitute.

She needed somebody to help her, to be all the things he couldn't be.

His gut stopped churning, calmed and spoke to him. *Seth Greene.*

He'd brought Bryn back and kept their family together for another day. The man had stood there with the bat that looked like a fence post and watched them all, but mostly he'd watched Mom. Let her be, but stepped in when he could help. He'd got rid of the cop, he'd persuaded Bryn to give back the shirt and he'd let Mom unload on him.

She'd talked to him, not all square-shouldered like when she was with the bank manager or caseworker, but with her hip jutted out and her hand mussing up her hair even worse, like she did when working out a problem with Daddy-R. Once, she'd touched his arm. And when Seth Greene had found out she was alone, he'd wanted to help. Mom had turned him down but…

His insides were settling now. No one could replace Daddy-R but someone like Seth Greene would work. That must've been why his gut wanted him to come to Spirit Lake. Because Seth Greene lived here.

Thunder vibrated through the wood and joined the beat in his gut. This was it. Things were supposed to go wrong so Seth Greene could make them right.

SPIRIT LAKE AT dawn was a kind of ground zero. As Seth drove the truck with Mel through the streets, the scene was of full-blown vandalism. A maple tree, a cloud of bright green leaves, had fallen across the street, and they detoured onto a different street where the truck tires crunched over twigs and broken glass and hail. They swerved around a kid's lawn chair and an overturned flowerpot, pink blooms strangely intact, bumped over a flagpole and vinyl fencing. Holes in siding and punctured windows made houses appear like the target of gang warfare. Every single parked vehicle was dented, every single windshield busted. One big plus for the underground parking at the two-bedroom apartment he rented with Mel.

"Think of the roofs," Mel crowed. "I bet there isn't one in town that doesn't need to be fixed, if not replaced."

His brother was right. They'd hit the jackpot. Worst hailstorm in sixty years, according to the news. Worse than anything in his lifetime or even at fourteen years Seth's senior, Mel's. Their dad would've been a kid during the previous one. About the age of Matt.

There he was again, thinking of the boy for no reason. He'd woken last night, hail pelting against his bedroom window, and immediately wondered how the family was doing. Matt, he figured, would be listening to the thunder splintering the air, scared but not wanting to show it in front of the others, curled tight with his knees to his chin, blanket drawn so only a breathing hole remained, an animal playing dead. The other three had probably burrowed under the covers with the mother on her big mattress. Only the mattress, Seth had imagined as he lay alone on his king-size bed, because she probably hadn't had the time to assemble the frame. She must've been bone tired. Hard enough to take care of four kids on a good day but on a moving day…at least on a night like this, he'd concluded, sinking back into sleep, they had a decent roof over their heads.

"After Tim Hortons, we'll swing by the lumber store and place an order, okay?" Mel said. "There'll be a run on materials, let me tell you."

For Mel, a coffee was incidental to a trip to the coffee shop. It was all about the captive audience. Sure enough, as soon as Seth had them in the drive-through lane, Mel hopped out. "Get me my usual."

Seth watched through his rearview mirror as his brother cut in behind the truck over to the driver's side and went two vehicles down to a gray crew cab. It was Pete, owner of Pete's Your Man. The handyman lived seven miles west of town and could give a detailed damage report. Seth eased the truck forward and the vehicles bumped along behind him; Mel walking beside Pete, their voices mingling with the idling motors.

Weather permitting, Mel scouted for information this way most days, and most days, Seth didn't mind. It gave him a few minutes of solitude and satisfied Mel's addiction to facts and figures, and every tradesman eventually got used to Mel's tap on their window.

But today it felt…wrong. It was one thing to fix a roof at the end of its days, but another to profit off struggling folks, insurance notwithstanding. It wasn't like Mel to feel so excited about making money off the misfortunes of others, yet he'd been raring to go from the second his feet hit the floor. Hadn't it occurred to Mel that they'd have to work harder at a job Seth had long ago lost interest in?

Maybe that was it. Maybe the problem was him, not Mel.

Him lying awake, thinking about a nameless widow and her scared kids, instead of how to make himself some real money.

At the outdoor menu board, he placed the order. "One large coffee, dark roast, one cream." Then he drew breath and let it rip.

"Extra-large iced cappuccino. Half the ice. Double the sugar. Whipped cream. Caramel and chocolate swirl. Spoon, no stirring stick. And twenty Timbits. At least four need to be cream filled. None with icing sugar."

To the clerk's credit, she didn't ask him to repeat it. Memorizing Mel's morning order was probably part of national training to work at the chain.

Seth checked his mirror again. Mel was trotting over to another truck in the queue. Ron's Siding read the lettering on the truck door. He and Ron had exchanged plenty of customers over the years. Seth rolled up the line and opened his Facebook to see pictures of golf ball–size hail in town and north, a grainery toppled south, a horse struck dead by lightning east eight miles.

And one person dead. Frederick Stephensson. Struck in the head by a hailstone the size of the baseballs Seth had tossed around last night. His niece had posted the news, and it had been shared and shared again until it was now in Seth's feed. Seth didn't know him.

But he knew the brother, Stephen Stephensson. He was the one who'd hired his dad to roof his house. The roof his dad had fallen from and broken his spine.

Now, twenty years later, there had been another death out there.

Seth was overcome by a sudden urge to get out. Get out of the truck, get out of the line, get out of the work piling up like the vehicles behind him. He pressed his fist to his temple. He started, stopped. Three more vehicles. Start, stop. Two more. *Keep it together, Seth. This line will end, you won't be trapped forever.*

At the take-out window, Mel hopped back into the truck. "Isn't just the town," he said as he flipped open the box and examined the donuts.

"Hail's flattened everything between here and Pete's. Broke three windows and took out his wife's garden. Ronnie said there isn't a stalk of grain standing between here and his place. Some storm. Get this, they've both had calls this morning, people needing repairs done. Ronnie said we should keep in touch, work together. This could go big. You get any calls?"

Seth shook his head and swung out of Tim Hortons onto the street to Tim-Br-Mart. "Frederick Stephensson's dead. You hear that?"

Mel stopped with his spoon of whipped cream halfway to his mouth. "Really?"

"Hailstone to the head. I saw it on Facebook."

Mel stared out the windshield. "Isn't that something?" He brought the spoon to his mouth. There must've been something revelatory in it because he smacked his lips and said, "You know, Stephensson's roof will need redoing. Especially now that he's selling."

Seth braked the truck so hard Mel had to scramble to keep his donuts and drink. "What's got into you? The guy has just lost his brother by an act of God. Two deaths out there and all you can think about is how to profit off him?"

Mel stared back as if Seth were the crazy one. "I don't know where old Frederick died but it wasn't on the farm. The two of them moved into town last winter. The farm's been on the market ever since."

Well. Mel would know. "At any rate, I will never get up on that roof again. Got it?"

In answer, Mel took out a cream-filled donut but didn't start to eat it. "I was already thinking with all the extra work this summer we could buy a place. And if Stephensson sells—you know, him and Dad—"

So this was why Mel was so excited to make money. Their dad had once planned to buy the Stephensson place and was actually doing the roof at cost as part of the negotiating price. Twenty years on, Stephensson, for whatever reason, was only now selling…

Seth hit the gas with enough force for Mel to once again grab his food.

"Yes, I know about him and Dad. I'm not buying a place. Especially that one."

Mel righted his food and spoke more softly than he had in a long time, "Didn't mean you. I could. But it would be ours, you know that."

That hurt. Hurt worse because Seth knew Mel was trying to be nice about it. After their mother died six months ago, Connie got the house, Mel got the money, and Seth got enough money to bury her. "Fact is," Seth said, "the last thing I want to do is tie myself down to one more responsibility."

Up ahead, he could see a truck turn into the lumber store. "How early do you have to be to get a jump on the day?" Seth said, hoping the question was enough to change the topic for Mel. Usually his half brother would've taken the bait but today he said, "What do you want?"

Not this. Not fixing old, broken, warping, leaking, crumbling roofs. Where you were exposed to whatever drops from the sky— bird poop, snow, rain, waves of blistering heat. Roofs that, once laid all new and solid, would be taken for granted until replaced two decades later—the time it takes for a baby to grow to an adult. Where one wrong step on the job can pitch you over the edge to injury—or worse. Where the only alternative is to wear a harness that ties you down, lets you swing like a monkey in a cage.

Seth parked the truck alongside two others and switched off the engine. "I want whatever I want, whenever I want."

"Yeah, well, don't we all? You need to be more specific." Mel shook the donut box. "Which one do you think is cream filled?"

CHAPTER FOUR

ALEXI SAT WITH the kids in a semicircle in front of her, still in their pajamas, on or in their sleeping bags. She was divvying up the three remaining juice boxes, a small bag of plain potato chips and two slices of pizza from last night's delivery among them. Breakfast. That and their bottles of water she'd filled from the outside tap.

She'd have to find a way to cook food today. Maybe she could get the fire pit working. If, she stretched a kink in her neck, she could get her body working first.

"Amy. Bryn. You share the apple juice. Amy, you go first."

Amy took the box and gave a suck and swallow. Good enough for Bryn, who stripped the box from her hand and sucked it flat in four gasping gulps.

Amy kicked him with her prosthetic foot. She purposely used that foot when she wanted to avoid feeling the pain she was delivering. "Bryn! You were supposed to share."

Alexi closed her eyes, stinging from lack of sleep. She'd kill for a coffee. "Amy. I know you feel wronged but kicking won't make it better."

"Yes," she said, her eyes fixed on Bryn. "It does."

"Well, I was thirsty," Bryn said and raised his finger. Matt and Amy groaned. Once Bryn started ticking off arguments on his finger, he had to use all five before he'd stop. "Second, I couldn't see the bottom so I didn't know to stop. Third, it's hard to stop when you get started. Fourth, fourth…"

Alexi handed Matt the second box. "Here. Share this with Callie." He took it and smiled at her. A wide, relaxed smile she hadn't seen for a year. Her breath caught. What had brought this on? Last night, he seemed so sad and tired…and small.

"You look happy," she commented.

He jabbed the plastic straw into the box and held it out for Callie to sip first. "Yep. I am happy."

They heard the front door suddenly open, followed by heavy footsteps.

Finally, the landlord. Except wouldn't she

have knocked? Alexi hadn't thought to lock up last night after moving back inside. And from the kitchen it was impossible to see down the stairs to the entrance. It could be anyone. The kids stared at her like owlets.

"Hello?" A man's voice.

"Seth Greene!" Matt jumped to his feet with the juice box and ran for the top of the stairs. Amy and Bryn followed, while Callie vaulted into Alexi's arms. Alexi pulled herself to her feet and limped after them.

Seth stood there, looking up at them. In jeans and a T-shirt and wearing heavy boots, he looked ready for work. He also looked annoyed, his jaw tense, his gaze fixed up and away as if counting backward.

"You should've knocked first," Bryn pointed out.

Seth still looked as if he were counting as he explained, "Habit."

Perhaps it was falling unconscious on a wood floor or lack of liquids or the weight of another day starting bad, but he made no sense. His presence made no sense. She hefted Callie up higher on her hip. "It's habit for you to walk into other people's places without knocking?"

Seth tilted his head to where she stood a

little off to the side at the half wall. His eyes narrowed, neither looking nor not looking at her.

"I lived here once," he said.

"You did?" Matt said. "Cool!"

Seth turned to Matt, and his expression softened. Matt, in turn, smiled back. Alexi felt a flutter of panic. No way did she want Matt getting any false hopes about a man who'd no intention of sticking around. A man she didn't want sticking around. She stepped behind Matt, put her hands on his shoulders.

"Strange you didn't mention that yesterday," she said.

His gaze rose past Matt to hers. "Wasn't important yesterday. Thing is, I got some time this morning. Thought I'd come over and help. To be more *specific*," he continued with an odd spitting emphasis on the last word, "I thought I'd see if I could get the water inside working for you. I know which hoses go where."

Matt twisted to look up at her with his old happy grin. "That'd be awesome, wouldn't it, Mom?"

No. It wouldn't. "Thank you, but this is a problem the landlady needs to deal with. I'm not sure how it will affect our agreement if you come in and fix it."

But come in is exactly what he did. He walked up the stairs, stepped into the kitchen, no doubt taking in the sleeping bags. He moved to the living room and strolled down the hallway, checking out the bathroom and bedrooms as he did. All the baseboards were gone and the floors were stripped to the wood, baseboards included.

He returned to where they stood in a tight group. "Your landlady already affected your agreement."

"Yes, and so she should be the one to deal with it. I don't want you involved. Though again, thank you." Could she be any clearer?

"What are you going to do in the meantime? You can't live in the tent."

How did he know about that? The phone on his belt rang. He glanced at the screen. "Need to take this. Hello, Greene-on-Top."

From Seth's side of the exchange she gathered someone was inquiring about getting a roof repaired. Bryn and Amy dashed back in the kitchen and reappeared with pizza and juice boxes, resuming their place as if her conversation with Seth was a TV show they didn't want to miss. Matt took three short sips from his box and handed the rest to Callie, his eyes on Seth the whole time.

After the call, Seth started to type a message. A good opportunity to get him turned around and out the door.

"Looks as if you're busy from the storm," she said. "I don't want to keep you. I'm sure something will work out."

He reattached his phone to his belt. "How do you figure that?" He looked at her, grimaced and glanced away, doing that looking while not-looking thing. Was there something on her face?

She was shifting Callie in her arms to check when Matt piped up. "But, Mom, the landlord won't talk to us. Your phone is dead, anyway. And we can't afford to fix it."

Alexi felt her face grow hot. It was bad enough that a stranger knew she couldn't afford a repairman, but that he had to learn it from her kid was even more shameful. It meant she couldn't hide her poverty from her own kids.

"And Seth Greene offered to do it. This is the right thing to do." He squared to her. "I feel it in my gut."

Her own gut screamed something else. If Matt had got it in his mind that Seth was who they needed—heaven help them all. She needed this man out of her house now. But how? She couldn't even call the police. And what did it matter? He was chummy with them, anyway.

He pointed to his temple. "What happened to your head?"

What? She touched her forehead and discovered a huge bump and, as she felt more carefully, a cut. Dried blood flaked onto her fingers. That explained his odd way of looking at her.

"I guess it was a hailstone. I—I was out getting the sleeping bags."

"You didn't know you got hit?"

"I felt something. It was dark. It didn't hurt, really. I thought it was rain, not blood." Why was she explaining this? She felt the wide eyes of the kids on her like bright bare bulbs. Why hadn't they said anything? "It looks worse than it is, I'm sure. I bruise easily."

"What were you doing in a tent with a storm forecasted?"

"It was my fault," Matt interjected. "I suggested it because the place stunk so bad."

"You suggested it, not decided it. Therefore, it's not your fault," Seth said.

Which implied it was hers. "You're right," she said, her voice squeaky with frustration. "I should've checked. It—it was a good thing it worked out as well as it did."

Seth stared at the bruise on her head as if it were an enormous, hideous wart. "Why is your phone dead?" he said, jumping to another deficiency.

"The battery ran down and she can't find the charger," Matt explained.

Were there any more ways to display her incompetency? "I'm sure it'll show up," Alexi said.

Seth tipped his head down the stairs. "It's in the box by the front door."

There were ways. "I—I forgot that I'd brought it in."

"I'll go get it," Amy said, running down the stairs.

"I get to plug it in," Bryn said.

Callie slid down about to follow, then reconsidered and wound her arms around Alexi's left thigh. Matt didn't budge, and there was no subtle way of dismissing him.

Seth turned to her. "I hate—no, *loathe*—home renovations. Frankly I've got better things to do with my time."

And she had better things to do than hear him gripe. "Then get doing them."

Matt gasped, but she was beyond caring how rude she was. Could he think any less of her, anyway?

Seth merely shrugged. "I was until I saw your busted tent from the roof I was on. And I saw the roof here I'd put on three years ago, banged up but still good and I'd wondered why you'd chosen a tent over it. Then I remembered you saying it stunk inside and then I wondered if you got the water running. I'll be making plenty from this storm. I figured I'd take a few hours to help out before it gets crazy. Like Matt said, it seems like the right thing to do."

So. He saw her as a charity case. A victim in need of services. Exactly what she'd been for a third of her life. From age seven to the day she turned eighteen, she'd lived in foster care. Only when she'd married Richard had she been someone else. A wife. A mother. A full member of society. With him gone, she'd reverted to her childhood status.

Except now she had four children under her care. Their well-being, not her pride, was what mattered. As for how Matt's proximity to an adult male would play out, well—well, no water was also a complication she'd have a hard time explaining, too.

She swallowed. "Okay, I do need help. I accept your offer. Thank you."

"Yes!" Matt jabbed his fist in the air and tore into the kitchen, shouting the news to Amy and Bryn. The solid pressure of Callie disappeared as she broke away to join her brothers and sisters.

Seth grimaced at her swollen temple, and she touched it self-consciously. "A man died last night from a hailstone," he said quietly. "Him and my dad…knew each other. So when I see you like that—" He broke off. "It can end so fast."

Old familiar pain, the never-healing bruise on her heart from Richard's death, swelled inside her. No, this was not the time, not the place and definitely not the person. She looked him in the eye. "I know that."

He went still, then worked his jaw from side to side, shifted on his feet. "I don't think I caught your name."

He hadn't? Had they overlooked introductions yesterday with everything happening? No, she'd learned his name and then not extended him the same courtesy, the man who'd brought Bryn back, kept her day from crossing into a living nightmare. Now he was here again today, willing to help someone he didn't know the name of from the goodness of his heart. His grumpy heart, but still...

She dropped her hand from her temple to hold it out to him. "Alexandra Docker. Alexi, for short."

"Alexi," he said and gave her hand a quick, hard squeeze before letting go. His own hand felt warm and solid—and gritty, like a sand-paper block.

"Alexi," he repeated and then added what made no sense at all given that he was the one doing her a favor. "Thank you."

SETH RESTED THE drainpipe against his shoulder as he wrestled to get the fitting on, one shoulder brushing against a stud, his head bent to clear a copper intake pipe that ran across the utility room. This was a two-person job really, but the only handy person was Alexi Docker and she was the last person he wanted to face.

Literally, to face. Seeing her all banged up had rattled him, and then when he'd heard how it had happened, it felt like the fresh death of Stephensson was there before him, and he'd come off—well, a little harsh. He'd made it worse with his boneheaded comment about losing others suddenly. She'd shut down just like yesterday when the subject of her dead husband had come up. No room there to explain that he understood how she felt, that his own father had died unexpectedly, too, even if it was twenty years ago, not one.

"Hello?"

At the sound of Alexi's voice, he jerked, which shot the pipe out of place.

"Sorry," she said. "Didn't mean to sneak up on you." She stood at the entrance to the utility room, her long legs set apart enough for Callie with her pink-framed glasses to peep through. The second Seth made eye contact she slipped from view. That one was either really shy or she didn't like the looks of him, or both.

Alexi pointed to the pipe. "Can I help?"

It made no sense to refuse her, now that she was standing right here. Right here in a T-shirt that fit real well. He snapped his focus back on the job at hand. "Yeah, actually. Could you hold this pipe here? I need to put on a fitting and cut the pipe to the right length."

She angled in beside him and steadied the pipe exactly where he wanted it.

"Thanks," he said, for the second time in this visit. At least this time, it made sense.

"It's me that should be thanking you."

That was true.

"I didn't know it would be so involved," she continued.

Anything involving Connie got way more complicated than necessary. "Turns out that I just can't clamp off the valves," he explained. "Looks as if the entire waterworks is getting revamped so I have to install a drainpipe first."

"Oh, I heard you leave. You went for supplies?" Was there reproach in her voice, as if he should've checked in with her?

"I didn't know I was supposed to tell you." Despite his attempt at politeness, he could hear belligerence in his voice.

Her eyes were on the pipe as she replied coolly, "I didn't know I was not supposed to wonder where you went. After all, wondering about us was what brought you here this morning."

He didn't answer because she'd made a couple of good points he wasn't about to concede. He chalked a line on the pipe.

"Excuse me. I need to use the cutter," he said instead. Rather than let her back out and exit before he followed with the pipe, he tried to edge past her, which forced them into shuffling around each other, dodging pipes and each other's body parts.

Could his time with her be more awkward? Free of the tight quarters of the utility room, he headed straight for the cutter he'd had to rent, but that would be a conversation with Connie, and fired it up. Two minutes of noise and he was done. This time Alexi gave him plenty of room to get around her, but that didn't stop her from following him in. Callie lingered at the entrance.

"Since I am in a wondering state of mind," she said, steadying the pipe for him again, "I was wondering if, since you lived here before, if you know the number of the landlord. I got her cell number but she's not answering. I thought there might be a landline I could use."

Seth took his time lining the pipe up with the fitting to buy himself a few seconds of fast thinking. "Landline won't do you much use. She's in Las Vegas."

"Las Vegas? Are you sure?"

"Very."

She looked over her upraised arm and pinned him with her full blue gaze. "How do you know this?"

Seth fiddled with his end of the pipe. "How do I know this?"

"Yes." The faint hiss at the end of her one word conveyed her opinion of his delay tactic.

"I was at a ball game last night and a guy there knows Connie. Said she was in Vegas." There, not a word of a lie. He slipped the fitting over the freshly cut end of the pipe. Perfect.

He slid his hand along the pipe to hers. It was a beautiful hand. Large and capable and smooth, like his favorite hammer and with a good heft to it. "I got it," he said.

She dropped her hand and it immediately strayed to her back pocket. She'd already done that three times since coming downstairs. Strange habit. "I will have to find out what my rights are," she said. "I didn't sign up for this. I should've asked the officer what I could do when I had him on the line."

It would serve Connie right if Alexi took legal action. Hadn't he warned Connie just last night? But if history was anything to go by, his sister would go down dragging as many as she could grab hold of—like Mel and him. "She might come around yet."

Alexi shoved her beautiful hands into the tangled heap of hair. "Meanwhile, what am I supposed to do? What about the kids? I can't go back. And I've nowhere else to go."

She clamped her mouth to a thin line and looked away. If he was anybody other than being a practical stranger to her, he could've hugged her, told her everything was going to be all right. If he was anybody other than who he was, he could make things right. As it was, he stood there, holding the pipe, clueless about what to say or do. No, he knew what to do: attach the other end of the pipe, but he wasn't about to restart another round of shuffling that would bring him alongside her body parts.

Her hand went to her back pocket again, and it dawned on him what she wanted. Her phone. That's where she carried her phone, which was charging now. The world was addicted to phones but her case was severe.

"I'm sorry," she said. "It's not your problem, and you are being so kind."

Kind? Hardly. He didn't want to lie to her. It made her think she had to be grateful to him and from the way her voice had gone tight, she hated depending on him. He understood; he didn't want her to depend on him in any way, shape or form. He decided to set the record straight. "Not doing it for you. It's for Connie."

She frowned. "For the landlady?" Her eyes widened. "I mean—of course. I didn't realize you and she might be…" She trailed off and took a step backward, which brought her up hard against a stud.

He now had room to move to the other end of the pipe but no way did he want Alexi thinking he actually chose Connie. "She's my sister."

"Your sister?" Her eyes narrowed. "So yesterday, when you asked about the landlady, you were really asking if your sister had contacted me?"

He took his time to get to the other end of the pipe. "Yep," he said, his back half-turned to her. "I didn't want to get involved in her business." He shoved the other end of the pipe into a fitting. It went in easy and straight. Good. So long as he used his hands and not his mouth, things went well. "Still don't, but she's a bad habit."

He felt her slide behind him and out of the

room. At the door, she paused. "You think helping others is a bad habit?"

Seth had long ago lost track of the number of people he'd been obliged to help during the past couple of years, all because he had helped the wrong person. "Yeah," he said, "I guess so."

A smile played at the edge of her mouth. "So you're saying that I shouldn't feel guilty that you took time out of your schedule to help me?"

Guilt. He knew too much of that. "You can only be guilty for your own choices, and it was my choice to come here today."

It was the truth. He'd really done what he wanted, when he wanted.

Her hand moved and he supposed it was going to her phantom phone. Instead it rose to her cheek, her hair, to wrap around the back of her neck, as if she didn't know what to do with it.

"Thanks," she whispered. "I needed to hear that."

Whaddaya know, Seth thought, he'd made her feel better. His bad habit had finally done some genuine good.

CHAPTER FIVE

Two DAYS LATER, Alexi shouldered open the front door of the house, Callie in tow, carrying the last box from the U-Haul trailer, a plastic tub of cloth scraps and stuffing for her craft business. Matt sat on the stairs to the main level, his shoulders slumped.

Poor kid. She'd relied on him to carry load after load and then help her wheel and lift the furniture when not four days ago he was packing it into the trailer. She set down the tub and sat on it, suddenly aware of how good it felt to take the weight off her sore ankle. "I'm sorry, Matt. You must be exhausted."

Callie sat beside him, her way of showing sympathy. He shrugged. "I'll live."

His answer recalled what Richard would say to the kids whenever they howled about a scrape or a bruise. He hadn't. He was killed on impact in a head-on collision on the highway south of Fort McMurray on his way home after a twenty-one-day stint in the oil patch. Since then, only Callie cried over a scraped knee or a bruised elbow. Alexi wished they all would. Tears were normal.

"Listen, I'd like you to treat yourself. Go on up to Mac's. Get yourself a slushie, okay?"

"Should I ask Seth Greene if he wants anything?"

Seth was jury-rigging the kitchen sink with planks and sawhorses and running pipes underneath. Time he could be profiting from his jobs that she knew from the calls on his cell were stacking up. Yes, she didn't want Matt getting chummy with Seth. He was a good part of the reason she'd kept Matt busy with unpacking. The last thing the already complicated adoption process needed was the introduction of a relationship between Matt and this man, but no sense making a big deal out of a small courtesy, either.

"Yes," she said. "You should. Make it clear that I'm paying and it's my pleasure." She couldn't resist adding that last bit, knowing full well Mr. Grumpy could hear every word.

Matt shot up the stairs while Alexi headed outside to sweep out the back of the U-Haul, Callie right behind like a devoted puppy.

She barely had broom in hand before Matt

popped his head in. "He said thanks but he's okay. Should I get him something anyway?"

Richard again. He'd always get her a treat even when she specifically said she didn't want one because he didn't want to ever leave her out.

"It's enough that you offered."

She handed him a twenty, and told him to make sure he pocketed the change before taking the drinks. She skirted the house into the backyard, Callie on her heels. Amy was riding a stick with her posse of imaginary friends, her bow legs for once looking appropriate. Callie broke away to join Amy, while Alexi scanned the yard for Bryn. Where, oh, where, oh, please—

There. Under the weeping birch, lost in the shadows with Seth Greene's old baseball bat. He was pounding it into the ground with a rock. She was about to call to ask the reason for that when her phone sounded. It was a number without a name. The landlady?

She tapped the green bar. "Hello."

"Alexi. How are you?" It was the measured voice of her caseworker.

She was so not prepared to take this call. She climbed the stairs, careful with her bad ankle, to the back deck, so the kids didn't

overhear. Callie—miracles of miracles—
watched her leave but turned back to Bryn
and Amy when Alexi stayed within sight.

Alexi drew breath and aimed for a tone
of airy confidence. "Oh, hi, Brenda. Fine.
And you?"

"I must admit to a little confusion. Weren't
we supposed to meet yesterday?"

Shoot, she'd forgotten to reschedule, which
would've bought her time before having to
officially notify Brenda of a change of address. "Oh, yes, right. That's my fault entirely. I forgot to tell you that I wouldn't be
able to make the meeting."

"Did you also forget to tell me that you'd
moved?"

How did she know? Alexi turned away
from the open kitchen window where Seth
was working and kept her voice low. "No. I
mean, yes. Yes, I did move. To Spirit Lake."

"Spirit Lake. I've heard of it. Near Red
Deer, right?"

"Yes, about ten minutes west."

Brenda groaned softly. "Oh, Alexi. This
is not good."

Yes, it was. It was. It just didn't look that
way. Stay confident, she ordered herself. "I
told you that I needed to get out of that house

for Matt's sake. He bolted every single week. The house was toxic for him."

"Given time—"

"I gave it almost a year! It was only getting worse."

"But a move? Not just to another house but another community? What will be the effect of that, Alexi?"

A question she'd asked herself a million times and every time she'd consoled herself with the answer she now gave Brenda. "Since the day I promised him we were moving, he hasn't run off. That was two months ago. I had to keep my end of the bargain. And he hasn't run off here, either." Alexi wasn't about to tell her Matt was out of sight and off the property right now.

"But, Alexi, this triggers new questions. How will you manage your business from a new location?"

"Nothing changes. It's a home-based business. I still have my own website. I'm still on Etsy. That doesn't change. It's business as usual."

"And how is business, Alexi?"

"It's business as usual, Brenda. I was paid last week and I'm expecting payment on two more orders today, as a matter of fact."

Which was the truth. The other truth was that they'd barely cover the minimum payment on her credit card.

Brenda's sigh felt like a puff of cold air in Alexi's ear. "I hope things go well for you. I really do. However, the consequence of your change is that we will have to reopen parts of Matt's file. Likely do a new home study."

What? No one could see this wreck of a house. Alexi pressed her fingers to her temple, forgetting that her head bruise was there. She bit back a squeak of pain. "When?"

"I'm not sure. You're out of my territory. I will send the paperwork to the Red Deer office, and a new caseworker will be assigned. Today's Monday, so…perhaps as early as next week."

There was no way this place would be in shape by then. She drove her fingers into her hair, bunching it so hard it hurt. "Listen, Brenda. This is the thing. The house here is still being renovated. There's a—a—man working on it even as we speak but if the new social worker sees it like this right now, without knowing who I am, it won't look good. Is there any way you can delay the transfer?"

There was a loud thud from the kitchen. Alexi whirled to see—nothing. Then Seth rose from where she guessed the sink was. She wondered how much he'd overheard. Her voice had risen, and now there was silence on Brenda's end. Alexi was about to ask if she was still there when the woman who had guided her and Richard through three adoptions, was taking her through the last stages with Matt, who had championed their cause time and time again, who knew Alexi's life story and hadn't judged, finally spoke. "I can't stop what will happen. And I'm telling you now this process is only going to get worse. The office up there has some good people but there are others—others who might not be as sympathetic."

"What do you mean, not as sympathetic?"

"I mean that there are people," Brenda spoke slowly in a clear effort to be diplomatic, "who are more concerned about filling in the paperwork and putting in the hours than the lives they are affecting."

Great, all Alexi needed. A caseworker who wouldn't listen.

"I have no control over who will be assigned your file. But, as you know," Brenda went on, "I have a heavy workload and transferring your file may take longer than I originally anticipated."

Alexi breathed out. "Thank you, thank you, thank you."

"Don't thank me," Brenda said. "I am doing this for the sake of your family. And for Richard. To be honest, I don't know if he would've approved, Alexi."

As soon as the call ended, Alexi opened her phone photo of Richard. All she could see was Richard's smile and open face. "I was right, wasn't I?" she whispered.

All he did was smile at her. It was all he'd done for the past year.

The door opened and out came Seth. "Sink's in," he said with his usual verbosity.

"Thanks." Would there ever come a time when she wouldn't have to say that to him?

"All it does is drain. You can't run water into it yet. There's a plug."

"It's an improvement. Thank you. Now you can get back to your real job."

He grunted, whether in agreement or not she wasn't sure. "You okay?"

He'd overheard. She smiled. "No worries. Just sorting details out with the caseworker. Comes with the territory."

He frowned and pointed to her head. "I meant that."

"Oh! Ah. Yes. It's fine. Thanks for asking." Honestly, he must think her touched in the head.

"See you're still limping. You got ice for that?"

When had he noticed? "No point. It would melt anyway. Remember? No freezer."

"That'll change soon. Connie will be back Wednesday."

In two days. If they could survive that long.

"She'll take over. Bring in the trades." Seth spoke with a kind of grim optimism, the kind she knew all too well, the kind that believed the burning house could be saved with enough buckets of water. Then again, what else could he say? What else could she say?

"Oh, good," she said casually, as if what he said was a given. She glanced at the kids who were screaming at each other in excitement and fear, the way kids playing do.

Seth was looking at them, too. Frowning, probably thinking the worst if she was on the line with child protection. She made herself say, "I'm adopting Matt. That's why I was talking to the caseworker."

"Where is he?"

He was frowning, not because of who the kids were but because one was not there.

That was touching, except for how he'd immediately zeroed in on Matt. "I sent him off to Mac's to get himself a treat. His wages," she joked. "He said he'd asked you if you wanted something and you said no."

Seth didn't smile back. "He didn't say he was doing it alone. Does he know where to go?"

"He knows. I trust him." *Please, Matt, don't let me down.*

As if he heard her, the gate swung open and in walked Matt. He carried a tray of three medium slushies and one large one. In the other tray was a large one and an extra-large one. So much for any change.

The kids spotted Matt and rushed him, at the same time Matt spotted Seth on the back deck. "Hey, Seth Greene! I got you a slushie." He clutched the tray with the largest slushie while his siblings tore the other from his grasp.

"You guys get the medium ones, I get the large one," he advised them in no uncertain terms as he snatched his. "Because I worked the hardest," he added, shutting down Bryn before there was an argument.

Matt mounted the stairs to Seth. "Here's yours. I didn't know which flavors you like so I got a little of them all." He held out a monster-sized slush of rainbow colors and handed Alexi a mostly orange one. "I know you said you didn't want anything but it didn't seem right."

Alexi took it and thanked him. Seth looked set to refuse and Alexi held her breath. Part of her wanted him to blow Matt off to stop any attachment from developing. The rest of her didn't want Matt to face one more rejection.

Seth must've looked too long into Matt's puppy eyes because he took the drink so enormous his own large hand was stretched to grip it. "Thanks. You shouldn't have."

He wasn't a very good liar, and he seemed to know it because he straightened and tried again. "I appreciate you thinking of me."

The mighty Seth Greene had twice thanked a child for something he didn't want.

"No worries. We really appreciate all that you're doing for us here," her far-too-mature son said. Yet again, pride and sadness twisted in her heart.

Not thinking, she took a long, restorative slurp on her slushie...and got instant brain freeze.

Seth gave Matt a long look. "Glad to be

of help, Matt." He took an extended slurp on his rainbow drink. From his sudden grimace, Alexi knew that he, too, had contracted her present condition.

Matt grinned at them. "Pretty good, eh?"

Seth eyed his ten-inch-high drink. "You betcha."

He slid Alexi a secretive look that conveyed his real thoughts on the matter, and she quickly clamped her lips around the straw to hide her smile. Oh, boy. Mr. Grumpy had made her and her kid happy within seconds. Alexi could only imagine what effect he'd have if he actually tried.

Not that she wanted him to.

ABOUT SUPPERTIME THE next day, Seth and Ben were up on their ninth roof in four hours, preparing an estimate, when Ben dropped the news that Connie was back in town. "She was working tables at lunch."

Seth looked up from his phone calculator. Back a day early. "Did she say if she called Alexi? Her tenant?"

Ben stepped to the overhang with his tape measure and pulled out a good length, his back to Seth. "No. It never came up."

After a lifetime of friendship, Seth detected tension in Ben's voice. Why did the man keep beating himself up? Spirit Lake was small, but not so small that he had to eat where his ex-girlfriend worked.

"She's doing the dinner shift, too," Ben said over his shoulder.

Which was his way of telling Seth where she could be found without encouraging him to go there. Neither of them had brought up the issue of Connie since the ball game, and Ben already seemed of two minds about telling him she was back in town. So after Seth passed the estimate to the owner, who agreed unhappily to the underlined number on the bottom, he told Ben only that he was calling it a day, and they agreed to meet at the crack of dawn, as per every day lately.

Seth made straight for Smooth Sailing. Connie was behind the bar at the taps. She looked up with a customer-friendly grin, which vanished at the sight of him. She returned to leveling off a sleeve of beer she carried to a guy in a work shirt and a baseball cap on the other side of the bar. He glanced from his idle interest in a poker game on the wall-mounted television to notice his drink and Connie's chest.

It must burn Ben to see other guys take

their peeks. Seth wouldn't like it happening to his girlfriend. If he had one. Not that he was interested in having one, anyway. It was enough trouble helping out a random single mom.

Seth swung onto a stool beside the taps. "Hey, what do I have to do to get a little service around here?" Seth said loud enough so Connie couldn't pretend she didn't hear.

Her back to him, he knew from the way the guy's face split into a sudden grin that Connie had pulled a funny face. She turned and moseyed real slow over to him.

"You're here to nag me about the house, aren't you?" She pulled out a pricey foreign beer from a fridge under the bar. She popped off the top and set it square in front of him before he could stop her.

"I'm not getting that. I want whatever's on tap."

"You have to order something so it might as well be something that comes with a bigger tip."

"I can give you a tip, if that's what you want. Like how to keep a happy tenant. You been over to see Alexi yet?"

"Not likely. I'm into conflict avoidance."

"Well, I'm not." Seth picked up the beer

and read the label. A Scottish beer. He took a swig. It was actually not half bad, not that he was going to tell her that.

She turned away but he called after her, "She's living in a house that has no floor, Connie. No running water in the kitchen. Only one bathroom with a toilet and sink that work and that's because I fixed them. She has four kids. Don't you have any common decency?"

The guy had perked up, and the two office girls at the far end were tracking her, too. Connie spun and stomped back.

"I didn't ask you to go over there and fix it!" she hissed, her hands fisted into her hips.

"You didn't ask anyone to fix it. You let her move in, knowing what it was like."

"I tried to call her. It's not my fault."

"Yes, Connie. It. Is. How about you fix *your* house?" He took another pull on his beer. This really was good stuff.

"Yeah, my house, not yours, so butt out."

"You're incredible. Did you know your tenant is on the verge of suing you because of the condition?"

"Let her sue me. Renovations take longer than I thought. I'll just sue the contractors and she'll never get anywhere."

She strode off to serve a new customer, her smile wide and fake. He should finish his beer and let it go. Where had helping others ever got him?

Yet, as soon as Connie was within normal speaking range again, he couldn't stop himself. "Why do you bring trouble onto yourself, Con? Why couldn't you have just left things the way they were?"

Connie's eyes flashed. "Because it was old and ugly and nothing, nothing about it had changed. I tried to live there. I lasted four days. You've no idea how much I hate the house."

"I've got a good idea," Seth said.

"Mom gave me the place to get back at me."

Seth stared. "How can you possibly think that? She wanted you to have a roof over your head."

"Because she knew I didn't have the brains to get one for myself!"

Where did she get off with that attitude? "Maybe she was right."

His sister sucked in her breath. He did, too. They looked away from each other, at different spots on the bar counter. He had overstepped the line. No small part of his frustration with Connie over the years came from the fact that she wasn't dumb. She was brighter than him or Mel or most everyone he knew. But she wasted it. In her earlier years on drugs, alcohol and bad boys. Now mostly on bad boys. It was no use telling her how intelligent she was. She wouldn't believe him.

"That was uncalled for," he said softly.

She snorted. "Doesn't mean it's not the truth. Spent most of my life depending on others. Too dumb for school, too smart for the streets. Always doing some job that doesn't get me ahead."

Just as he figured, she didn't believe him. "You make enough money."

"You know what it takes to live? The bare minimum?"

He thought of Alexi with four kids. "I bet your tenant does."

Connie narrowed her eyes. "From what Mel tells me, you're going way beyond the call of duty with this one. How many times you've been over there to fix her pipes? Something you're not telling me?"

In his mind popped an image of Alexi's lips suctioned around the slushie straw, then spreading into a secret smile with him. One of those commonplace moments an intimate couple shared.

Nope, nothing to say.

"Point is, you own the house. You have a responsibility to keep it in working order. There are laws against renting a place that doesn't have running water, Connie."

She picked up a dish towel and began to buff the counter. "Look, I don't have the money to fix it. I bought the flooring and the countertop. It's all stacked in the basement. The fridge, oven, microwave are on order. I thought I could do it with some help but it didn't happen." She lifted her hand, palm out, as if testifying. "I tried, okay? I'm not keeping on with something there's no way I can do. So I tell you what. You fix it up, and you can have the rent money for the next six months. She can even write the check out in your name."

Exactly what he expected. Sticking him with her mess. "I don't need the money. I'm up to my eyeballs with roofing jobs. The storm has meant we're the busiest ever. I don't have time."

Connie tossed the towel aside. "Then I guess she's out of luck."

Seth stood. "You really are a piece of work,

you know? Don't you care about anybody except yourself?"

"Caring for myself takes all I got."

In that second, Seth envied Connie. She could walk away from her messes, not at all weighed down by any sense of responsibility. "Why do I bother with you when all you ever are is ungrateful and irresponsible?"

Connie leaned in. "You bother, big brother, because you're a class-A jerk who thinks he's above everyone else when all you are is a man with a hammer on somebody else's roof."

With that, she fixed him with her widest smile, one that didn't look the least bit fake to him, scooped up a menu and strolled over to the man who'd long lost interest in poker and looked ready to take a gamble on Connie.

Seth paid for his beer with a twenty and left without asking for change.

CHAPTER SIX

WHEN ALEXI SPOTTED Seth rounding the corner of the house into the backyard, she didn't know whether to hustle him away for Matt's sake or latch on to him for all their sakes. All four kids were there, Matt and Bryn having invented a game with the rebar and binder twine they'd found under the back deck. Matt had the hammer from Richard's toolbox and was building what looked from her view at the kitchen window like a very complicated cat's cradle. Bryn immediately launched into an explanation of the game to Seth, while Matt stopped pounding and regarded Seth with the same shy wondering look he'd reserved for Richard.

She came out onto the deck in time to hear Matt say to Bryn, "He's an adult. Maybe he doesn't want to play a kids' game."

"But he plays baseball. That's a kids' game."

"But he plays it with adults, so it's an adult game."

"Dad played kids' games with us and he was an adult."

Bryn, too, wanted a piece of Seth Greene. Loneliness. Here was a man in their backyard, exactly where a father hung out. Except the difference was that if Bryn got too attached it wouldn't result in him being taken from her.

Seth, for his part, began to sidle away from the boys toward her. "Hey, guys, I need to talk to your mom. I'll catch up with you all in a bit."

Not if she had anything to say about it. Bryn returned to the game but Matt watched Seth leave, his face bright with worship. Okay, time to nip this in the bud.

When Seth cleared the top step, he kept coming until he was right beside her, positioning himself so he could look at her and the kids at the same time, mirroring her pose. It unsettled her how naturally he did it, as if he was used to backing up others, being that second set of eyes—or hands.

"Connie's back in town. Just got through talking with her."

From his clipped tones, Alexi surmised it hadn't gone well.

Seth continued. "She basically said she can't afford to carry on with the renovations."

Alexi's heart sank. She slipped her phone out of her back pocket and held it tight. She'd found that if she simply did that during the rough spots throughout the day and if she slept holding it, she could trick herself into feeling connected to Richard. And yes, she knew she was no better than Callie with a stuffie.

Seth's green eyes flicked to her phone. "You need to make a call?"

Trust him to zero in on her weakness. "Uh…no. I—" She returned her phone to her pocket, its hard flatness pressing through her shorts into her backside, and engaged her hand with the string ties on her blouse. There, she thought, satisfied?

Apparently he was because his focus was on the kids when he said, "She did make me an offer. Said that if I did the work you could pay me your rent check for the next six months."

"My rent money as wages? That wouldn't cover it." Providing she could even produce a rent check.

"That and I'm already swamped with work," he added. "I told her as much." He grimaced. "It didn't end well. Thing is, I help you, I help my sister. And I don't want to help my sister."

"So you're saying you won't help."

At least he had the decency to look uncomfortable. "Yeah, that's what I'm saying."

"I understand." And she did. "You've already done more than I could've hoped for." The truth again, even if it wasn't easy to live with.

Seth said nothing. Instead he frowned at the kids, like a foreman not pleased with the progress at a construction site. Matt was directing his siblings on how to crawl or step or jump or hop through the laser beams of binder twine, a construct he'd dubbed "The Matrix."

"How will you manage?"

His sudden question threw Alexi, not the least because she detected an undercurrent, as convoluted and frail as the orange strings in Matt's maze, of genuine interest. He kept his attention on the kids, so there was no way to tell. As for his question, she couldn't even see her way beyond August. She needed his help but he'd flat out told her he wasn't going to give it. Living here wasn't an option so...

"I'll start looking for a new place." Just

saying it made her sag. Wouldn't that please the new caseworker? Another move. Another strike on her file.

"Not many places with a yard like this one," Seth commented.

"I know. It was the clincher for me," Alexi said. "That and the fence. It was…perfect."

Seth made a noncommittal sound, a kind of grunt that probably meant he'd heard and that was enough. No long conversations into the night with him. Not that… She felt herself grow even hotter in the daytime sun. She just missed Richard so much. Her hand strayed to her back pocket where her phone was.

Seth caught her in the act. "You can't live without that thing, can you?" Another question with an undercurrent she couldn't quite figure out.

She pointed to the one attached to his belt. "Who can?"

"Yeah, for calls or music. To hear it ring or sing. You hold it like a kid with a stuffed toy."

Her breath caught. He'd nailed her dead-on. "Yes, I expect I do," she mumbled.

He took the hint. "Not that it's any of my business." He looked back at the kids and shook his head. "All the twine's going to fall to the ground the way Matt's got it knotted."

He removed his baseball cap, scratched his hat-flattened hair, set the cap back on, a classic gesture of agitation. He clearly wanted to get in there and sort things out for Matt. Not for his sister, not for her, but maybe…

No, it was a sneaky idea, one she instantly hated herself for. Then again, what was a little self-hatred to one as desperate as her?

"Can I be honest with you, Seth?"

He slanted her a look. "You haven't been so far?"

"Yes, of course. But I need to tell you something that right now is none of your business but that I would like to make your business."

He eyed her phone.

"No, it's Matt."

"What? Matt? What's wrong with him?"

Just as she thought, Seth liked him. "Nothing. The thing is, Matt is the oldest but really he's our fourth child. He came to us about a year and a half ago. Richard found him. Or Matt found Richard. That's another story. Anyway, we decided to adopt Matt, just like we adopted the other three.

"Matt's case was complicated to begin with. There was other family involved that took sorting out. And we needed to prove our eligibility. The usual paperwork. Then Richard—then there was Richard's accident."

"They said you couldn't adopt because you're a single mom?"

"No, no, that's not the issue." A single mom without an income was, however, not that Seth needed to know that. "But more paperwork meant a delay, then Richard, when he…" Why couldn't she spit out the word? "Richard's passing was hard on Matt, and his behavior caused more delays. I decided to move because it was what Matt wanted, and what I believe he needs. I knew that would translate into more delays in paperwork, and that there would be a new caseworker. What I didn't count on was showing her this reno wreck."

She sucked in her breath. "There is a very real chance that if she sees this mess, she'll order us to leave immediately because it isn't safe for Matt. Frankly, I've no place to go."

Seth looked past her and through the kitchen window. "When's she coming?"

"I don't know exactly. My old caseworker was going to hold off on the paperwork but likely in the next couple of weeks."

Seth pulled off his cap, scratched and replaced it. "Exactly how good does this place have to be?"

"It's mostly Matt's living space. His bedroom, the kitchen. It doesn't have to be perfect but—"

"Running water might be a good idea," Seth said, his mouth twisting with sarcasm.

"Yeah. Something less…Third World," Alexi said. "How about if I help? I don't know how to tile or anything but you could—"

"I'm not tiling. Tiling's a big job. You know how much cutting has to be done in a kitchen? You need a tile cutter and which one of us is going to pay to rent one?"

She didn't answer his questions because she didn't think he was really asking. Another awkward silence fell between them. Short this time. "Look, I want to help you out but what you're asking is a full-scale intervention."

"I wouldn't ask if I had any choice. I know I could never repay you. I mean, I would try but—"

Seth waved his hand. "No. You've got nothing to give me."

He might as well have slapped her in the face. The sad truth was she had nothing to offer a man.

"Don't you know anyone to help you? Friends from Calgary?"

She didn't. She knew people, of course. Parents of her kids' friends, members of the craft group she'd belonged to when Richard was alive, a few of the neighbors but no one well enough she could turn to for help. The one thing worse than asking for help was having no one to ask.

She shoved her hands into her front pockets to stop herself from reaching for her phone. "I wouldn't be asking you, if I did."

He crossed his arms, shifted on his feet. He was getting ready to reject her.

"I'm not asking it for my sake," Alexi said in a rush. "I'm asking it for Matt's sake. If Matt has to leave us, I know for a fact he'll run."

"Run?" Seth looked at the boy who was manning one string after another, reefing on them so they were stretched tight so his siblings could skip between them, all the while shouting and gesturing like a coach with his team.

Yes, she saw what he must see, too. A boy who built a game so his brother and sisters could have fun. A boy who watched over his foster mother when strangers like him came near. A boy who bought his family slushies. A boy who, if he ran, it was to rescue his naked bro. She had to make Seth see what would happen if Matt lost this home.

Time for more truth. Truth she wasn't supposed to share. "Seth, Matt ran from his mean drunk of a mother to his father, a three-hour drive away, by hiding in the back of four different pickups. He was seven. Then when his father was stabbed to death in a drug fight, he hitchhiked to his grandfather's place in Calgary. When his grandfather died, he was placed in a foster home. When he had enough of that, he found Richard in Walmart.

"He followed Richard and me and the kids out to the van, and got inside as if he was already part of the family. Buckled himself up and waited for us to take him home. All he'd tell us was that he wasn't going back. So... so we took him home."

She touched his arm and it immediately tensed. She didn't remove her hand. "Seth. I hate, hate asking for charity. Maybe even more than you hate giving it. I have no one else."

Her hand was suddenly off his arm and in his hand. Her fingers held by his in a tight, full grip. This was nothing like his handshake. This was the hold of a man who felt her pain and wanted to bring her through it. "I'll do it," he said, his voice raw. "I'll help. Just—just don't beg me. I don't want you thinking that I'm anybody other than a guy with a hammer."

What a strange thing to say. He was more than that. Anybody could see that. She gave him her biggest smile. He cleared his throat. "Besides which, Matt's a good kid. You don't have anything to give me, but Matt—well, you're the only one who can give him what he needs."

For a solid year, she'd had to prove that to teachers, caseworkers, neighbors, the police. And on the worst nights, she'd lain curled on her side of the bed, knees to chin, with only the light from the phone, wondering if maybe she was wrong. To hear it now from a man who hardly spoke and when he did, it wasn't ever complimentary, well…she bit her lip.

"Thanks," she whispered. She forced herself not to say it more than the one time.

He nodded once, released her hand and crossed to the stairs. "Hey," he called to Matt, "let me show you how to make a knot that lasts."

As Seth closed the distance between Matt

and him, Alexi watched the consequences of securing Seth's help unfold. She saw Seth take the string easily from Matt's fingers, saw them crouch together, knee to knee, the smaller hand pulling, the larger tying, one holding the rebar, the other pounding it solid. She'd given Seth reason to become attached to Matt. Worse, she'd given him the right.

It also didn't help that she still felt the warm pressure of his hand as if he'd never let go.

As soon as Seth left the house in the early evening, he called Pete, the handyman, and brokered a swap of a rush kitchen reno job for a rush roof job on Pete's house and barn, for which Mel gave him no end of flak the next morning on their new job.

"We've already made commitments elsewhere," Mel said and paused from mounting an anchor on a ridgeline to take out a sheet of paper from his front pocket. "Here, take a look."

Seth angle-walked from his anchor point on the roof of a five-thousand-square-foot house in Spirit Lake's exclusive lakefront community, the owners being willing to pay the hefty rush job fee Mel had just implemented, and took from him what turned out to be a spreadsheet. It itemized the customers, the estimates, the approved jobs, the projected expenses, and the expected start and completion dates of twenty-two jobs.

Seth didn't even know Mel could navigate a computer beyond calling up The Weather Network. He didn't even own a phone. "You did this?"

Mel finished driving an unnecessary screw into the anchor clip before answering. He always built the safety system strong enough to support elephants. "No choice. We've got to get ourselves organized. And you—" he shook his hammer at Seth "—aren't helping."

"I'm helping our sister," Seth said.

Mel started to drive in one more pointless nail. "Not from where I'm sitting. No love lost between you and Connie. Looks to me as if you want to help a pretty widow."

"I didn't say she was pretty."

Mel squinted up at Seth from underneath his cap. "Is she?"

Long legs, a life-loving smile and the best pair of eyes he'd ever stared into. "Not bad. Anyway, it's not her I'm doing it for. It's her oldest kid."

"How's that?"

Seth said nothing, not wanting to betray Alexi's confidence.

Mel grunted. "I rest my case. We're not running a charity here."

"If there's anyone who has a right to complain about money, it'd be me."

In the six months since their mother's will was read, Seth and Mel had not discussed how the funds were distributed. Now, in less than a week, they'd each brought it up.

Mel pulled another screw out of his belt.

"Enough with the screws," Seth snapped. "Hope you factored their waste into your pricing." He scrunched up the spreadsheet and tossed it at Mel.

Mel caught the paper ball against his chest and smoothed it flat. He nodded once, his head down. "Okay," he said quietly. "I get it. You take whatever time you need."

Now Seth felt like a jerk. "I don't need time. I need…"

Mel looked up, waiting. For specifics, probably.

Seth spun away. "I need to get back to work."

CHAPTER SEVEN

ON EACH OF THE NEXT seven days, Seth got a call from Alexi, updating him on the progress Pete and his crew were making. She continued to thank him—she couldn't seem to stop herself—the way you would with a stranger, but surely by now, he had to count for someone different, someone you'd not feel in debt to for every single act of kindness.

No way could he explain that to Alexi without sounding as if he was coming on to her. Which he wasn't. He took her daily calls because he was interested, and not because of the soft roll to her words or the fact that she was using her most treasured possession to talk to him.

In the early morning of the eighth day since promising to help Alexi, a solid roof of thick clouds rolled over Spirit Lake and let loose thick rain.

"Guess I'll get caught up on some paperwork," Mel said, firing up his laptop at the dining table. "You might as well go to Tim's by yourself, seeing as how it's too wet for networking."

Fine. This way, he wouldn't have to explain why, in addition to the regular order, he was picking up four lemonades and a large coffee.

When Seth returned with Mel's whipped coffee and Timbits, he set them on the dining table and turned to go.

"Where're you going?" Mel asked.

"Out," Seth said and left before his nosy brother shot off another question.

This time at the house, Seth remembered to knock. Matt opened it. "Hey, Seth Greene. Mom!" he yelled up the stairs. "Seth Greene is here."

Seth had never noticed before that the boy called him by his full name. Weird. Then again, he hadn't made it clear how he wanted to be addressed.

"Hey, Matt. You can just call me Seth. Or Mr. Greene, if you prefer."

Matt shrugged. "I haven't figured out what to call you, actually. Until then, I prefer to stay on a full name basis."

"I'm not sure—" Seth began when Alexi called from the kitchen, "Seth! Come, look!"

There she was, modeling the kitchen like a

game show assistant. Her hands flared open to the cupboards, caressed the countertops and flicked on—"It's magic!"—the water taps in the fully installed sink.

Matt jumped in. "Look at our new fridge!"

Seth hadn't taken it in, seeing as how his eyes were riveted on Alexi. But now he saw the behemoth. Stainless, double door, freezer drawer on the bottom and—

"Look, Seth! An ice maker!"

So this was why Connie couldn't afford contractors. Wasted it on something way beyond her price range, while he was having to do favors to get the work done. Then he caught Matt's expression. He wore the wide-eyed, hopeful look of someone who had pinned their happiness on making sure the other was happy.

"Do you like it?" Matt asked.

"Yeah," he said. "I like it. It's…awesome."

Matt beamed. "It came yesterday. You can have ice cubes or it'll crush the ice. Last night I made everyone smoothies with juice and old bananas. It was as good as you get at a restaurant."

"Those lemonades for us?" Bryn cut in.

"Yes. And the coffee's for your mom."

"Oh!" Alexi said. "Thanks." Her blue eyes

lifted to his, and it hit him again how *blue* they were. She must've gotten a ton of compliments about them. He wondered if Richard had paid any attention. Yeah, he would've, because looking into them would make a man forget everything else.

"My pleasure," he said. And meant it. He got coffee for Ben and Mel and the temporary help because that was the right thing to do. With Alexi's bunch, it was like playing Santa Claus. "Double cream, no sugar. I hope you like it that way."

Matt looked up from his lemonade. "Whoa. That's exactly how she has it. How did you know?"

He hadn't. It just felt like what she'd want. "I lucked out. Good thing. Otherwise, I would have to keep bringing her coffee different ways until I got it right."

"It would be easier to just ask her," Bryn suggested.

Seth and Matt exchanged quick smiles of understanding. When Seth turned to include Alexi, he caught her frowning, the corner of her mouth down turned. What had he done wrong?

She smiled again, though now it looked

like a superhuman effort. "What brings you here today?"

"It's raining. Thought I'd see what I could do."

"It's all good. The guys seem to have a handle on it. They'll probably come by in a bit."

Was she trying to brush him off? "No, not today. I already told them I could get a few things done, so they can move on to other jobs."

"Well," she said, with a sweep of her hand around the kitchen, "as you can see, most everything is done."

She had to be kidding. Sure, there were cupboards but the doors were stacked. There were no tiles on the floor, so the subfloor was still exposed.

"When's the tile getting laid?"

"Not sure."

"The rest of the appliances?"

"Maybe tomorrow. The stove is on back order."

"For how long?"

Her face tightened under his barrage of questions. "Okay, I could do with help."

"I'll help," Matt said.

"No," Alexi said at the same time Seth said, "Sure."

"Why not?" Matt challenged. Good question.

"It… I…" Her gaze collided with Matt's and she stopped. Seth knew she was feeling the exact same way he had with the fridge. She couldn't refuse his happiness. "I guess you and Seth could pull up the carpet in your bedroom."

Matt shot off. Seth lingered, wanting Alexi to give a straight answer to Matt's question. Instead she got busy with a box of what looked like rags to him. "While those two are busy," she said to the other three kids, "how about we sort out my business materials?"

Seth took the hint and headed down the hall. Matt's bedroom turned out to be his old one. To be exact, the one he'd had for the first dozen years of his life before moving to the basement. What an unholy mess. It looked as if Connie had tried to pull the carpet up herself. In one corner, slabs of carpet were piled high with most of the underlay rolled away to expose the old subfloor. The boy's mattress was tucked into a corner. Beside it was a storage tub with a flashlight and the book, *Guinness World Records 2013*. Put the whole setup under a city bridge, and it would make sense. No way was this place going to be ready for any caseworker anytime soon. They needed another two weeks, at least.

"Time," Seth said, "to get started."

Matt turned out to be not a bad worker, even if his job consisted of hauling pieces of carpet out front to a large disposal bin Seth had ordered the day he promised to help. He could write it off as a company expense.

In between trips, Matt kept the conversation rolling. "How many roofs have you done, do you think?"

"A few hundred."

"Wow. Aren't you scared to be up that high?"

Seth lifted a corner of the carpet underlay with a box cutter blade. "No reason to be," he said, because that was the truth. "There's a harness to keep you safe." The harness Mel had insisted they must all wear right from the day of their dad's accident. Harness with rope that tripped him up a half-dozen times a day.

"I'd be scared anyway."

"I'm not up there alone," Seth thought to point out. "I work with my brother and a friend."

"You have a brother?"

"Yep. An older one. His name is Mel."

"Cool. Let me get this out to the Dumpster, and then you can tell me more."

Seth smothered a smile at Matt's adult-speak, and let him go. He took a mighty heave on the underlay. To reveal dark rotted boards. Crap. Where had this come from?

He called from the doorway, "Hey, Alexi?"

"Yes?"

"Can you come here for a minute?"

As soon as she entered the room, he pointed to the floor.

She groaned. "What does it mean?"

"It doesn't look like mold," he said. "I'll need to lift off the rest of the underlay to check that the damage is contained. Then I'll have to cut out and replace this section of the sub-floor."

"That'll take time, won't it?"

"More than you got."

"Couldn't we just lay carpet over top for the time being? Until after the meeting?"

"And then have to redo it? Let me see what I can get done today. With Matt helping—"

"I don't want Matt getting in your way." She pulled out her phone and set it tapping against her chin. Her worry signal.

"He isn't. He's actually a help." Seth

dropped to his knees and tugged on some more of the carpet. More rot but not as deep, so maybe it was contained.

Alexi stood there still, phone tapping away. Maybe he hadn't sounded sincere enough. He'd been accused of that before. He sat back on his haunches and looked squarely at her. "I'm happy to have him around." Her mouth twisted.

"I'm sorry, Seth," she said. "But you're not to have anything to do with Matt, understood?"

In her tremendous blue eyes, filled with fear and resolve, he didn't forget everything but remembered. He tumbled through life events, bounced and skittered past his good deeds, his organized parties, his "good guy" business breaks for widows and low-income seniors, his upkeep of his mother and the house, past every time he rescued cats and dogs and bumblebees, past all that to the one stain on his life he could not erase and what she, new to town and too busy to become involved, must've discovered through her government connections.

She had found out about his criminal record.

"IT's NOT WHAT you think."

Alexi and Seth stared at each other, each

having spoken the same thing at the same time. Alexi had watched the sadness wash over Seth's face when she demanded that he stay away from Matt. She hadn't expected that powerful a reaction, and she'd only wanted to reassure him that it wasn't personal when he'd blurted out the exact same thing.

Only he couldn't have meant the same thing, right?

He gestured, like a gentleman holding open a door, for her to explain first. She plunged in, needing to convince Seth before Matt returned.

"You know Matt runs but he doesn't run *away* as much as he runs *to*," Alexi said in a near whisper in case one of the kids overheard. "When Matt ran from his father it came out later that he'd already planned to go to his grandfather's. When his grandfather died, he didn't have a plan. He told me later that it taught him to always have one, or otherwise other people could control where he ended up. The foster home turned out not to be ideal. There was—"

Alexi stopped. No need to go into that.

"At any rate, it gave Matt time to figure out a plan. We discovered later that Matt didn't happen upon Richard, that he'd been scouting for months before he found Richard."

The front door opened, and Alexi paused, waiting to see what Matt would do.

"Hey," Seth called out. "Your mom and I are working some measurements out here. Could you haul out the pile Pete left in the kitchen?"

"Okay!"

"Thanks, bud."

As soon as the front door closed again, Alexi hurried on. "The point is, he'd already planned to come to Spirit Lake. He'd already found this house from Kijiji. The reason I packed us all up was because I knew Matt would come here anyway."

Seth looked dubious. Alexi pushed on.

"It's not just that. There's a pattern. Matt wants a father in his life. He left his mother for his father who wasn't any better than her with his drinking. When his dad died, there was a cousin, a good woman, single but with two adopted kids from Haiti. She wanted him, but Matt wanted a father, so he went into the foster care system. The father there was absent or if there, never talked to the kids. At all. Matt found Richard because Richard was a father."

"Yeah, but the pattern stops here. Connie had the place for rent, not me."

"Look at the two of you. You can't tell me that you haven't seen him attach himself to you."

He frowned, which meant he was seeing it. She pressed her point. "He's targeting you as his next father. But that won't help his adoption process. It'll raise questions about this new man in his life. I'm asking, and I know I've already asked a lot, but I'm asking you to keep your distance with him. For his sake, for all of our sakes."

Seth reached down and gave another tug on the underlay to reveal more water-darkened subfloor. Both of them groaned. Seth held firm to the huge triangle of underlay as he spoke. "So let me get this straight. You talked me into doing these renos for you so Matt wouldn't be taken from you, but now you're saying that I'm the cause of his problems."

"Not the deliberate cause."

"Because you want me to do something for you and the boy but not get anything out of it. No money, no contact with the boy, nothing."

Did he have to put it that way? "It's not you. Anybody close to Matt right now would catch the wrong kind of attention."

He gave the underlay another strong pull, lifting it so close to her feet she had to hop back. He didn't seem to notice as he glared at the floor. The wet boards were now a lighter shade. The damage was contained.

"Point is, it is me. Point is, he chose me. Why don't you ask him to back off until after the adoption? Keep quiet around the caseworker. Seems like a smart kid."

"That's tricky. Because they can ask Matt point-blank if I've told him not to say anything."

Seth nodded his understanding. "Can't leave well enough, can they? Haven't you all gone through enough?"

A rush of thankfulness passed through Alexi. He did understand. Impulsively she said, "So that's why it's so important to me that he become adopted. For him. For the other kids. And yeah, for me."

He paused. "A hard kid to say 'no' to."

She held her breath. "But you will, won't you?"

Her cell rang. The Government of Alberta. What now? She was happy to ignore it but Seth had already turned away to tear off the carpet in the closet. As usual, bureaucracy interfering at precisely the wrong time.

"Is this Alexi Docker?" The voice on the other end was broad and rough, female.

"Uh, speaking."

"Okay, this is Marlene." She also gave her last name. "Don't try to remember that. Legacy from my ex. Remember Marlene. I'm with the agency here in Red Deer. So I hear you moved in on my turf, and we need to meet. How about the day after tomorrow? Friday, at nine?"

Wha—? "I have some work deadlines coming up. Next week would be better."

"Work? What kind of work do you do? Says here in the file 'Little Wonders.'"

"Yes, I do custom work. Mostly...stuffed toys."

"That's nice. You make enough to pay the bills with that?"

Yes, this was definitely the one Brenda had warned her about. "So far, so good."

"Ha. That's what I say when they ask about my plan for immortality. I won't keep you long. About an hour. How about you pick a time and I'll clear my schedule?"

Alexi offered what she knew every government worker would say no to. "How about Friday? Say quarter to four?"

"Sure. I could wrap it up in forty-five. Sounds good."

The moment the call ended, Alexi's mind started to race. How was she going to get things in shape by the day after tomorrow? True, the appointment was in the afternoon, so she had the morning to tidy, but what about this room?

The thump of carpet behind her made her spin. Seth jerked his head at the cell tapping her chin. "You do that a lot, you know."

Alexi grimaced. "I have reason. That was my new caseworker. She insisted on coming this week. Friday at quarter to four."

Seth shook his head, long steady swings of absolute certainty. "Not a chance. Not even close. There's no way we'll get it done."

"What can we get done?"

Seth regarded her. "You don't give up, do you?"

"That's not a choice I get to make."

Seth continued to regard her, except in an entirely different way. The corner of one eye narrowed, crinkled, into something like a wink, and in so doing, the corner of his mouth lifted into an upturn that might with the slightest encouragement break into a smile.

She responded with her own lip upturn. That was all it took for him to break through with a full-on grin.

It was the first time a man had smiled at her since Richard, not because she was a customer or a seller or a mom with paperwork. Yes, she had Richard's smile on the phone but it was nothing compared to Seth's very real one.

"Okay," he said, still smiling. "If you can't give up, then I guess I can't, either." He looked around. "We could get the carpet laid, I suppose. I'm going to cut out that rotted part of the subfloor. That'll be some job right there." He picked up his measuring tape and zipped out a length of it, ready to get to work.

The front door opened. "One more load, Seth Greene, and I'm ready to help."

"Okay!" Seth called back. Alexi's smile faded. Had he forgotten completely their conversation about Matt? He retracted his measuring tape, the metallic hiss and twang of it scraping on Alexi's nerves.

"Seth. I need to know if I have your cooperation."

He looked up from his kneeling position

on the wooden subfloor. "What does it look like you got?"

Was he being deliberately obtuse? "I mean with Matt. She sounds…tough. Brenda—the other caseworker—warned I might get assigned to someone not entirely sympathetic. You can't be here when she comes, okay?"

Seth shrugged. "I hear you. I'll be gone by Friday at noon at the latest."

"And between now and then? Will you play it cool?"

Seth sat back on his haunches. The smile was gone. "How exactly do you see this happening? Any second now, he's going to come here, expecting to help me. Do you want me to tell him to get lost?"

Alexi had a sneaky suspicion that Matt wouldn't be so easily deterred. Seth picked up a hammer, tested its heft, and then switched it for one with a larger head. "Because," he said in answer to his question, "I'm not going to be rude to him. He'd see it as cruel, and there's no way I'm going to hurt a kid who's already lost three dads.

"So, this is what I'll agree to. I won't go looking for him but if he comes to me now and again, I will treat him with the respect he deserves no matter what some bureaucratic busybody wants to make out of it. Deal?"

Not exactly what she was hoping for. Still, in his own pigheaded way, he was sticking up for Matt, and that meant he was on her side. "Deal," she said, and added, "Thank you."

He grunted, selected what looked like a sort of chisel, set it against the nail-studded strip of wood and tapped it with his hammer. The strip sprung away and Seth shuffled forward to continue his work along, from what she could see, the entire perimeter of the room.

Clearly, their conversation was done. Time for her to intercept Matt. She was at the door when she remembered.

"Oh, what did you mean when you said to me that it wasn't what you think?"

Seth hit hard with the hammer and the wood strip snapped. "Not much," he said. "Only that I wasn't trying to interfere."

That sounded...off. Especially given his almost devastated reaction. She might've pressed it, except that the door opened and Matt sang out, "Coming, Seth Greene!"

Seth popped out a length of stripping.

"You going to take care of that," he said, not stopping, "or am I?"

She left without a word, because they both knew the answer to that.

CHAPTER EIGHT

SETH WAS ON the roof of an apartment complex with Ben and Mel by seven the next morning. A real tough seven because he'd only rolled into bed six hours earlier, having stayed at the house to work on Matt's bedroom floor, which, like every reno job since the dawn of time, took way longer than he'd figured.

Right at ten when the sun had fully set, he had finally finished prepping the floor and was ready to quit when in came Alexi, Matt having crashed on her bed, who thanked him, cut the ties on the underlay and began to roll it out herself. Nothing for him to do except to drop to his knees beside her and get 'er done.

"You look warmed over," Ben said, as he and Seth set up the rope anchors under a steady wind. Mel had landed this new job, no small feat considering Greene-on-Top was a small company. Didn't help that the wind was strong enough to trip a person up.

"Yeah, I was carpeting at the house until twelve thirty," Seth said.

"You going back there today?"

"If it rains. She's got a social worker coming over tomorrow. She's in the middle of adopting and it won't look good if the kid doesn't have a decent room."

"Which one?" Mel asked from his seat on a pallet of shingles where he was scarfing down his daily twenty-pack of Timbits. "The naked one?"

How had his brother heard them from that far away and over the wind? "No, the oldest one. Name's Matt."

"What's the naked one called?"

"Bryn. And he's not naked anymore."

"I know that," Mel said. "But since I didn't know his name was Bryn, I couldn't call him that, could I? What are the names of the others?"

Seth told Mel because it was easier than explaining why he didn't need to know. His older brother liked to know the names of everyone he met, and the thing was he actually remembered them all.

Mel flattened his empty donut box and walked to them with short, concentrated old-man steps. He was always stupidly careful when he didn't have his harness on. He ran the ropes through his hands, checking for any fraying. Every new job he tested them, as if they'd unloop themselves from one site to the next or shred on the way over. Drove Seth nuts.

Mel pulled a section of rope taut and squatted. "You know, I should take her over a Welcome Wagon basket. It comes with coupons and brochures and whatnot. Her being a widow and all."

Ben shrugged on his harness. "This your idea of giving a woman a gift?"

"Just because I'm nice to a woman doesn't mean I want to date her."

That's what Mel said, but not what he felt. More than once Seth had watched Mel reach out to a woman and be shot down. If he were Mel, he'd have given up long ago. "She's not looking to date," he said.

"How do you know? Have you asked her?" Mel said.

No point. She still loved her dead husband. All the while she told him about Matt, she'd rubbed the base of her ring finger with her left thumb as if her wedding band was still there. He'd never loved a woman as much as she loved Richard. His relationships were short, friendly arrangements, not unlike his jobs.

Hooking up with Alexi would be a whole lot messier. He wasn't even sure how she could go out on a date, what with all the kids to find a sitter for. If she would even leave her kids to go out. His mind strayed to her in a short blue dress to match her eyes and to show off her legs, out alone with him, maybe down by the lake, each of them the center of each other's world for just a bit...

"No, I haven't."

"She might, then," Mel said.

Irritation flared inside Seth. "She doesn't need you harassing her."

"I wouldn't harass. I'd help."

"I'm already doing that," Seth snapped. "I don't need you interfering."

Mel's eyes widened and he looked over at Ben. Seth couldn't see what Ben communicated, but Mel suddenly bent his head to his rope testing and nothing but prepping the site was done for the next two hours when down came heavy rain with hail mixed in. The perfect reason to see Alexi.

Matt opened the door a split second after his first knock. "Hi, Seth Greene!"

One look at the boy's excited face and Seth

felt as if a chunk of wood was wedged in his throat. Playing it cool around Matt was going to be harder than he thought. But absolutely necessary. No way did he want to give the caseworker the slightest reason to dig into his history.

He swallowed hard. "Hey."

"I got everything set up in my room to finish the baseboards."

Before the boy had gone to bed last night, Seth had vaguely agreed to let him help with reinstalling the baseboards, and then promptly dropped it from his mind. Bad move. He glanced over at Alexi who, from her frown, had no idea what was going on.

"How about," she said, "you help me hang cabinet doors in the kitchen?"

"We can do that later after Seth Greene is finished with the baseboards," Matt argued. "I know how to fill in the nail holes. Otherwise he has to do it and that isn't making efficient use of his time."

Alexi darted Seth a pleading look, her wild hair looking especially electrified today. Caught between their two sets of puppy eyes, he chose the blue pair. "I'll get the baseboards on, Matt," Seth said. "You help your mom.

There's plenty to do. You can always fill the holes after I leave."

The boy's face fell, and Seth felt himself sink, too. He handed Matt a plastic bag. "Here. For your mom."

Matt pulled out a pair of knee pads and beamed as if it were a bag of money. "Mom! Look. A gift."

"Not exactly," Seth clarified. "Usually I do better than knee pads."

"You've only known her for a couple of weeks," Matt said, "so this is an appropriate gift." It sounded as if the boy expected the gifts to keep rolling in, bigger and better.

Alexi must've picked up on the same assumption because she quickly said, "We'll certainly make use of them. Thank you." Her eyes widened pointedly at him, as she tilted her head down the hallway.

Time for him to step into his role as kid-hater handyman.

"Yep," he said. "I better get at it."

During the frequent pauses when his power tools fell quiet, he tuned in to the sounds of Alexi and her kids. She and Matt had settled on extracting or pounding flat the exposed nails in the living room. Based on the commentary from the boys, Amy was playing minigolf, while Bryn played a mock version of Minecraft on the disconnected computer. Years and years ago when his mom and dad talked in the same living room, their low conversation drifted like background music into his room as he fell asleep.

The sounds coming down the hallway today put him in the same state of mind. Not that he was about to fall asleep. Not that they were his family. It was just that…well…he liked this family, despite them being an odd bunch. Connie, for the first time in a long while, had made a good decision renting to them.

Seth was driving in the last nail when the doorbell rang. He didn't pay much attention beyond registering Alexi's footsteps on the stairs. Then the visitor replied back to Alexi's hello.

"Good day. I'm Mel. Seth's brother. Did he tell you I'm with the Welcome Wagon? Also, I brought donuts for you all. You like donuts, don't you?"

ALEXI BLINKED AT the huge smorgasbord Mel was displaying. "Oh, wow. Thank you. I… uh…"

Beside her, Matt was already doing the

arithmetic. "We could each have at least three. But there's also Seth Greene."

Bryn piped up before she could stop him. "Are there any gluten-free ones?"

"No, there aren't," Alexi cut in. "But I can get you some later."

"You mean he can't have these?" Mel said.

Bryn sighed at the lineup of plump doughnuts. "I have sensitivities."

"Oh," Mel said. He looked as crestfallen as Bryn, and Alexi immediately liked Seth's older brother. Not that she could see much family resemblance. Seth was taller and more muscled, and—well—better looking. Though from the expression on his face as he appeared beside Bryn and Amy at the top of the stairs, not in better humor.

"Mel, what are you doing here?"

"Showing a little hospitality, is all."

"He brought these," Amy said. Mel held the box out to her and she took a sprinkled one and quickly bit it before Alexi could say no. Not that she planned to. No way would she deny the kids a treat. Or ruin it for Mel, who shifted the box to Matt. "My brother's been telling me all about you," Mel said.

"No," Seth said, "I haven't."

Mel said, "It's just an expression."

Seth spoke through gritted teeth, "You come to help out?"

It was Mel's turn to look peeved. "I first gotta get the boy some gluten-free donuts."

"Dairy-free, too," Bryn specified. "They're at Sobeys. In the freezer. They come in cinnamon sugar or chocolate. I prefer the chocolate. I'll show you. Let's go."

Bryn hustled down the stairs and stepped into his rubber boots, as if it was settled. Alexi sucked in her breath. How to explain to Bryn why this wasn't a good idea in a way that wouldn't insult Mel?

Amy stepped in. "Bryn, you can't go with him. He's a stranger. He won't know what to do if you freak out."

Thanks, Amy, Alexi thought, *for doing my dirty work.*

"No, he isn't," said Bryn. "Why would I freak out when I'm getting donuts?"

"I don't freak out, either," Mel weighed in. "But I agree with Amy. You shouldn't ride with strangers."

Amy pointed at Mel. "Wait a minute. How do you know my name?"

"Seth told me."

Alexi could well imagine what Seth said. She was a strung-out mom who lost one of her kids the first day here, took them camping in a storm, rationed juice boxes and relied on him, a stranger, for running water.

"How about," she suggested, "we all go? A little trip. Mel can come with us and Seth can stay here."

"You mean I stay here by myself and do the work?" Seth said. If Alexi didn't know better, he sounded downright sulky.

"Yep," Mel said.

"What about Callie?" Matt offered. "It'd be bad if she woke up and there was only him here. I should stay, too."

True. Callie hadn't even allowed Richard to touch her. Someone had to stay behind. But leaving Seth with Matt—alone—was not part of the plan, either. What was she thinking? Now she'd have to cancel the trip, and Bryn would make her pay.

Seth frowned at her and then gusted out his breath. "Amy stays, Matt goes. Matt, you deserve a break. It's Amy's turn to pull her weight around here."

Good grief, her girl was only six. How much weight could she pull? Then again, he did have a point.

"Yes!" Amy pumped her fist in the air, took Seth's hand and made a face at Matt.

Ah. A competition among the kids for Seth's attention. Lovely.

Alexi sighed and slipped her phone back into her pocket, only then realizing that at some point she'd brought it out. Which probably explained Seth's frown. She slid him a look, and he smiled. A quiet, confidential one that suggested a history between them.

She felt herself grow hot. She wasn't blushing in front of her kids and the men, was she?

The worst was confirmed when he said in a voice as intimate as his smile, "Take your time, Alexi. You deserve a break, too."

He noticed her. Not that she'd wanted him to. No, more that she hadn't expected him to, but he had. His simple words of awareness shot her through with a warm, fluttery updraft of pure well-being she hadn't felt since…in a long time.

It carried her through her chat with Mel as he rode in the passenger seat of her van with the kids in the back, through them trooping up and down the grocery aisles, buoyed her as she shopped for a carton of milk, cheese, carrots and animal crackers in case Callie woke and Amy couldn't soothe her. On impulse, she threw in a watermelon, much to the squealing delight of the kids.

Mel went through the checkout first with his box of donuts, chatting with the cashier about the hailstorm and finishing by handing her his business card. During her turn, she read the headlines on the celebrity mags while her groceries were rung through. Her eye was half on Bryn wandering to the exit when the debit machine declined her card.

"Do you want to try again?" the cashier said.

"Yes," said Alexi. "There should be money."

The cashier went tight-lipped, probably having heard that before. But there really should be. She still hadn't seen the money in her PayPal account but Connie's rent money should still be there. She'd told Seth she wasn't going to charge rent, right?

Mel was following Bryn out, and Alexi willed the machine to display the approved message. Declined. Panic kicked aside her joy. At her side, Matt watched.

"I...uh..." She scanned the pile of groceries. "...I guess I won't be..." A customer behind her started plunking groceries from his heaping basket onto the conveyor belt.

"There a problem?" Mel had returned with Bryn, who began to load the bag with the watermelon into the cart.

"Wait, Bryn, no." She hated, hated this. "I—I brought the wrong card with me. I thought there was money in this account but I guess not." She turned to the cashier. "I'm so sorry—"

"Nah, nah," Mel said. "I'll pay for it."

"But, I—" She stopped. She couldn't refuse him. Like with Seth, she'd swallow her pride and let Mel pay for the sake of her kids. "Thank you. I'll pay you back."

"You bet," Mel said, already handing his card over to the cashier.

Seth's brother seemed to think she would. But how, when she didn't have a cent to her name? She went cold at a sudden thought. What if Mel told Seth about paying for the groceries? If Seth confronted her, she'd have to lie, and if he could already read her face, he wouldn't believe her. Despite him stating that he felt she was right for Matt, who in their right mind would allow a mom to keep a child she couldn't support?

Especially a child he liked.

Especially when he could arrive at the exact time the caseworker was due tomorrow and expose the absolute truth.

ONE LOOK AT Alexi when she returned from the grocery store, and Seth knew something was wrong. Sure, she was all smiles as she cut the watermelon into triangular slabs for the kids, but from where he stood at the kitchen entrance, something in the high pitch of her voice, her darting from drawer to dish to sink as if on a timer, and the hardest to take, the way her eyes dodged contact with his, put him on edge.

Mel must've said something, though Seth had no idea what. Nothing about Seth's record. Mel wasn't a model of discretion but even he knew that some lines weren't to be crossed. Probably made some buffoon remark that had made Alexi uncomfortable.

He hadn't asked her out, had he?

Might explain why Mel had left within minutes of their return, saying he needed to pick up a few things for the Lakers-on-the-Go event tonight. Seth had told Mel to start without him because he was too busy at the house. Alexi had insisted he attend, said she'd manage the rest, and said it all while looking everywhere but at him.

Uh-huh. He pushed his shoulder off the frame of the kitchen entrance and turned to the bedroom to install the bifold doors when Matt caught his eye. The boy's look was intense, his focus switched to Alexi and then narrowed on him again. Matt's meaning was unmistakable.

"Hey, Alexi," Seth said, "I could do with some help putting up the closet doors when you're done here."

"Oh. I, uh, I…"

"Never mind. I can always ask Matt."

Full, blazing eye contact there. "Fine."

Now that he had her alone in the same room (Callie sat in the hallway, hosting a watermelon tea party with her stuffies), the finicky bifolds killed any chance of a friendly chat.

Seth shoved the door's top metal peg into the sliding bracket. "Hated these things when I lived here, and my feelings haven't changed."

Alexi didn't answer, occupied with easing the bottom post into the floor bracket without popping out the top peg. This was their fifth attempt.

He felt the door make a satisfying give as it dropped into place. "Finally. I'll keep holding it and you rotate the peg to lift the door up."

Alexi's mouth flattened with concentration, as she contorted her body to see under the door. Her T-shirt rose to expose the naked curve of her waist. It didn't take much imagination to see how that curve trailed up to other rounder, softer curves.

"Got it," she said.

Seth shot his attention back to the top of the door. "Good. You hold the door here and I'll get this last peg into the spring."

It took a flat screwdriver and three attempts but the snick of it snapping into place was like opening a tab on a beer can. Alexi reached for the other bifold door.

Enough was enough.

"Look, I'm sorry I played the Matt card, okay? But he gave me a look, like he wanted me to talk to you."

She tried to lift the door into place, obviously ignoring how impossible that was. "I don't know why he would've. You must've misinterpreted him."

That was a lie, and it burned him that she even tried to pull one over him. "Was it something Mel said? You can't listen to a word he says or it'll drive you nuts."

She met his eyes. "I like Mel. He never said anything wrong."

"What's the matter, then?"

"Nothing."

"No. There's something."

She gave up on the door, let its long hard

weight fall against her shoulder. She stared at the opposite wall. "Fine. There is. But it's none of your business."

Exact same words he'd used on himself the day he met her, and look how that had worked out for him. She was his business from the day she'd asked him to help with the house. "How about you tell me and let me decide?"

She pulled her gaze to his, her lake-colored eyes as bright as ever but rimmed with tired lines. "How about you help me with this door instead?"

He could've pushed her. Could've tracked down Matt and found out from him, but that would only prove he was someone she couldn't trust. And if there was one thing he wanted from her right now, it was her belief that he was there for her, no matter what she was hiding.

He reached for the door. "Okay. Let's do it."

CHAPTER NINE

ALEXI AND MATT might be off-limits for getting answers, but Mel definitely wasn't. Seth beelined for his brother the second he arrived at Stephensson's pasture, a couple miles west of town. Mel must've seen him coming, because by the time Seth had crossed the field he was standing ankle-deep in low-lying water, out of reach. "Hey, Seth, can you feed me more wire?"

Seth unwound wire, checking out the rest of the course as he did. It was all part of this evening's Lakers-on-the-Go event, a short one-mile obstacle course Seth and Mel had been working on between jobs the past few weeks. Seeing Matt's backyard matrix had spurred Seth to insert a few additions, additions that justified the waivers new members signed when joining the Lakers rec club. Barbless wire was stapled to staggered fence posts to form crisscross patterns, short wooden stakes with binder twine zigzagged at the top to give two feet of clearance, rubber tires were roped over the corner of a slough, square straw bales were stacked at the end of a relay race.

At the far end about half a football field away, Paul was teamed with a couple of regulars pouring water onto dirt in preparation for the final event in the obstacle course: a mud flat where participants were forced to roll under the overlying wire. The kids, in rubber boots and rain gear, were itching to start.

Seeing them made Seth drop the wire. "I forgot the prizes."

"Got 'em," Mel called. "Tim cards. Donated, too. Now, come on and help."

Seth picked up the wire. Mel was acting like an older brother. Made things seem normal between them, like a family should be.

Seth saw a lot of family that evening. As he timed the relays, watched kids weave and dart through the course, forget where they were and double back amid calls from the sidelines, watched parents piggyback their squealing children as they stepped through tires or ducked under wires, watched the parents alone take the course, forget where they were and double back.

He wished Matt was there.

The boy would've been all smiles to see his crazy game played—and loved—by so many. Seth had planned to bring Matt and have them run the course together. Not as father and son. Just as…a man with a kid. Before Alexi had nixed any contact.

Then again, maybe he didn't want Matt here. A few people here knew that Lakers-on-the-Go was a front for his community service requirement. Last thing he needed was for Matt to learn that the man he wanted for a father was a criminal.

By the time the game was finished, prizes awarded and the field taken down, it was nearly ten. Seth drove back into town with the lights on.

"Good of Mr. Stephensson to lend us his pasture," Mel said, swirling the last of the melted ice coffee in the take-out cup.

"I guess," Seth replied. "Good choice." Mel was in charge of venue booking. That was the deal the two of them had struck when his community service sentence was served. Mel seemed to think he had to help with every bit of work, despite Seth explaining over and over that his interference cost him hours he could clock against his sentence. Then again, he was nearly done. Thirteen hours left after tonight. A thought occurred to Seth. "You're not still thinking about buying that place?"

Mel hitched himself in his seat. "Nope. Given up on thinking about it."

"Good." Seth reached the intersection marking the town line, the brightness of his headlights diffused as he passed under the glow from the street-lights.

"You know," Mel began, "it's been twenty years…"

"Don't tell me to get over it. I was sixteen when it happened."

"And I," Mel said, his slow, easy voice going as low and hard as Seth had ever heard it, "was thirty. And let me tell you that a grown son feels the loss of a dad no less than a kid. I should know. I lost one when I was ten and then our dad."

Their mom and Mel had never talked about his real dad. It was a kind of unspoken pact among the entire family not to mention him, so Seth was quiet when he said, "I didn't know your first dad died."

"He didn't, but might as well have." Mel gusted out a growly kind of sigh. "Anyway, enough. You don't want to talk about what happened twenty years and I don't want to talk about what happened forty years ago."

"Fair enough," Seth said and waited a couple of respectful moments before asking, "What did you do at Sobeys to get Alexi so upset?"

"Me? Nothing. I like her. And her kids, even if there's not a right one in the bunch."

"There's nothing wrong with Matt."

Mel twisted in his seat to look at Seth. "He's the oddest one."

"What do you mean by that? He's a good kid."

"They're all good kids. But he's got that stray-dog look about him. Never sure what he's thinking."

Seth straightened in his seat. "I don't know about that. Alexi said there's a problem because he's getting attached to me."

"Why's that a problem?"

Seth tended to agree but he gave Alexi's line. "Because she's trying to adopt him and it'll look bad with the caseworker if it's seen that the boy's getting attached to someone who's not intending to be part of his life. She needs to prove that she can give him stability."

"Nobody more stable than you."

"I'm a bachelor and the handyman and I haven't known them for more than a month.

Not to mention my record, which she knows nothing about."

"Still, you'd think she has more problems when it comes to stability than having you around."

Now they were getting somewhere. "What do you mean?"

Mel flipped open an empty donut box and began to collect the loose sprinkles on his fingertip. "You ever wonder where she gets the money to live if she's at home with the kids all the time?"

Seth had, but decided it was none of his business. "Maybe she's got life insurance. No idea."

"Anyway, it got me thinking after I ended up paying for the groceries today."

It was a good thing they'd pulled into the underground parking of their apartment because Seth lost total concentration at the wheel. "What?"

"Her card was declined, so I paid for them. You passed our parking stall, you know."

Seth threw the truck into Reverse, struggling to recall what was in the two bags. "There couldn't be more than fifty bucks' worth."

"Thirty-four, twelve. To be exact," Mel

said. "She said she'd pay me back, not that I care if she does. Just worried that she can't pay other people, is all."

That explained her sourness. Money problems would worry anyone. Especially if four kids depended on you. What it didn't explain was why she didn't tell him when she must've known Mel wouldn't keep it a secret. She'd already asked him for his time, why not money? If she didn't have anyone else, why wouldn't she turn to him?

"You might want to finish parking," Mel suggested, and Seth eased forward. "Just letting you know, seeing as how you've taken an interest in her."

"Not in the way you think."

"You mean I got a chance, then?"

Seth was about to tell his brother exactly how unlikely that was when he saw Mel's grin.

"Yep," Mel said, "you're interested in exactly the way I thought."

Seth could explain a hundred different ways how wrong Mel's thinking was but when something got stuck in his head, there was no way to budge it.

When Mel got out, Seth kept the truck idling. "I'll be back later."

Mel's grin was still plastered in place. "Tell Alexi not to worry, that you'll figure something out." He closed the truck door before Seth could answer. Not that one was forthcoming.

Seth first parked at his bank and withdrew his maximum daily limit. Only when he pulled the thick stack of twenties from the ATM, a stack with real weight, did he see he'd become an idiot for Alexi.

ALEXI MEANT TO bring in the laundry she'd draped along the deck railing. She meant to set up her sewing equipment downstairs to make it appear as if her business was operational. She meant to bake banana bread to offer the caseworker the next day. She meant to unpack the bakeware so she could actually bake the banana bread.

But when all sound had muted to only the soft breathing of four sleeping children, to the hum of the new fridge and creak and whirr of the old rotating fan, and to the murmur of friends around a neighbor's fire pit, Alexi could not move.

Hot and tired to her core, she slumped down against the side of the kitchen island facing the back door. The fan, as it swiveled, cuffed her damp face with gentle, warm air.

She should have a shower and go to bed.

Yeah, right. She'd lie there and wonder how to feed and house her kids.

She opened her phone to Richard's picture. He smiled at her as always. He didn't frown, cross his arms, point at her bruises, question her, rescue her child, buy her a coffee, tell her she was a good mother, fix her home or ask her to tell him what was wrong after taking one look at her when she'd come back from the grocery store, his voice low and his face creased with worry. She'd wanted to unburden herself on Seth so badly her chest had hurt.

"Richard," she began and stopped. For the first time in a year, she had nothing to tell him.

Nothing more to feel. This was nothing other than the picture of a dead man she loved.

She felt pain as acute as when he'd first died. She was losing him again, this time her need for him as her daily sustenance. If she could no longer draw solace from him, then who?

Yes, she had the kids but their love existed

on a different plane. It wasn't that solid, intimate pact of two people taking on the world together.

A little like what she and Seth had, working together to give Matt a home. Except she was using him, something she sensed people had done all his life, and who wouldn't? He was the generous type who deserved more than she could give him, which right now was absolutely nothing.

She should've pursued an income more seriously the past year. Instead she'd pocketed the cash pooled by Richard's coworkers at the oil company. They'd been hugely generous. Almost Richard's yearly salary in cold hard cash. But there'd been a funeral to pay for. Van repairs. Rent, food, the usuals. No life insurance, and no income other than the few hundred dollars here and there from Little Wonders.

Besides, where would the kids have gone if she'd been working? She couldn't put Callie in day care. It would've destroyed her already fragile emotional state. Not to mention Bryn and his rigid routines. Or Matt and his tendency to bolt. Amy might've been okay but only if placed with the other kids, and how likely would that have been?

A quiet knock on the back door jerked her to attention, but before she could react, in walked Seth. He wore the same cargo pants as before, a green T-shirt and a blue baseball cap with the Lakers baseball logo. And he wore sneakers. She'd never seen him in anything other than his work boots. They made him more energized, more…alive. If that was possible, because whatever else Seth was, he was very much alive with eyes on her, for her.

She scrambled to her feet and then to her utter shame, she ran to him and he, as no small part of her knew he would, opened his arms and drew her in.

To be caught in his arms was a beautiful trap. He held her tight against his warmth, one arm around her waist matching their hips together, another across her back. She tucked her head against his neck and clung to him, and he let her, for how long she couldn't tell.

After a time, she began to order herself to step back, to break the hold. But it was like coming out of a deep sleep in the early morning.

It was Seth who loosened his hold and said softly against her hair, "Mel told me what happened."

She lifted her head from the warm bank of

his shoulder. "I never meant for any of this to happen."

His hold tightened. "We never do."

Her throat thickened with tears. She swallowed. For what she had to say next, it was only right that she break free of his arms but she couldn't bring herself to do it. Instead she braced herself against his chest and whispered, "I understand the position this puts you in. And I understand how you are totally justified in doing something about it, what with the caseworker coming tomorrow—"

Seth's arms dropped away from her. She hadn't realized how much of her weight he was bearing until his withdrawal caused her to stumble forward a step, nearly falling against him again.

"Why do you think I should do something about it?" His voice was harsh, suspicious. She floundered about her tired mind, searching for the key point he seemed to think she knew.

"Because of Matt...you like him...you wouldn't want him in a place where he wasn't taken care of...so you'd do something about it."

He shoved his hands in his front pockets and nodded slowly. "You read me right. You know, on the way here, I was thinking how stupid coming over was, but then I opened the door and…you came to me. It felt great. You and me and no other reason."

Alexi caught her breath. Exactly what she'd lost with Richard. She looked at Richard on her phone.

Seth snorted. "Yeah. Him. Why else would I be here except to do the job he no longer can?"

Alexi shook her head. He wasn't making any sense. Then he pulled a wad of cash out of his pocket and tossed it on the island, the green twenties splaying across the surface. She stared at the cash, at him.

"Are you giving me money?" She had to state the obvious because it was so incredible.

"Yes, I am. Isn't that what you wanted me to do?" He'd shoved his hands back into his pockets where she could see they were balled into fists.

She fisted her own hands into her tangled hair. "No, it isn't. I didn't want you to do anything. I'd only hoped that if Mel told you, you'd think it was none of your business and let it go."

"You think I'd ignore the fact you can't pay for food?"

"No, no, no! I didn't think you would. I thought you'd tell the caseworker because you wouldn't want Matt to live with me because I couldn't provide for him. I was hoping you wouldn't, that you wouldn't care. But—" she gestured at the fan of twenties "—of course, you do. I didn't think you'd show it this way," she finished weakly.

It was his turn to look confused. "So you think that I'd turn you in, force Matt to lose the home he chose because you'd run into money troubles?"

How had she not seen it his way? "All I'm saying is that I could understand why you would."

"Then you don't understand me at all, Alexi."

He was at the door before she stopped him. She reached for his hand but it was with the hand that held the phone, so only her last two fingers could touch his. "Wait, Seth, wait. Let me explain."

He waited but she couldn't find the right words, like when she talked to Richard. She had a million for Seth, all in the wrong order. "I'm sorry. I don't understand. I don't understand how anyone can give so much, and expect so little in exchange."

There was the slightest hesitation, and then he took her hand in his and raised the phone so that the glowing image of Richard was beside his face.

"How about in exchange," he said softly, his expression both tender and challenging, "you set down this phone and kiss me?"

SETH BRACED FOR Alexi's reaction. She set the phone on the kitchen table, screen down. She came to him, not in a rush like when he'd opened the door, but slowly. Her glorious blue eyes, dark in the shadowed room, were pinned to his, and she settled in front of him. He banded his arms around her. She cupped his face in her hands and brought his lips to hers. A peck only, she retreated, the swell of her lower lip all that touched his mouth, and then she returned, her kiss deepening.

He kissed her long and thoroughly. When continuing meant taking it to a level he was pretty sure she'd no intention of going, he pulled away and then dived back to her kiss-swollen lips for another taste. He eased away and returned twice more before he could stop. Not wanting to break contact completely, he wrapped his hands around hers.

Her gaze dipped to his chest. "Thanks," she whispered.

Now was not the time to tell her how much he detested her constant gratitude but he was curious. "Why thank me?"

"Because I can't help feeling that once again you've given me something."

He chose to believe she meant the kiss and not the money. "I think we both came out winners," he said.

Her gaze slanted toward the phone and his hands squeezed involuntarily on hers. She said quickly, "I've had a hard time letting go."

He could almost hear her searching for the right words to tell him what they'd just shared was going nowhere.

"No deadline on missing someone," he said, all the while wanting to wing the phone against the wall just to wipe the smile off good old Richard's face.

"Yes and…only… I want you to know…"

He didn't want her to stumble on trying to find a nice way to end what had barely started. He stepped out of her touch, let his hands drop from her and pulled open the door.

"How about we don't say anything more

this evening so there's nothing more we'll need to fix?"

She raised her hand as if to stop him again, then froze. Her shoulders slumped. "Okay."

It was just as he'd been afraid of. A dead man still had her heart.

CHAPTER TEN

MARLENE THE CASEWORKER rolled in like a tank. A tank encased in sweatpants and a paisley peasant top. She mounted the stairs and from that vantage point, surveyed the kitchen, living room and down the hall to the bedrooms. She let loose a long, low whistle and then advanced in green high-top sneakers toward the bedrooms.

Alexi hurried after her, Callie cinched to her leg, all Alexi's prepared explanations scattering as she tried to keep pace. Marlene poked her head into the room Amy and Bryn shared and then turned right.

"This is his. Matt's, that is," Alexi babbled as Marlene took in the bed and chest of drawers minus the bottom drawer which Alexi remembered belatedly was being used for Callie's stuffies. "That's new carpeting. Laid yesterday so things are still in a bit of uphea—"

Alexi broke off as Marlene opened a closet

door, the bifold sticking in the track, so she gave it a sharp pull and out popped the entire door.

Alexi couldn't suppress a groan.

"Not my fault," Marlene said. "Bifold doors are the devil's work."

A woman after Seth's heart. Not that she was thinking of Seth or his heart or any of his body parts, for that matter. Marlene bowled past Alexi back up the hallway and then pounded down the stairs to the basement. Alexi trotted behind, as quickly as she could with Callie. Thankfully the other three were in the backyard.

Marlene powered around the basement, no doubt recording every little horror. The bank of unopened boxes. The scraps of pipes and boards from the renos. The bathroom with the missing toilet. Looping electrical wires from which dangled Amy's skipping rope tied into a noose. What had the kids been up to?

Another long low whistle, and Alexi with Callie were pressed to the wall as Marlene ascended to the kitchen. The second she entered, Matt came through the back door.

"Hello, I'm Marlene," she said as she eyed the kitchen table with the cake platter of banana muffins Alexi had risen to bake while dawn was still gray. "You Matt?"

"Uh, yeah." Matt sidled over to Alexi, his eyes round. Alexi smiled at him as if everything was just peachy.

Marlene took a seat and a muffin. "Here, have one," she said to Matt and pushed the plate toward him.

To Alexi, she said, "I know what you're up to with the muffins. You aren't the first one to use that trick. Let's face it, they'd have to be packed with hallucinogens not to make me see what a wreck of a house you're living in."

Matt stopped unpeeling the wrapper from his muffin. Brenda had never spoken this openly in front of Matt.

"Yes, certainly you caught us in a bit of a transition…" Alexi fumbled. "We've made… A number of improvements have been made… Look…a fridge and stove." As soon as the words were out, Alexi realized her mistake.

And so did Marlene. "You telling me," she said around her muffin, "that when you moved in there weren't any?"

Alexi waved her hand, aiming for nonchalance. "Oh, a few days. We adapted well. Life is all about adapting to circumstances. Isn't it?"

Could she sound more idiotic?

Marlene swept crumbs off her chest and stood, brushing more crumbs off her lap. "Looks as if you all adapted to living like rats."

She stood and walked to the fridge, opened its door, and again emitted her whistle. "Oo-whee…a regular Mother Hubbard cupboard in here." She turned to Alexi. "Please tell me you got more food than almond milk and watermelon around here."

Never had any caseworker gone through her stuff with such authoritative gusto. Marlene must be what Brenda had meant when she referred to the unsympathetic workers at the Red Deer office. In a way, she was the kind of caseworker Alexi wished she'd had when she was a kid in the system living with people who kept their fridge that empty all the time.

She'd packed everything, absolutely everything inside her Calgary pantry, so she was able to swing open its door and show all the baking essentials and dry stuffs like rice, beans, flour, sugar…the whole lot.

Marlene grunted and turned back to the fridge. "How about the freezer?"

No, no, no. Marlene slid open the drawer

and stared into the cold emptiness. "Not even a popsicle. What do you do for meat?"

"I just moved in last week," Alexi said, thinking fast. "I'm buying fresh until I source out a local supplier and get a side of beef. It's cheaper and healthier."

"Where will you keep it all? I didn't see a freezer in my travels around this disaster zone."

"It's still in storage," Alexi lied flat out. What else could she say? Marlene didn't pursue it, probably because she had too much else to occupy her thoughts.

"And you talked to your landlord about this state of emergency?"

"Landlady," Alexi said. "I've already been reimbursed for the rent, and I've been assured that the work will be finished in four to six weeks." She didn't add that the reimbursements and reassurances had come from the landlady's brother.

"Professionally?"

"Yes," Alexi said. If "professional" meant Seth received payment, then she'd placed a deposit last night—on his lips. She felt her cheeks heat at the memory and hoped her color wasn't visible to the eagle-eyed Marlene.

"He used to live in this house," Matt added, "so it's easy for him to fix it."

"Oh?" Marlene leaned against the island counter, all chummy-like, her broad back forming a wall between Alexi and Matt. "Used to live here? Before the renovations I take it?"

"He grew up in this house. Actually, he's lived here all his life, except for when he moved out," Matt carried on. "The landlady is his sister. He's fixing up the house because his sister won't."

Alexi slipped behind Matt to include herself in the caseworker's line of sight but not Matt's. "Not won't, can't. Lacks the skill. Other tradesmen—qualified tradesmen—completed the kitchen cabinetry and floor…" Alexi trailed off, realizing that once again enumerating the improvements only confirmed how substandard the place was at move-in.

"Looks to me the landlady's lacking in a lot of areas," Marlene opined and turned to Matt. "Hey, can you get me my bag? Left it at the door. It's the one packed with bricks."

Matt scooted a look at Alexi, who shooed him off with her hand. She resisted the urge to go with him. "Can I get you anything? Tea? Coffee?"

A hopeful look appeared on the caseworker's face. "You don't have Dr Pepper hidden away, by chance?"

"Uh, no."

"Too bad. Something else quick and easy and legal."

"I could get you a slushie," Matt volunteered as he entered the kitchen, dragging the bag, black and fat like a potbellied pig, across the rough boards. "I can get whatever color you want."

"A slushie? Haven't tackled one of those in a dog's age. Thanks," Marlene said, taking her bag from Matt. "Sure, get me one, please. Something green and glowing."

Matt was dispatched to Mac's, Alexi making sure that Marlene saw her peel off a twenty from Seth's stack of cash.

After the door thudded shut behind him, Marlene said, "You're not worried about him running off?"

For the first time in the visit, Alexi experienced real fright. Of course, Marlene had read the file. The woman might dress like a flood victim but she knew her job.

Alexi dropped into the chair across from

Marlene and pulled Callie into her lap. She needed to pay attention—better attention—to her every word from here on in.

"He'll come back," she said, and then halted at any further explanation. Everything she'd said up to now only seemed to dig herself a deeper hole. She repeated, "He'll come back."

Alexi glanced out the window at Bryn and Amy. Unaware that company had arrived, they sat in the wading pool, their heads bent over a collection of floating leaves. Who knew what that was all about? She could only hope it would last until Marlene left. Callie shifted and reached for the bowl of pink Play-Doh, her go-to comfort activity.

From her bag, Marlene pulled out a long triplicate form, dated it and got to the point. "You got problems, Alexi Docker."

No kidding, Alexi nearly snapped back. Instead, she unleashed her prepared response. "Things look worse than they really are. Admittedly, the renos were unexpected but there is a plan in place and within weeks it should be better. I'm sure you'd agree it's not unusual for renos to take longer than planned."

"My point, exactly. What I don't get is why

you moved into the house when it looked even worse than it does now."

Alexi was glad Marlene didn't know that there was once no water. "I saw it before the renovations and I wasn't advised that it was undergoing renovations at the time I made the agreement."

"Didn't you have some kind of walk-through?"

Why was the woman fixated on the house? "I'd thought there was going to be one but the landlady was out of town. We had a mix-up with the move-in dates."

"Why did you decide to relocate here?"

"I researched the area, and it had what my family needed."

"Researched? You mean you hadn't been to this part of the country before. No family, no friends?"

"No."

"You saw this place and decided to leave Calgary and come here?"

Alexi made the mistake of hesitating, and Marlene pounced.

"Did you even see it before coming here?"

Callie was having trouble flattening the dough so Alexi helped her, her hands over Callie's little ones. "I saw pictures."

"So you never physically saw this place before moving in?"

"No."

Marlene wrote a line in sprawling black ink.

"There a reason for that? You had a job starting immediately?"

"No. I work from home."

The pen was poised over a blank section. "That's right. Little Wonders. Tell me about that."

"I sell plush toys online."

Marlene fixed Alexi with a shrewd look. "You make a living from that?"

Alexi said what she had to say. "I do."

"You realize you'll have to back that up at some point?"

Callie was pressing the cupcake cutter into the dough but not nearly hard enough. Again, Alexi helped, hand over hand. "I do."

"So why did you decide to leave Calgary?"

Explaining herself to Seth had been so much easier. He'd accepted her explanation that she'd gone along with Matt's gut instinct. Marlene would think her an airhead.

Alexi tugged the extra Play-Doh from the edges of the cutter. "As you know, if you've read the files from the past year, Matt has bolted several times since the death of my husband. He could no longer stand being in the house. He told me that. The place was emotionally damaging to him."

"Why not get another place in the neighborhood, then?"

"Matt wanted to leave and come here. As you probably know from his file, Matt can be very decisive."

"You do everything he tells you to do?"

"I listen to everything he tells me."

"There are plenty of towns like this around Alberta. Why did he choose this one?"

She couldn't tell Marlene that it was all done on the gut feeling of a boy with a history of running on instinct. "I don't know. Maybe because he once lived here for a time?"

Marlene grunted and tapped her pen against her pad. Tap, tap, tap. She righted her pen, ready to note something, halted and returned to her tapping. Clearly Marlene didn't like what she was hearing. She grunted again, except this time she flew her pen into action. She scribbled a note in the margin and drove a hard circle around it. Then she set down her pen.

"Okay. Let me get this straight. You leave

the home you and the kids have lived in for the past five years to come to live in a dive in a town you know nothing about to make toys, which you could do just about anywhere. Because your kid said so."

She leaned forward, her heavy breasts pressing on her notes. "This is the thing. You don't seem like a nut job. Your previous caseworker makes you sound like a saint. Only, I'm seeing a whole lot of things that don't add up. Unless—" she leaned even closer "—you insert a man into the equation."

Alexi squeezed the Play-Doh until it oozed out the bottom of her hands. "I'm not sure what you're talking about."

Marlene cocked an eyebrow at Alexi's Play-Doh. "I think you do but let's get explicit. You and the handyman. What's the story?"

Alexi plucked the tacky gunk from between her fingers. "There's nothing between us."

Marlene sighed. "Uh, right. The landlady's brother does all this work out of the kindest of his heart."

"Actually, yes, he does."

Marlene gave her a skeptical look. "Uh-

huh. Listen, do you intend to have a relationship with him?"

"Of course not," Alexi said, and instantly
wished she'd said nothing. It sounded so lame.

Marlene flipped to a clean page. "Does
this handyman have a name?"

"Uh… Seth Greene. He owns a roofing
company in town. Greene-on-Top."

Marlene started to scribble like mad, line
and lines pouring down, completely dispro-
portionate to Alexi's dribble of info. The
caseworker clearly didn't believe her. Alexi
strived to appear unconcerned as she handed
Callie little brown Play-Doh bits, the chocolate chips for the pink cupcake. Except she
dropped the same brown bit three times her
hand was shaking so bad. Had Marlene seen?

"Here, your turn. Let me watch you do it,"
Alexi said to Callie, and slipped her hands underneath the table. Alexi searched her brain
to think of the right words to tell Marlene.

Just as she'd searched—and failed—to
find the right words last night with Seth.
Their kiss had been…miraculous. At least
for her. She'd lost herself with Seth, and yes,
her gaze had strayed to the phone, as if she'd
arrived back from a journey and was center-
ing herself on an old familiar object.

She missed Richard but what she felt for Seth was real and new and important, yet at the same time of such incredibly poor timing. Nothing could happen between them until Matt's adoption was final. And who knew when that might be?

The Beatles' "A Hard Day's Night" went off on Marlene's phone. "And that," said Marlene, shutting her phone off, "is a wrap." She began shoving her papers together into her bag. "Sorry, I have to hurry, otherwise the Blue Jays will start without me."

"So where do we go from here?"

Marlene spared her a glance. "Nowhere fast. I need to shuffle paper around. But I can tell you right now, there'll be a few more visits before I'm done."

Alexi blew out her breath. So much for watching her words. Marlene had also watched. And judged.

At the door, Marlene paused. "Can you believe it? I'm leaving before I get my slushie. Funny how that worked out. I guess the boy gets a treat for all his trouble."

SETH CALLED ALEXI from his room after nine that night, having taken a shower and pulled on a clean T-shirt and shorts. He'd logged in a full twelve-hour day on a hot roof, and not one of those hours went by that he hadn't thought about Alexi's interview. He'd held off calling until now because he hadn't wanted Mel or Ben or a supplier or any of the four kids to interrupt.

He wanted to talk just the two of them like last night, no competition. Of course, talking to her on the phone meant Richard would be there, too. Still, in this rivalry with her dead husband it had to count for something that he, at least, had a pulse.

He stared down from his third-floor window at the traffic, at how the setting sun aimed harsh light off windshields, walls, the deck railing. The phone rang six times, and he had begun to wonder if maybe she was calling it an early night when she answered.

"Hey there," he replied. "How did it go today?"

"Oh. Okay." Her voice was low and tired and most definitely not okay.

"What happened? Do you want me to come over?"

"No!" He could hear her exhale. "Here's how it went. Matt said there was a handyman— you—helping to fix up the place, which was fine. The caseworker needed to know something was being done. Then it came out that the handyman was the landlady's brother... and Marlene—the caseworker—began connecting dots. In her mind, why would I come to a new town into a house I hadn't seen and needs work unless I knew someone already? And why else would you volunteer your time to fix up a house, especially one you grew up in, unless you were involved with me? I told her the truth about why you're helping but, Seth, you have to admit the truth sounds weak."

Except he'd spent the last few weeks believing it, and he needed this caseworker to believe it, too. "She thinks it's weak to help out a widow and her kids?"

"Seth—" She stopped, and when she restarted, it was with great care. "You have to know how thankful I am for you. But you are one in a million. In this day and age, to this extent...yeah...I don't blame Marlene for thinking there's an ulterior motive."

There was an ulterior motive. He did want something out of this. Last night's kiss proved that.

She'd nixed that idea.

"The thing is...the thing is that—" he could hear her draw in her breath "—I might have given Marlene the impression that there was something between us. I mean not now. But that there will be."

The sun shifted down to an angle straight into Seth's eyes. Blinded, he turned away from the window. Blinded and blindsided. "What?"

"She asked if I intended to pursue a relationship with you after the adoption and I said no, but I don't think she was convinced."

It hurt that she talked about her rejection of him with a perfect stranger. He blinked. "Yeah, I got the point last night. So why wasn't she convinced as much as I was?"

"Because…because I think Marlene saw the truth."

Seth had never felt more confused. "Which is what?"

A few excruciating beats passed and then she said, "I want us to be together."

He actually experienced vertigo as he stumbled and dropped to his bed, the bounce of the mattress throwing his balance off further. He closed his eyes against the motion.

Alexi wanted what he wanted. Only—and the realization spun his head faster—not if she knew the truth about him.

"Seth? Seth." Alexi's voice pierced through his senses. "Are you there?"

"Alexi," he said, eyes still shut. "You didn't mention my name to the caseworker, did you?"

Something in his tone must've struck her, because her answer was quick and nervous. "Yes, of course. She asked for it. I said you owned a company. You were well-known in town. What, Seth? What's going on?"

"She'll run a background check on me, right? A criminal record check?"

"Yes. That's standard. Seth, tell me. What's going on?"

Seth opened his eyes to see the perfect white of the ceiling. The apartment had been completely repainted before he and Mel had moved in. He still remembered the smell of the fresh paint, the carpets so clean and new his feet left prints, the appliances spick-and-span like no one had ever touched them.

A brand-new start.

Except he'd continued to work at the same job with his brother, who still roomed with him. Everyone still knew him. Some like Ben had known him since he was a kid, others like Paul for less but still far too well.

He could barely push the words out past the dry lump in his throat. "Alexi, I'm coming over. I've got something you need to hear."

CHAPTER ELEVEN

"POSSESSION OF A controlled substance with intent to sell?"

It was the third time Alexi had asked the same question since he'd made her sit at the kitchen table and he'd delivered his news from his seat at the far opposite end. For the third time, Seth gave the same answer, "Yes."

Her face contorted with disbelief, hurt... betrayal.

It was that last emotion that made him blurt, "For what it's worth, I didn't do it."

Her face contorted more. "You're innocent?"

"Not on paper. I confessed to it but I didn't do it. I took the blame instead of Connie."

"Connie? Your sister? She was trafficking?"

"Yes and no. Cocaine and meth. A few grams of each. She was doing a favor to get the real trafficker off her back. It turned out he knew the police were going to show up.

He set her up, except I was there, too. I'd come along in case things went wrong. I was expecting a fight or a knife, not the cops. So I passed off it was me because at that point in her career, Connie didn't need a criminal record."

"But you did?"

Something in her tone made Seth pause. Did she think he'd made a boneheaded move? Because not a day had gone by since then that he hadn't wondered the same thing. "I knew it would go easier on me. It did. I guess. I was released on my own recognizance for the first year until my court date, and then the judge just handed me two hundred and fifty hours of community service, is all. Me and Mel, we were already running Lakers-on-the-Go so the court allowed me to count one hundred hours toward my service. And Paul has tracked my time, but everyone just thinks he's there for the fun. Which he is."

"Lakers-on-the-Go?"

"Yeah, it's a club me and Connie and Mel came up with two, three years back in the summer. We set up a Facebook page, then we send a call out on Tuesday for what's happening Thursday, and everyone shows up at wherever. The lake, the ball diamonds, school yard."

That first summer of Lakers-on-the-Go had been one of the best summers of his life. He'd never felt closer to Connie and Mel, especially Connie. Then the druggies had gotten their hooks back into her and not a month later, he was arrested. And nobody had had a good relationship with her. "I've been running my community hours through it the past year."

"But if Connie was there, didn't they know it wasn't you?"

Yes, they had. Paul, tight-lipped and cynical, had glared at Connie the whole time Seth talked. "I confessed. She didn't."

Alexi's expression transitioned into outrage. "That was a real scummy thing for her to let you do."

"She was going somewhere. She was accepted into nursing school, you know. Had a stable relationship. Was actually turning things around for herself. I figured it would be worth it if she kept it up."

He couldn't go on. Every time he thought about what had happened next, it made him sick, and his stomach already wasn't doing too well.

"But she didn't," Alexi prompted.

Might as well lay it all out there. "No. She let it all go. Withdrew from nursing school. Spent her savings. Cheated on her boyfriend so he tossed her out. She says I backed the wrong horse. Thing is, Connie's bright. Brighter than me and Mel put together. Growing up, she could do my homework, and she's four years younger. I swear sometimes she did it to spite me."

Alexi snorted. "That's a lot of spite."

"You haven't met her."

"Maybe I should. Just to see the look on her face when I punch it."

The pure venom in her voice startled Seth. He'd expected her anger to be directed toward him, not *for* him. It made what he had to do now even worse.

"Problem is damage control," he said. "Now that the caseworker knows—or will know soon enough—you're going to have to come up with a good explanation."

Alexi took up a clump of Play-Doh and began to pinch and poke it. "I'll tell her the truth."

"It's like you said, the truth sounds weak."

"How would I know you had a criminal record? We've only known each other for two weeks."

"Yeah, but that's not what she thinks."

Her hands stopped over her work, and she lifted her blues eyes to his. "Why didn't you tell me, Seth?" she said softly. "Given me a heads-up, so I knew to avoid talking about you? I could've warned Matt. You knew how important it was to me and...I thought it was important to you."

"It *is* important to me. I honestly didn't think it would come to this."

She tore off a piece of Play-Doh so hard it came away with a short plucking sound. "No, Seth. Don't lie. You knew it could come to this. You just didn't want it to come to this."

Not since he'd viewed his father's dead body, wearing a suit and tie, in the coffin, had truth hit him so hard that he felt winded. He had not wanted this and yet once again, by his doing, it had come.

"I guess... I guess..." He took a breath and kept going. "I knew that telling you about me would blow any chance of us being together. And I wanted that very much. Too much."

She lifted her face to his and for a split second, he was granted a sight of how much she wanted him. Then her mouth thinned and her gaze dropped. "Well, you're right. You and I—" and now it was her turn to draw breath "—are through."

She'd made the cut he thought he'd have to do, what he'd doubted he had the strength for.

He creaked his mouth open to speak but as halting as her speech was she beat him to it.

"There's still the question of the house," she said. "You can't come here anymore."

Cut.

"I've got the numbers of the contractors so I'll contact them if necessary."

Cut.

"And please don't pay for anything. Payment implies assuming responsibility, and responsibility implies attachment."

Cut. Completely off.

He bowed his head, and at last got his mouth working enough to say, "I don't know what to say or do, Alexi."

Her mouth twisted downward. "There's nothing you can do, Seth. Nothing I want you to do."

He nodded, searched for the right thing to say. All he could come up with was, "I'm sorry, Alexi. I'm really sorry."

Perhaps because the memory of his conviction lay freshly exposed, Seth's mind reeled back to a time weeks after his sentencing. Connie had shown up at the house, dead drunk, blubbering about how sorry she was. *Sorry, sorry, sorry*, she'd slurred on and on, gripping his shirtfront until he'd thought she'd tear it clear off him. He'd pried her away, set her down on a kitchen chair, feet from where he sat now, and told her to shut up.

Now, as he sat on the hard kitchen chair and waited for Alexi to hand him her own kind of verdict, he realized how wrong he'd been not to forgive Connie. He'd chosen to assume her crime, yet he'd resented it and stewed over it every day since then. He'd done it from duty, not love. Or maybe it had been love and he'd treated it like a duty. Either way, he made Connie carry a terrible burden these past two years.

Alexi fiddled and fiddled with whatever she was making with the Play-Doh, then finally spoke. "I know you are, Seth. And I know I'll forgive you. I might've already. But it doesn't change what we need to do."

Which was for him to once more get up and leave. He pushed back his chair, pressed both hands to the table and raised himself in a slow unfolding, his every muscle tight and unwilling.

He did the only thing he could do, what he should've done right from the start, and left her alone.

CHAPTER TWELVE

THE NEXT MORNING, Alexi tapped the submit button for the online government survey and waited for the results. They were as expected. She qualified for six different government subsidies, income support being the most significant.

She dropped her forehead to the hard edge of her phone. She'd never been on welfare. Never received a single government dime since she left the foster care system fifteen years ago. Even when Bryn received his diagnosis of autism, she resisted applying for support for children with disabilities.

She couldn't bear the questions, the paperwork, the interference. She'd done enough during the adoption process. But now...now there was no other choice.

But to go on welfare meant to accept that adopting Matt was at an end or a good long postponement. She couldn't see Marlene recommending adoption into a single-parent family on welfare with no prospects. Right now, she was an unfit mother.

Not just for Matt. For them all.

Matt appeared at her elbow. "I was thinking maybe I could go with the others around the block."

Matt, alone with them all? Callie, too? Her youngest loved being in her stroller, but if Bryn got to be a handful, then what?

"How about Bryn stays home with me while you three go out?" Alexi suggested.

Thankfully, they all agreed to that, especially Bryn because he got to help her make pizza crust. Oddly, kneading the dough grounded her. Doing one good thing for someone she loved and who loved her for doing it lifted her into action.

She made a list and got busy. Was it true, she asked *The Red Deer Advocate*, that they were looking for newspaper carriers? "Oh, you are! Yes, in Spirit Lake… Oh, filled… Sure, put me on your waiting list."

"Hi there, I'm looking to start a home day care through your agency…Yes, I have four kids. Three are school-age…A single mom… I rent…Okay, I see. Well, thank you anyway for your time."

Once again, Alexi pressed her head to the

phone. Now what? Maybe she could work at a call center. For eleven bucks an hour. That wouldn't work out to much more than she was earning now through her stuffie business and she'd have less free time with the kids. She certainly couldn't afford child care unless she applied for government child support, which brought her back to square one.

Bryn wandered over. "Mom, where's everyone else?"

She checked the time. Nearly an hour had gone by. Where were the kids?

No, not this, not today.

As if on cue, Matt burst through the door with the others right behind. "Mom, we got fifty-five dollars! Fifty-five!"

Sure enough, a clutch of bills—blue, purple, one green—were waving in her face. "How did—"

"Found them," Matt said quickly. "Over there, on the grassy place, along the path. It must've dropped out of someone's pocket. But if we left it there someone else might take it, right?"

Alexi gave Matt a long hard stare and stayed silent. She'd used it to great effect first on Richard and then the children. It had never failed her. But Matt stared right back with his solid brown eyes until finally she sighed. "Congratulations, all. You'll have to think carefully about how to spend it."

"Oh, no," Matt said, handing the money to her. "You have it. We don't need anything."

That's when Alexi knew for sure Matt was lying. What kid gave up perfectly good money to their parent? Money they didn't believe they deserved. She looked at the others, and read the guilt there.

"Okay. I'm going to ask some questions and I want straight yes-no answers. Understand?"

They exchanged looks.

"Amy, did you or Matt steal this money from anyone?"

"No!" She said it with such indignation that Alexi knew it was the truth.

"Did you take it from someone's property?"

She frowned and glanced to Matt. "I don't think so."

"What do you mean, you don't know? Was it lying on someone's property or just in front?"

Amy's frown cleared. "No, it wasn't."

"Matt, do you know who this money belongs to?"

Matt looked her in the eye. "Honestly, the only one I can think it belongs to is you."

There was some question she was failing to ask but it completely eluded her. She'd have to take them at their word. "All right. I'll keep an eye on the money."

They all cheered, even Bryn. Alexi almost smiled herself. The kids, except for Callie, headed out the back door to play. Alexi lifted her youngest onto her lap. "So, Callie, what do you think Mommy can do that people will give her money for?"

Callie surprised Alexi by actually answering. "Look pretty."

Yes, there were jobs where that was helpful. Unfortunately, she didn't qualify for them. You have supermodel eyes, Richard had told her. You could do makeup commercials, he'd said. But pretty eyes wouldn't cut it.

By lunch, she hadn't gotten much further. As she threw together peanut butter sandwiches, carrots and water-weakened juice, she forced herself to act normal, to smile every time she sensed Matt looking in her direction.

Whether or not he had talked to the others, Alexi didn't know, but that afternoon the kids were as good as gold. While Callie napped, the rest played together outside, and after Callie woke, Matt offered to take her and Amy out for another walk. Bryn wanted to come, too, and he looked so eager that Alexi relented.

"But just for a half hour. To the playground, a short play and then back again. Understood?"

As soon as they were gone, Alexi second-guessed herself. But the playground was less than two blocks away with only one street to cross. Matt was five months from turning twelve. He could handle himself. Besides, she had to begin to trust Bryn at some point.

Still, she stared blankly at her computer until thirty minutes later, they all returned, safe and sound, skipping into the backyard. She came out and leaned on the deck railing.

"How was your time?" she called down.

"Great!"

"Great!"

"We had so much fun!"

"I looked pretty!" Callie said.

What was it with her saying that?

She was setting out a supper of pizza and veggies when Seth called.

"Where are the kids?" No preamble, no

hesitation, like nothing had happened last night.

"Out back. Why?"

"Mrs. Pinkster, the lady five doors down from you, calls me this afternoon. Asks me if I know the family that's moved into the house. Apparently, your kids knocked on her door today. Told her that due to their various physical and mental disabilities would she care to donate whatever she could spare."

Alexi groaned.

"Also," he continued, "apparently you have brain cancer and need money for treatments."

This made her almost choke in surprise.

"Mrs. Pinkster asked if I knew anything about your situation, and if there was anything she could do. After the kids left, they carried on to the sixth door down."

Callie's comment about looking pretty now sounded degrading. It was horrible enough that she couldn't provide for her kids but that they knew and tried to help, and now the neighborhood knew… She hung her head.

"Alexi?"

"Yeah?"

"You don't have brain cancer, right?"

"No. Not yet, anyway."

Seth made a sound that could've passed for a short laugh or a grunt. "Alexi?"

She was about to answer but the front door opened to a woman in a pink minidress and pink stilettos and columns of sparkly bracelets that stretched halfway to her elbow on both arms. She was gorgeous. Gorgeous blond hair, gorgeous body, and a face that supermodels would envy...and just the oddest bit familiar.

Could her day get any worse?

"Hey, you must be Alexi. I'm—"

Alexi held up her hand. "I know who you are." Into the phone, she said, "I have to go. Your sister's here."

"TALKING TO SETH, I take it?" Connie swept up the stairs, as if—well—as if she owned the place.

Alexi ignored the question and asked one that seemed way more relevant. "To what do I owe the pleasure?"

Connie clicked on her heels into the kitchen, either not hearing or ignoring the question. Alexi bet it was the latter. After all, tit for tat. "Oh, wow. Look at the counters! I just knew this grain would rock."

She dropped her purse, a giant red thing

with gold clasps, on the island, and trailed her fancy nails along the surface. One, Alexi noted with glee, was broken. "And wow. Look at this fridge. Isn't it ah-mazing?"

She scooped a jar off the countertop and pushed on the ice spout and out clunked ice cubes. "Tons of houses have fridges like this. But really, isn't this totally decadent?" She opened the fridge. "Uh…okay…going for minimalism, eh?"

Why would anyone want to lift a finger for this self-absorbed woman, much less ruin years of his life?

Connie filled the jar with water from the sink and then held it up to the light from the window. She rattled the cubes. "Wow. Look at the patterns!" She set down the jar, stripped off one of her many glittery bracelets—she wore as many as some women owned—and slipped it over the rim of the jar.

Then with an affected regal walk, she came to Alexi, at the last moment, kneeling. What the…?

Connie held the water out to Callie. "Here you go, sweet pea."

Alexi was about to explain about the acute shyness, the public term she used for Callie's trauma, when Callie broke her grip on

Alexi's leg and took the jar, her dark hands tight on the clear glass. She squatted with it and began to play with the chunky beads on the bracelet.

Connie laughed and stood. "Look, a fashionista in the making. A girl after my own heart."

Alexi could only stare at the small miracle Seth's miserable sister had performed. "I... Callie doesn't usually open up to strangers."

Connie shrugged. "Bling is a great icebreaker." She glanced at Alexi's bare arms and hands. "Of course, it's not for everyone."

Connie began to play with the clasp on her bag. "The thing is, I talked with Seth a few weeks ago, and I explained to him that I was experiencing problems getting the work completed."

"Every 'wow' you see here is because of him."

"Yeah, well, it's still definitely not up to par. I take full responsibility for that. I will clearly have to bring it up to standard before I could possibly let you or anybody live here. So, the thing is, I don't think we can continue with our agreement."

It took Alexi a long moment to register

what the world's nastiest landlady was getting at. "Are you evicting me?"

"No!" Connie said. "Evicting implies you've done something wrong. You haven't. More like giving you notice." She flicked the clasp open and shut, open and shut. "Effective immediately."

It was a good thing Callie wasn't leaning on her, because Alexi's legs gave way and she had to grip the island for support. "You can't do that. I've paid rent."

"To the end of the month, which is like, in two weeks. So technically you've got until then."

"You've got to give me more notice than that." What were the legal requirements exactly? She and Richard had rented their place in Calgary, a quiet exchange of checks and routine maintenance that had continued for nearly a decade.

"Yes, for this month but the agreement was you had to pay first and last month's rent at the time of move-in. And you didn't, so technically, you're behind. That gives me grounds."

"I thought it was arranged between you and Seth that he'd do the renovations in exchange for you waiving the rent."

"I don't have the paperwork for that." Connie smirked. "Do you?"

Like last night with Seth, Alexi had a nearly unstoppable urge to punch Connie in the face. Hard to believe that this was the same woman who'd had a breakthrough with Callie not five minutes ago. "What if I pay you right now? All that's owing you plus next month's rent."

"Cash?"

"No, I don't have that kind of cash here. By check." Drawn on an account with zero balance.

"Ha!" Connie said and pointed her finger—the one with the broken nail—at Alexi. "I know that look. You don't have the money. I'd have to kick you out next month anyway."

"Look, it's like you said," Alexi said. "You couldn't rent the place out in this condition anyway. How about you let us stay until it's ready to rent?" At the rate of these renovations, it could buy her a year.

"That's not the point. Things have changed for me. I need a place to live, and since this house is mine, my choice is obvious."

Connie's columns of bracelets and her overstuffed bag took on new meaning. Maybe she was packing all she owned. Maybe desperation would make her compromise. Alexi was certainly willing. "Maybe we could all just share the place until—"

"Until one of us murdered the other in their sleep," Connie said. "No, I'm not bunking down with you and four kids, especially when I—"

"Own the house." Alexi was beat, and in her defeat she said something she wouldn't ordinarily have dared. "I don't know why Seth bothered to save you from prison."

Connie froze, and then she busied herself with one of the columns of bracelets, stretching one over another to rearrange the order. "Oh, he told you about that, eh? You two must be close. Or, this is another of his causes. A widow and her four kids are just up his do-gooder alley."

How dare Connie trivialize what was… what could've been between her and Seth? Alexi slammed a fist on the counter, a pale substitute for the face she wanted to drive her fist into.

"For your information, Seth can't be a part of my life, of Matt's life. He's the boy I'm trying to adopt and criminal records don't look good. Your kicking me out of this house isn't the only thing you've kicked out of my life."

Callie had abandoned her bejeweled jar to cling to her leg.

Connie swung up her bag and moved to leave, but she caught sight of Callie's wide-eyed gaze. She peeled off another bracelet and kneeled in front of Callie. "One more?"

Callie obediently stuck out one arm, the other wrapped around Alexi's leg, and Connie slipped it on. They smiled at each other, like friends in on a secret.

Connie rose and turned to Alexi. "As for you, don't pull the holier-than-thou stunt on me. I know what I am. I know what I'm capable of. But even I didn't ask him to take the rap for me. You, you know you're taking advantage of my brother. You're stringing him along, aren't you?"

Alexi shook her head. "He knew I needed his help because of the situation with Matt. We both knew we were doing it for him."

Connie gestured to the nearly empty fridge. "You really think the kid couldn't do better?"

There it was. The question that had wormed into Alexi's thoughts. Connie's pink-painted mouth twisted. "Your face is a dead giveaway, girl. You're in this for yourself."

"That's not true!"

"Answer me this. Do you intend to have a relationship with my brother?"

"I would if I could."

"Then you're not. You can have your reasons for doing what you're doing but at least be honest with yourself. Cut him loose."

"I did! Because you ruined it."

"Quit coming back to that stupid argument. Seth ruined it by taking the fall for me. That's a fact. But you're the one making him pay for it all over again. You won't take a chance on him, will you?"

Connie started a "gotcha" grin, then it wobbled and she bit her lip. "The fact is neither of us deserves Seth."

She spun away and left in a clatter of heels and bracelets, Callie holding to Alexi's leg, her eyes following the beautiful pink lady and her fake jewels.

SHE'D DECIDED TO give up on Matt, ditch the adoption and hand him over to Child Protective Services. The mean landlady was kicking them all out, and they'd nowhere else to go. They were basically homeless, and she'd spent all night and all this day thinking of another way out but she couldn't.

She told him this when the others were in bed and he'd gone with her to sit on the back deck stairs. Matt knew from her face that it was going to be important, but he thought it was about their money problems and he already had a solution. He'd followed her out into the dark and coolness, excited to share his plan with her.

Never had he dreamed she'd do this to him.

She sat with her arm around his shoulders and told him that it was her, not him, not ever him. The fact was, she said, she didn't deserve him, and he deserved to be with someone who could provide for him and love him as much as she loved him because she did, she really did.

"This is about money," he interrupted, "isn't it? I know what you can do. Ask Seth Greene for a small loan. Like a hundred dollars. Two hundred to make sure we're covered. Then we'd buy bread and cheese and lettuce and cold cuts—no listen, Mom!—and make lunches, and we could sell them to Seth and Mel and the guy that works with them and other people."

She squeezed his shoulder and began shaking her head. He rushed on.

"That'd make us some money, and we could gas up the lawn mower and I could go door-to-door, and you wouldn't need to take me because I could just push it. I can even do that after school. I could rake leaves in the fall—we got a rake already, we wouldn't need a loan for that—"

She squeezed his shoulder really hard this time and pulled him tight against her. "I don't want you to go, either," she whispered.

It was like she was squeezing a big lump of tears in his chest. He swallowed hard. "Homeschool me," he said. "I could be at home taking care of Callie while you work. I'm old enough."

She rested her cheek on his head, which squeezed the lump near to bursting. "You can't be learning if you're taking care of kids. Besides, I wouldn't be home to help you with your lessons, which I'm pretty sure the case-worker wouldn't approve of."

Matt felt the lump crack, his whole insides start to cave in, and this time he spoke just to get words out, any words, so as not to cry. "What does it matter what she thinks?

You couldn't do anything to make her happy. She's fat and ugly and stupid and I—"

"Don't, Matt. Don't let your sadness make you mean. That's not you."

This time it was him squeezing hard, squeezing his eyes and lips tight, squeezing his hands between his knees, because she had this way of making every wrong thing he did appear to come from a good place within him that he didn't even know existed.

She lifted her head and with her fingertips, turned his face to hers. "The thing is, Matt, you're not mine. And because of where I am right now, I cannot make you mine. Even though I want that more than anything else in the world."

To keep from crying, he looked up and away. The stars were coming out. There'd be more, and if you were out all night like he'd been more than once, there'd be so many they'd all blur together in places into a great dome.

Only it wasn't a dome. It was just the curve of the earth making it appear that way. Because really it was black endless space and faraway, dead places.

"Please," he said in his best, calmest voice, "please talk to Seth Greene. He will help you. He'll talk to his sister. I know him."

She shook her head. "He's a good man but even he can't pull off the miracle we need."

"Have you tried?"

She moaned softly. "Matt. Please."

He didn't push her because even though she was wrong about Seth Greene, he knew nothing he said was going to budge her. "When?" he said.

"I'll call Marlene tomorrow, and we'll go from there."

It wouldn't take long, he thought. Hours, a day or two at the most. He'd have to move fast. He leaned away from her, straining against her hand on his shoulder. "Could you leave me alone for a bit?"

She let him go, though she continued to sit on the step, her mouth twisting. She finally stood and walked to the back door. She paused. "Matt. You're not going to run away, are you? Promise me that much."

It hadn't even crossed his mind. "No. I promise."

"Thank you," she said, and he could hear the smile in her voice. That was the other thing about her. If he said it was so, she believed him.

He wasn't running away, but he wasn't going to let her give him up, either.

CHAPTER THIRTEEN

THE SECOND SETH entered the drive-through lane of Tim Hortons coffee shop with Mel, he spotted Matt crouched beside the speaker box. The truck clock read 6:21 a.m. Great start to a Monday morning.

"Isn't that Alexi's oldest?" Mel said. Matt must've recognized them, too, because he rose and came straight for them. His hair was every which way, and he wore a T-shirt, shorts and sandals. Okay for noon but at this time of morning, it had to be cool. As the boy drew close, Seth lowered his truck window.

"Seth Greene." The boy's eyes looked bruised, the eyelids heavy. He looked as if he hadn't slept all night. Had he run off? Alexi would be in full panic mode.

"Matt."

"We need to talk."

No kidding. Seth eyed the gap ahead of him, and the line piling up behind them.

Before Seth had a chance to respond, Mel

said, "Sure, open up the back door there." Matt didn't need to be told twice before he was in the passenger seat of the crew cab.

Mel turned to look at him. "What do you want for breakfast?"

"I don't have any money," Matt said.

"My treat."

"Okay. Thanks, Mel."

Seth felt more than his chronic low-grade irritation with Mel. The boy had come to see him and Mel was taking over.

What's more, why did Matt call Mel by his first name while he got the full name treatment?

"In that case," Matt said and drew a deep breath, "I'll have five hot breakfast sandwiches on an English muffin, five hash browns, a side order of bacon, four orange juices and a medium coffee." He paused and added unnecessarily, "To go."

"Got it," Seth said fast before Mel could get in another word.

At the take-out window, Seth put in their regular order, Matt's order, added six muffins, three grilled wraps, up-sized the coffee to a large with a double shot of cream, and threw in an extra box of Timbits.

No doubt Alexi would thank him, even though it wasn't her gratitude he wanted.

Not that he could ask for what he really wanted from her.

As bags and boxes and cups were passed into the vehicle, Matt tucked his family's share around himself, all the while his stomach squeaking and groaning like an eager puppy.

"Dig in," Mel said.

Matt looked longingly at the bag of hash browns but said, "No. I'll wait to eat with the others."

Mel, with a Timbit on the way to his mouth, stopped. "Good idea. I'll do the same."

Still sideways in his seat, he chatted with Matt about what grade he was in (grade six in September), what sports he liked (baseball and soccer and snowshoeing), if he'd been to the Calgary Zoo (of course), and since he had, which was his favorite animal (the penguins, same as Mel).

All well and good, but that got Seth no closer to finding out why Matt had tracked them—him—down. How had he even known to go to Tim Hortons? Had he just surmised from Mel's donut box and the fact that that was where most of Alberta's working population went every morning?

Whatever, it had to be something serious. Was it money? Had Alexi gone through his money already?

Or was it something Connie had said when she'd come by yesterday? Yeah, bet it was his charming sister.

He glanced in the rearview mirror at Matt to ask a few of his own questions, but when he saw the boy with warm bags of food and cold drinks, his head resting against the back of the seat, and a small smile playing on his lips as he listened to Mel rattle off random facts about Antarctica, Seth decided that all explanations could wait until they got to the house.

The door flew open as they came up the walk. It was Alexi and from the moment he saw her, Seth saw nothing else.

She was a wreck. She was in sweatpants and a gray T-shirt, her hair loose and wild, her feet bare, her shoulders slouched, her hands hung by her side. No phone.

This was not his Alexi.

"Matt." Her one word, empty and flat. Resigned, as if she'd expected him to leave her.

"I had to," Matt said, and she nodded, not surprised, not angry. Nothing.

There was something else missing about her. Of course. Callie. It was still early. He could take a moment to talk and find out what had gone so wrong.

But in the way of all kids who sense when the adults in their lives would like time alone, there was the snick of a door, a sleepy call, the sound of bare feet on wood and the whole crew was there.

After a quick connect with their mom, the kids clustered around Mel with his paper bags and drinks. He climbed the stairs to the kitchen, the kids encircling him like chicks around a hen, leaving Seth and Alexi alone together.

She hadn't thanked him or Mel for the food, but had quietly instructed the kids to do so. Maybe she didn't realize he'd gotten her breakfast, as well.

He wanted to open his arms as he had only a few short nights ago, have her fall into them, feel the rightness of her body against his and let them talk with nothing between them.

Two things held him back. One was the boy up in the kitchen. As much as it grated that some bureaucrat held the power to decide who was part of Matt's life based on some idiotic rule, he wasn't about to jeopardize the best thing that had happened to Matt: Alexi.

The second were the cups of coffee in his hands. He held out the large one. "Here. The way you like it."

Alexi stared at the coffee as if it were a foreign substance. Then in a slow, almost drugged way, she took it from him and held it. She didn't drink, just stared at the plastic lid.

This was killing him. "Alexi. What's the matter?"

She lifted her eyes to his. Her blue, blue eyes now dull and bloodshot.

"I'm giving up Matt."

Her whispered words floated around Seth, their meaning not settling on him. "What?"

"I have to. I've got no money, no job, no home—"

"No home? What do you mean? This place is coming together."

Twin frown lines appeared between her eyes. "You haven't talked to your sister?" There was a small, distinct spitting of the last word.

Connie. He knew it. He shook his head.

"She kicked me out. Said she was moving back in. Immediately."

His paper cup of coffee slipped a little in his hand. So that was why Connie had come over. He'd thought she might've insulted Alexi or laid out new rules, never eviction. If possible, she'd sunk to a new low.

He pulled out his phone, stopped. As if she'd answer at this time in the morning. Probably had it turned off.

"Mel!" Seth called. "Mel. Come here, okay?"

"Why? I'm eating."

"Now!"

Mel took a dog's age to appear at the top of the stairs, his cheek bulging with food, a half-eaten muffin in his hand.

"You two need to come. The food's getting cold." He turned to Alexi. "Seth got you a lemon poppy seed muffin, but you'll have to watch that the seeds don't get stuck in your teeth."

"Mel," Seth interrupted, "did Connie tell you she's moving back into the house?"

Mel's eyes grew round. He said to Alexi, "Connie's moving in with you and the kids?"

"No. She evicted them."

Mel took a bite of his muffin. "Oh." Like it was news about someone they barely knew.

Then again, how well did Mel know Alexi and the kids? It was him, Seth Full Name Greene, who was all wrapped up in their daily life, him who Matt came to when times were tough, him who was all torn up over them going hungry and having no roof over their heads.

Without a single clue what to do, he turned to Alexi. "We'll think of something. I know people in town. I can already think of a dozen people to call."

"No need," Mel said and popped the last of the muffin into his mouth. "I have a place."

"Mel, we can't fit five people into—"

But Mel was shaking his head. "Not talking about the apartment." He swallowed, his gaze switching to Alexi. "I bought the Stephensson place. You and the kids can move out there."

Then, as if he'd not just stripped Seth of the family he'd come to care for as much as his own flesh and blood, Mel took another bite of his muffin.

Seth felt a hot trickle on his hand. He'd squeezed the paper cup hard enough for the coffee to overflow the rim. He eased his hold, aware that Alexi had noticed. She was worried, yes, but in her eyes, he saw something else. A flicker of hope.

Mel had given it to her.

"Come on," said Mel. "Let's eat. I'll tell you what I'm thinking."

Alexi followed. Seth couldn't. Because once she and the kids moved out there, he'd only see them over his father's dead body.

MEL, SETH DISCOVERED from where he stood rooted at the entrance, had it all planned out.

"Me and Stephensson signed all the papers back in May."

May! Two months ago. Way before the hailstorm when Mel had first mentioned to him about Stephensson selling. Then, last Thursday, he said he was done thinking about it. Yeah. Because it was already a done deal.

"Technically, I don't take possession until the end of the month," Mel said from the kitchen, his voice muffled by a Timbit. "But I know Stephensson has already left, so I could check with him and see if he's okay with moving the date up. Or if he's okay with you just moving in without us having to go through the rigmarole of signing anything else."

Mel really had bought the place that had killed their dad.

What was he thinking? There were a dozen places he could've got. Why blow his inheritance money on this place? It was…morbid, was what it was. Morbid and sick and…and cruel.

Mel had betrayed him, just as Connie had, but at least with her it wasn't unexpected. With Mel… Mel knew exactly how he felt about the place, and yet he'd gone ahead and done it anyway. Yes, Mel had the right. Yes, Mel was a grown man. But by buying that property, Mel was deliberately going to a place where he knew Seth couldn't follow.

Seth stared at the dark brew in his cup, the same coffee he'd ordered alongside Mel's frothy concoction for years now, a little tradition to start their day together.

He'd lost it all. No Mel. No Connie. No Alexi. No Matt and the other kids. Everyone had made choices that didn't include him.

He wrenched open the door and left, chucking his coffee into the hydrangea bush he'd planted one Mother's Day years ago. As he drove away, his phone rang. Ben. Probably wondering why he and Mel weren't at the site. Seth didn't pick up. Ben would call

Mel, and Mel, who was showing himself to be quite the boss, could handle it.

THE FARMHOUSE WAS better than Alexi had expected. It was a two-story, old-time farmhouse, the kind found in calendars of prairie homes. Except this one looked far more solid and modern. Large windows, new vinyl siding and what made Alexi gasp, a deck that wrapped straight around the sides and front. Perfect for summer suppers.

"It looks good from the outside," Alexi conceded.

"Yeah, the roof needs replacing but it'll do for now."

Alexi squinted upward. Now that he mentioned it, the shingles curled and warped all across it. "I'm sure you and Seth will take care of that—"

Mel pulled on the beak of his cap. "Do you want to see the inside?"

The renovated kitchen had appliances that weren't top-of-the-line but looked like they actually might work. There was flooring everywhere, even hardwood in the living room. Sure, work still needed doing—unpainted walls, missing baseboards, no window coverings—but it was all manageable. At least Marlene could see she'd upgraded.

Callie gently released her leg as she began to explore the cupboards. A good sign. She could see the other three through the kitchen window, climbing the fence to the barnyard.

"Are there any animals here?" she asked.

"No," Mel said.

A safe yard. Another check.

"The brothers had their niece and her family come live here," Mel said, "so they'd started renovating. Then the niece's husband got a job in Saskatchewan so the brothers moved into town and put the place up for sale last winter. One brother, he died in that bad hailstorm we had. Remember that? Got a hailstone to the head and dropped dead."

Alexi touched her forehead, remembering Seth's intensity the morning after. His sadness—no, more than that—his helplessness at the quickness of life passing. She watched Callie open the cupboard door beneath the sink, climb in and close the door behind her. Almost immediately, the door swung open. "Welcome home!"

The sudden loud happiness of Callie's voice made both adults grin. Alexi decided to take the next step.

"So how much? For real, for what you think it's actually worth."

There followed much nudging and twisting about of the baseball cap. "Well, the thing is, you probably can't pay me what it's worth, eh?"

True, and yet her back stiffened. "How much would it be if I could?"

A shrug, another nudge. "How are you with a paintbrush?"

"What are you saying?"

"How about you pay me in labor? Paint the place, nail some boards on, handle a bit of the outside work. I need it done, and I don't have time to do it myself so I'd have to hire someone anyway. I know you have to work it around the kids and your other business but I trust you to do what you can."

It was something like the deal Connie had made with Seth. She stepped up and hugged Mel. "Thank you," she said and stepped back.

Mel turned beet red. He cleared his throat. "Seth'll come around. I surprised him with buying this place. He doesn't take well to surprises."

There was more to it, but it wasn't her place to pry. It would suggest an interest she'd no right to indulge.

"So, to be clear, you bought the place. Not Seth?"

"Yep."

She was pretty sure she knew the answer but she asked, "Are you and Seth going to live here, too?"

Mel scrunched his forehead. "Hadn't intended to. You want us to?"

"No!"

Mel gave a start, and Alexi revised her tone. "I mean, I just needed to clarify. It would be best if there was some distance…"

Mel's frown creased deeper. "I thought you two were together."

"No. We're not." She whispered the words, not because of Matt but because it was all she could manage. Somehow saying it aloud to someone else made it real and solid. It was like when she'd told the kids that Richard had died. Their crumpling faces meant it was true, and not a reality she could hide.

Mel looked far from happy. "I don't get him sometimes."

"It wasn't him. It was me. And it wasn't me, it was Matt." She sighed. Why had it become so difficult to love someone?

Sudden shrieks pierced the house. Alexi ran for the front door, emerging onto the front deck at the same time as the kids came running toward it from the barnyard.

Matt was in the lead, and didn't stop until he was right before her.

"Mom, guess what?"

Before she had a chance to reply, he said, "A cat! With kittens. Five kittens!"

A cat with kittens. More work. And on a farm, heartache. Yet, she couldn't stop a smile from starting and it grew until it was as big as the kids'.

"What do you know?" she said. "What do you know?"

But if anyone could be grinning more, it was Mel. "Wait until I tell Seth. He'll never believe it."

CROUCHED ON A SMALL hill in the pasture next to the farmhouse, Seth watched them. He had walked there from where he'd parked on a side road, coming across the green field where Stephensson had once pastured his cattle and where the obstacle course happened.

With each step through the coarse grass thickened with yellow clover and purple alfalfa, Seth had remembered. He remembered

Old Stephensson, who had already seemed old twenty years ago, tell him about how he always pastured a portion of the herd close to home—the cows with the calves born late, the yearlings with a lame foot or weak eyes, the heifers too young to be with the bull. The misfits.

Old Stephensson had told him this when he'd come with Mel and his dad to roof the house.

Instead of helping to rip off the shingles, Seth had hung out with Stephensson in the barnyard, firing off random questions about livestock management and crops, as cats and kittens wove patterns about his legs and meowed for their turn to be snuggled in the crook of his arm. Sixteen, old enough to drive, and yet he'd asked his dad the second he'd got on the roof if they could have a kitten. Dad had said, *"We'll see."*

From what he could see of the kids, there were still kittens. Who was taking care of them, if Stephensson was not there? Were they wild? Did Alexi know they could carry diseases?

Never mind. Not his business. Just like the farmhouse roof.

It was a steep roof, the steepest Seth had

ever been on. So steep, his dad said, a pigeon couldn't walk it, and he'd insisted they wear safety ropes. They were laying the starter row at the bottom, the trickiest because it determined the look of the entire roof. His dad was showing Seth how it was done, right from the setting of the chalk line to cutting the shingles. Seth was catching on, setting himself a rhythm whereby he measured, aligned, remeasured, cut and laid.

Finally, his dad had stood, said, *Yep, keep on, just like that*, took a step back and that was the last time his dad spoke to him.

He and Mel pieced it together afterward. The shingles were normally piled higher on the roof, but his dad had moved a short stack down to lay the first row, which he normally did himself. He had his own routine, but this time his attention had been focused on Seth. And the rope? He'd removed it, probably to maneuver more easily around Seth and the shingles.

One wrong step.

He remembered how for a second he didn't even know what had happened. There'd been no sound, just a peculiar thud and then a strangled yelp from Mel. He'd looked up from his shingles then, glanced around, then down.

His dad was sprawled on the front steps, cement steps, meant to last. He was angled downward, his head on the bottom step. Mel was crossing the front lawn in a stumbling run. He'd dropped his thermos of coffee and slid in beside their dad. Mel lifted his head, and a part of Seth silently screamed at him not to do that, something to do with the spine.

Their father died in excruciating pain from a broken back two hours later.

Seth remembered fumbling with the knots to free himself, knots his father had shown him how to make not an hour earlier to keep him safe.

All Mel ever said of their father's death was *If I'd a gun that day, I would've shot him.* Seth got back on the roof the next day. Mel had stayed at the bottom until he couldn't stand it and joined him. *Easier to catch you before you start falling*, he'd said. The two of them finished it in one day, and went back home to help with the funeral. He'd spent twenty years avoiding even looking at that house, and now some of the best people in his life were going to make it their home.

He stood, turned his back on the old house

with its old roof. He still couldn't bear the sight of it, though now it was for a whole family of other reasons.

CHAPTER FOURTEEN

THE SUN WAS FIRE on his back when Seth got to the top of the apartment roof and strapped on his harness. Mel was working the nail gun, while Ben installed flashing.

Seth didn't know if Mel had said anything to Ben but after a glance from each of them, they kept their heads down and said nothing.

Which suited Seth just fine. They all stayed on the roof straight through lunch and into Mel's siesta break before calling it quits. By then, they wore gloves, even though their hands were sweating, otherwise the metal was too hot to handle, and the shingles were like slabs of hot rubber.

As soon as Ben's boots hit the ground, he informed them he wouldn't return until four and left in his truck.

"Wonder what that's all about," Mel said, sliding into the passenger seat beside Seth and maxing the air conditioner. "How about Taco Time? I've got coupons." It was part of their routine to grab lunch at one of the fast-food places in Spirit Lake.

"If it was our business, we'd know, and yes," Seth said. Mel was always poking his nose where it didn't belong, which was doubly annoying given that he'd no trouble clamping up about buying the Stephensson property.

Seth couldn't take it anymore. He turned in his seat to face his brother. "Why didn't you tell me you bought the place?"

"You know," Mel said. "You're not the only one who's stood on that hill the odd time or two."

How had he known? "Today was the first time back in twenty years. You been there more than that?"

Mel stared out the windshield. "Can't count the times."

"So why buy the farm, Mel? Why do it when all it does is bring back bad memories?"

Mel shifted in his seat. "Because Dad wanted me to. Last thing he said I could make sense of."

Seth remembered Mel cupping their father's head. That's when his father must've spoken, because by the time Seth had wrestled free of his harness and come down the ladder, their father was incomprehensible from the pain. "Why?"

Mel gave Seth a rare, square-on look. "For your sake, Seth. He was worried about you."

"Me? What do you mean? I was fine."

"Nah. You were about like how you are now. Looking for things to fix. To take care of. He figured the farm was a good place to start. Animals, pets, crops, machinery breaking down all the time. Something to tie you down because you liked being tied down. Still do."

"No, I don't."

"Yes, you do. But you don't like to admit it. That's what Dad said and he's right. Look at you with Alexi."

"She's not a charity case to me. It's more than that."

"Know that," Mel confirmed.

Yeah, Mel had known all along it was more than that. Crap, how long now had he not seen how together Mel was?

Which made Seth realize something else. "You like the business, don't you?"

Mel shrugged. "Hard to explain. I like the view from a roof, I guess. Means you're still with people but they can't get to you."

So that was it. Coming to a strange place at age twelve, not quite fitting in and on the run from his past. The roofing business would've been a way in with people. Still was, if his early mornings at Tim's drive-through were any indication. Seth turned down the air-conditioning. It was cooling off fast enough.

"You telling me that Stephensson waited all this time to do it now? That doesn't make sense."

"I guess he carried on, kinda like we did. Family moved in and helped out but they all went their ways, and so him and his brother moved out, and put it up for sale. As soon as I got the money, I went to him."

"You know, just because Dad wanted the place, doesn't mean you needed to follow through. Despite what he said."

Mel shifted about as if sitting on a ball. "I liked this roofing business well enough. But I didn't want to do it on my own. Back when Dad died, you were happy enough to help out, and with the way Connie was acting out, our Mom and I decided that maybe it was best we stay where we were at."

Seth thought of the warm, earthy smell of the pasture this morning, how even in his anger and disappointment, he remembered how the cattle were kept. "I guess...I guess you two made the right decision."

"Back then we did," Mel said, "but your mother didn't forget. Last winter, she got wind of the sale and she...she was pretty sick by then, but she made me promise that I would follow through. That's why she gave me the money, so I could buy you the farm."

Seth stared at Mel, stared out the windshield at nothing in particular, back at Mel. "You got to be kidding me."

"Do you think," Mel said in a quiet, reasonable voice, "if she'd given it to you, you would've purchased the farm?"

"No! I'd have rather burnt every last single dollar."

"Well then, our mom and I made another good decision."

"But I don't want it!"

"I think you still want it."

All the suppressed emotion from this morning welled up. "No, I don't. Because of Dad. And because of Alexi and the kids living there."

Mel did his rolling-on-a-ball shift again. "Alexi said you two aren't together because of Matt. How's that?"

Seth bit off the obvious retort about why

Mel was asking what was none of his business, because when had that ever stopped Mel?

"She's in the middle of adopting Matt. The caseworker would see me as a person of interest. Especially given my record." Seth couldn't keep the bitterness from the last word.

"Would it stop the adoption?"

"Not necessarily. It might. It's not worth the risk."

Mel frowned. "I'd say it is. You want her, and the kids need you."

Seth felt a rush of—yeah, all right—love for his half brother who'd spent his inheritance to make things right, despite the absolute wrongheadedness of it all. "I'm not going out there, Mel."

"Okay. I'll help her out, then."

Seth knew from the way Mel said it in an overly casual way, his gaze out the side window, that he was deliberately goading him. He knew exactly how much Seth hated the idea of Mel being there and him not being there, and Mel was banking on his interest in Alexi to drive him out to the farm, despite his hatred of the place.

Except this was one plan of Mel's that wasn't going to work.

Seth pulled away from the curb. "You do that."

THE WEEKS THAT followed were manic for Alexi. After the two-week slapdash flurry of packing, moving and unpacking, there was adjusting the kids to their second home in roughly a month and then starting school with a bus to catch, teachers to meet and paperwork to shuffle. Not to mention she had a new job of repairing and renovating the house and yard. And wonders of wonders, a pre-Christmas promotion to her existing customers brought in orders that had her bent over her sewing machine until midnight every night. By the time she stretched out in her bed, Alexi was a limp mess.

Mel was her saving grace. She was in daily contact with him, either through visits or texts on his newly purchased cell. His visits had to do with the renovations, either checking her progress or bringing out supplies. Often as not, he timed it with a pizza or a barbecued chicken from the grocery store, which led to an impromptu meal, regardless of whether or not she was already cooking and often the kids dived in before thanks was given or hands washed.

Not that she was complaining. Money was still tight, and a free meal was a gift.

He also brought news of Seth.

She never solicited it but she still gathered up every mention of him like a fan girl with a star: how long his day was, which roof he was on, where and what he'd eaten, the pickup ball game he'd gone to, the minigolf he'd organized for the seniors.

It helped that the kids were as hungry for information as she was. Not a visit went by that they didn't ask Mel where Seth was and if Mel could ask Seth to come out because they'd like to show him the kittens and the barn loft and their rooms and he could have supper with them, too, or breakfast. Or any time, really.

Only Matt didn't ask. Alexi had explained to him that she and Seth had agreed not to communicate until his adoption came through to avoid jeopardizing the case. Matt had agreed, his eyes wet with tears. Whenever Seth's name came up, Matt pretended not to hear or, if he could, got out of earshot.

Alexi's heart broke every time. But it paid off. Mid-September, Marlene paid her first home visit, having allowed Alexi and the kids plenty of time to get adjusted to their new home. She was an hour early, which didn't surprise Alexi.

"The place has floors. Very modern of you," was her assessment after inspecting every room in the house, including under Matt's mattress for whatever kind of contraband she thought an eleven-year-old boy might have.

Inspecting the property occupied most of her time. Good thing the kids were in school. Marlene marched to the barnyard, tested railings, flicked the switch to see if the grain roller was disconnected (it was) and poked her head into every stall in the barn. Alexi, holding Callie's hand, was pressed to keep up.

"No livestock?"

"No. Unless you count the mother cat and her kittens over in the manger." Alexi pointed to a wooden partition against the far wall of one stall. Marlene crossed over and peeked inside. Her frown lines melted away and a soft smile appeared.

"Cute little guys," she said. She reached through a wood slat and plucked out a black-and-white one and held it out for Alexi to take. She did and knelt so Callie could pet it, too.

Marlene picked up a second one with different black-and-white markings and tucked it into the crook of her arm, its tiny claws clinging to Marlene's hockey jersey. Alexi had never before met a bureaucrat who didn't care about looking like one.

"Tell me how Matt's doing."

Alexi began her rehearsed speech, one that was the absolute truth. "Good. He started school week before last, and seems to be doing well. I spoke to his teacher on Friday, and she said he's a hard worker and gets along well with the other kids." Alexi hadn't really expected anything different. Matt was a good kid.

"How about that Seth Greene? Does he still come around?"

Alexi had worked out a plan for this. She steeled herself and her voice. "No. I discovered that Seth has a criminal record. Drug-related. I cut off any contact between him and my family, including myself."

Marlene studied Alexi as she gave the kitten slow and easy one-finger pats. "And is he staying away?"

"Yes. Neither Matt nor I have had any contact with him in about two months." And still missing him like crazy.

"You're sure about Matt?"

"Yes. The bus takes him to school, and after school, the bus brings him back."

Marlene nodded and returned to her petting. Alexi showed Callie how to pet gently, head to tail, Callie staring, lovestruck, into the kitten's dark eyes.

"Shame about that record, really. Absolutely clean and then hit with that big-time charge."

Just as Seth and she had feared, Marlene had found out. At least, Matt's caseworker was doing her job. Such a good job that Alexi decided to say nothing.

"His sister is another story," Marlene continued. "Your landlady is a real piece of work."

Wasn't that the truth? Alexi responded as noncommittedly as possible, "I've had no contact with her, either."

"But your current landlord is still a member of the Greene family."

"No criminal record, though," Alexi pointed out.

"Nope. Good as gold, that one."

Again, Alexi said nothing, a state Marlene soon discouraged.

"What would you say your relationship with this Mel Greene is?"

Finally, a question that she was happy and fully prepared to answer. "He's my landlord. He's an employer that I do small jobs for. He's friendly enough with the kids. They nor I feel threatened by him."

"Even though he has a key to the place."

"Yes."

"Seth have one?"

"No."

"But the two of them live together."

How did she find this stuff out? The kitten was about to plunge off her bent leg, so Alexi placed it against her chest, the tiny feet kneading her hoodie, the claws flexing. "I can't control who Mel keeps in contact with." Or who Mel talks about.

Marlene unhooked the kitten from her jersey and returned it to the manger. Alexi took that to mean their barn talk was nearing a conclusion and did the same. The two women watched the kittens totter to their mom, who touched her nose to their heads and administered licks that teetered them about.

"You'd tell me if Seth Greene tried to contact you, right?"

"Yes," Alexi said confidently because she knew Seth would never do that.

Marlene straightened. "Well, then. File closed on Seth Greene. Time to move on."

Marlene stepped out of the barn into the bright afternoon, and behind her back, Alexi gave a short fist pump in victory.

That night, tucking Matt into bed, she told him the good news about the caseworker accepting that Seth was not part of their lives.

Matt didn't smile. His mouth twisted. "Bryn and Amy miss him."

"They have school. And Mel. They'll be okay."

"You miss him still?"

About a hundred times a day. "I've got too much to do."

"Callie has his baseball cap," Matt said. "He left it here when he was working inside. She keeps her necklaces and stuff in it."

Alexi didn't know that. She swallowed. "She's okay."

"It's all because of me that he can't come over. And they have to suffer."

Alexi scooped his hair away from his face.

"They'd suffer much worse if you weren't part of their lives," she said quietly.

"But it's because of me that they have to choose. That you have to choose."

"It was my choice, and I made it, so don't you go feeling guilty. Understand?"

It took a long while, his face fighting to hold back tears and arguments, but at last, he gave her the nod she needed.

She bent and kissed his cheek. "I love you."

He looked out the window to the dark, star-bright sky. "I love you, too," he said tiredly.

WHEN SETH'S PHONE jingled an incoming text, he ignored it. He needed both hands to install these roof anchors, and two screws had already slipped out of his grip and bounced down the roof and over the edge. One more and he'd have to retreat to the ground for more, and then climb back up, harness-free. Safety equipment wasn't required to actually install safety equipment. Better than not having any equipment any of the time, but it made setup a real pain.

He'd barely put the drill to the screw when a second text came in. It had to be Mel. Not a week after Alexi and the kids moved to the farm, he finally got a phone and it had become his latest toy.

Seth drilled in the screw and was pulling out another when the sudden chiming of an incoming call jarred him enough for the screw to slip out of his fingers and roll off the roof. Seth let loose an exasperated growl and snatched up his phone. "Mel, I swear—"

"Hey, Matt there?" Panic sharpened Mel's voice.

"No. What's up?"

"The school called Alexi. Matt's not there."

No, Matt. Don't do this.

"What makes you think he's here?"

"Last night at supper, I said we're done at the apartment and moved to a site down the street from the house. He might've come there." Mel paused. "The kids miss you. Matt, especially."

As if he could do anything about it. Seth stood and straddled the ridgeline to look down the street. Nothing either way. "If he's coming, he's still on his way."

"You up on the roof by yourself?"

"Yeah. How else are the anchors getting in?"

"It's against regulations."

"I think you've got bigger problems right now."

Mel grunted. "Okay, I'll drive between the school and you, and try to see him."

Seth plotted the possible routes in his mind. "Come by Mac's. That's the one he might know best."

"Alexi's already doing that. I'll come up along Forty-Seventh."

Alexi. He dragged his hand across his face. Not a day had gone by these past two months that he hadn't wanted to see her, but never under these circumstances.

He scanned the street again. "Okay, I'll stay here. In case he comes a different way."

He descended the ladder against the back of the house and checked the alley. Nothing. What was the boy thinking? He hadn't run off, had he?

Better get back on the roof. If Matt was looking for him, he'd be looking up. But up there, he felt helpless, and so he did the only thing he could do, which was to get back to work. He had to have the safety gear in place before Ben showed up, and who knows, the boy might be with Mel and Alexi already.

He was securing the brass plate of the last

anchor when from right behind him he heard, "Hello, Seth Greene. It's me."

Matt was on the roof without a harness. He looked steady enough, his rump on the shingles, his feet pointed downward.

"Matt. What are you doing here?"

Seth hadn't meant to speak so sharply, and Matt's small smile vanished. Seth calmed his voice. "You've got Mel and your mom looking for you, you know that?"

"Yeah, I know. I was going to have you text Mom as soon as I got here."

"I'll text Mel. He'll get ahold of her."

Matt's shoulders slumped. "I'm the reason you haven't come out to the farm, right?"

Seth finished his text, which bought him a few seconds before he had to reply. "Your mom explain about me?"

"She said you being there would make the caseworker think you were going to be part of the family. Which isn't the case."

Seth felt a rush of thankfulness that Alexi hadn't told Matt about his criminal past. It mattered more than he cared to think that the kid thought well of him.

Except now he'd have to tell the boy that, indeed, Seth had no intention of being part of the family.

He sat down, like Matt, and within arm's reach. He pulled down on his cap to beat the angling sun. Good thing he wore shades so Matt couldn't find the truth in his eyes. "Yep. We didn't want any…confusion."

Was that the best he could come up with? And from Matt's frown, he seemed to be thinking the same thing.

Seth kicked at a curling shingle, lifting it off a few more inches. "Timing's bad," Seth offered. "Maybe we'll get together a few months from now, when the adoption's a done deal. Until then, things are pretty good, aren't they?"

"Mel's okay but he's not you."

"That's what I tell him, too."

Seth was rewarded with an upturn of Matt's mouth, but that soon faded. "It wouldn't be so bad if it was just me, but everyone's missing you. Even Callie. She keeps her treasures in your ball cap."

"Oh." Seth had to clamp his lips tight together to stop himself from confessing that he missed them all, too. Missed their noise. Missed their smallness. Missed Alexi with her blue eyes and the feel of her against him…

"I wondered where that hat had got to."

"The thing is, what if…" Matt turned sideways so he was tilted with the slant of the roof.

"Sit properly," Seth barked and didn't care how it sounded. Matt returned to his former position. "The thing is, if I…if it was decided that instead of me getting adopted, I just stayed a foster kid, then it wouldn't matter so much if you came around, right?"

"No, Matt," he said quietly. "You get yourself adopted by your mom. You want to be hers and not theirs. You hear?"

There was the crunch of tires on gravel in the back alley, and then Alexi's van rolled into sight. She stopped and hopped out.

"Matt!" she called as she rounded the hood. "Are you okay?"

One look at Alexi and his heart revved up. It was as if he'd been in standby mode the past two months and the sight of her flipped a switch. She wasn't even that close, but he knew that tumble of dark hair, knew how her length fit against him, knew the face she now lifted to where he sat beside Matt.

It hit Seth that he must love her, and how depressing was that? Between Matt's adoption and her living where his father haddied, she might as well still be married to Richard, his chances with her were so hopeless. Seth put his hand on Matt's shoulder. "You go back down, eh?"

Matt nodded but didn't move.

"Go down, the way you came up. Feet first, your front down. On all fours."

Matt started to go, then stopped. "Seth—"

Seth couldn't stand to hear it, couldn't stand to disappoint the boy anymore. "Go on. I'll watch."

Matt went then, keeping himself safe. Alexi walked toward the ladder, disappearing from Seth's line of sight. At the ladder, Seth coached Matt on how to get on it, and then he disappeared and Seth relied on the vibrations of the boy's feet on the metal to know that Matt had made it down safely.

He stood and watched Alexi walk across the yard, her arm around Matt's shoulder, her head bent as she talked to him. At the gate, Matt stopped and turned. He waved.

Seth waved back. A simple gesture that on any other day and certainly if both feet had been on the ground, wouldn't have mattered. But there, half-turned, his left foot slipped and he adjusted with a step backward that caught his heel on an upturned shingle.

All at once, he was falling backward, off the highest part of the two-story roof.

No, he thought, his arms and legs instinctively reaching even now to fix his mistake. Not in front of them.

CHAPTER FIFTEEN

AFTERWARD, ALEXI was struck by how quietly Seth's body hit the ground. It should've sounded like thunder, sent shock waves through the ground and up into her body.

Beside her, Matt screamed. "Seth Greene!" He broke away from Alexi and ran for Seth, as she followed.

He was flat on the lawn, face up, his legs twisted. Matt dropped to his knees by Seth's head. "Seth Greene, please, are you okay? Please, please?"

It didn't make any sense to beg but Alexi knew the desperate place it came from. Seth stared straight up at the blue sky, didn't move, didn't answer.

No. No.

She knelt beside Matt and leaned over until her face was above Seth's. "Hi. It's me, Alexi."

He gave a cranky frown. "No kidding," he said in a winded, hoarse answer.

Tears of relief rushed to her eyes, and his frown deepened. "I'm going to call the ambulance, okay?" She fumbled for her phone.

This time, she was able to provide more information than with Richard. Yes, she was with him. Yes, he was conscious. No, she didn't know the address but would ask him. Then after she relayed that message, the questions continued. No, she hadn't moved him. No, he hadn't moved. Yes, she would stay on scene, remembering then that Callie was strapped in her car seat in the van.

All the while Matt's pale face was fastened onto Seth. As soon as she ended the call, she touched Matt's shoulder. "It'll be okay. The ambulance is on its way."

His dark eyes lifted to hers, and then beyond to something behind her. She heard a choked sound. It was Mel. Coffee and donuts fell as his eyes locked on Seth. In an instant, he was crouched at Seth's other side.

"I've called the ambulance," Alexi said. "He fell. From the roof."

Mel pinched his mouth and nodded once. He cupped his hand over Seth's forehead as if checking his brother for a fever. "You'll be okay."

Seth's green eyes cut to Mel. "Get your gun."

Alexi watched in bewilderment as fury flooded Mel's face. He snatched his hand away and looked ready to wrap it around his brother's throat when Seth's eyes suddenly rolled backward and he passed out.

ALEXI STARED AT her phone on the kitchen counter, willing it to ring, but all she got was the picture of Richard and the kids at the playground. She really needed to update her wallpaper.

"Can't you just call Mel?" Matt asked from the kitchen table where he sat with the homework he wasn't doing.

She'd brought him and Callie home when the ambulance left with Seth and Mel. Matt wouldn't have functioned at school. She left Bryn and Amy in class. Let them have their day unburdened.

She forced herself to step away from the phone and go to the stove to start the grilled cheese sandwiches for lunch. "Mel will call when he can. He said he would and he will."

"If he remembered, but maybe he forgot," Matt countered.

No, he wouldn't have forgotten her tight

squeeze on his wrist, the promise to call she wrung from him before he'd got into his truck to follow the ambulance.

After a silent lunch, Callie went for her nap, snug among her stuffies. Matt was wiping the table but stopped when she appeared in the kitchen.

"Can't you—"

Alexi held up her hand. "I'll phone."

Her call went to voice mail. "I know you might not be able to return my call right away," she said, "but I wanted to know how Seth is doing. I…if you could call me if… when you can, that would be good. If there's anything you want me to do, I will. Just call me. Please."

Fifteen minutes passed without a call and Matt declared he was going out to check on the kittens. She agreed because there was nothing like the soft warmth of an animal to bring comfort and because worrying was hard enough without appearing not to. A year of it had worn her out.

With Callie still asleep and Matt outside, silence stole around her. She hated silence. Always had. She had filled it with kids and when the kids were asleep, she'd filled it with Richard.

Talking to Richard.

Talking, talking, talking him to death.

Richard had his handset on and she'd put the kids to bed a half hour ago. An hour away from home, he was tired and she was talking with him to keep him awake, telling him about all the things they were going to do during the next ten days he was off. She was saying how they should all go to the zoo because she got half-price coupons when suddenly he said, *No.* Not in fear or anger. Calm and a little sad.

For a split second she thought he was talking about her idea, and then there was the most horrible noise, a great crushing. It went on and on. The sound must've lasted for seconds really but she heard it all.

The truck phone system was totalled, so she never knew if he heard her frantic shouts to him. He was dead by the time the paramedics came.

Seth was still alive. But the paramedics were worried about his back, about the possibility of a concussion, especially because he'd fainted. For sure he'd broken an arm and a leg. Ribs, too.

Had they found more problems? Was his back fractured? Would he walk? She couldn't imagine Seth in a wheelchair. No, she thought, her phone pressed to her chest, she could imagine it and was terrified.

She swallowed her panic. She would not go down that path. If it wasn't death, it was life.

Her phone rang.

Mel.

"Hi." She paused to let him work past the obviousness of his opening line and get on with the real news.

"Well. Well, he's a bit broken up."

"What do you mean exactly?"

"There's a test or two to come back and then we'll know everything."

It occurred to Alexi as she gripped the sink to prevent herself from screaming at Mel's vagueness that he was being deliberately so. He was trying to protect her from bad news, just as she had with Matt. Only she wasn't a child who needed protecting.

"Okay, Mel. I'm away from the kids. I know you're not trying to upset me but I'm already worried sick. Please tell me what's going on."

"His right arm and right leg are broken. His left shoulder was dislocated, so his left arm needs to be in a sling for the next few days at least. And he's got a couple of broken ribs."

Alexi sagged with relief. "Is that it? No head injuries?"

"No. Well, a concussion but they don't seem too worried."

A concussion and not worried? People died from them. "What did they say about him passing out?"

"He stayed conscious the rest of the time."

"Did they run any tests?"

"Yes. I made sure of that."

Alexi wasn't certain exactly how Mel could make sure of that but she'd take his word for it. "How is he doing otherwise? Is he awake?"

"The painkillers were starting to kick in and he was about to rest. They'll wake him in a couple of hours. I thought I better leave so he could sleep. Say, did you know that they have nap times in the hospital?"

Trust Mel to make time in the hospital seem enviable. "I'm sure it'll be the first one Seth will have taken since he was a baby."

"He didn't take them then. Hollered right through them."

Alexi laughed, her pent-up anxiety making it come out short and wheezy. She felt the pressure of someone watching her and glanced around to see Matt standing there. She waved and smiled, and his worry softened to relief. She turned back to the phone. "Please tell him we're all glad he's okay. Are they keeping him in overnight?"

"Yeah, well, that's the thing. The doctor will release him tomorrow, if it all works out, but he'll need some home care."

He paused.

He meant her.

She couldn't. It would only jeopardize the adoption. Marlene was only proceeding with the paperwork predicated on the understanding she'd severed contact with Seth.

Seth wouldn't want to come here, either.

But Seth was the reason Matt was still with her. He'd helped her with the house when he didn't even know her. How could she refuse him now that she did know him? More than know him.

Alexi closed her eyes. She'd experienced the same terror when Seth fell off the roof as she had with Richard's crash. And she'd loved Richard. Did that mean then…?

She hardly knew. All she knew was she couldn't turn her back on a man that hours ago she'd felt sick at the thought of losing. "Okay, yes. We'd love to have him stay with us."

And, heaven help her, she meant it.

MEL TOLD ALEXI that he would tell Seth the precise location of his convalescent home, and though Alexi had some reservations, she'd gone along with it because after all, Mel was Seth's brother and could probably talk more openly with him.

She heard exactly how open their conversation was when their company truck pulled into the yard around the time for a morning coffee break. She stepped onto the broad front porch and could hear their voices, especially Seth's, coming loud and clear through the window.

"I may have got a concussion but you're the one who's lost his mind!" came Seth's not-very-muffled voice. "I'm not staying here."

Oh, dear. She needed to intervene.

"Callie, could you wait here? I'm just going to get Seth, okay?"

Callie set herself on the front step.

Alexi stepped up to the passenger side of the truck and from the driver's side, Mel lowered the window. Seth stared steadfastly out the windshield. His right arm was in a cast; his left, in a sling. He wore a neck tensor bandage, and his seat was laid back to accommodate his broken leg. And those were the injuries she could see.

Okay, she'd handled troublesome kids, she could handle one grumpy male. "Hey, Seth. How are you?"

He kept staring straight ahead. "Did Mel make you do this?"

"No, Seth. I wanted to."

"That's stupid, and you know why. I'm not arguing with you when I've already had it up to here with Mel."

"Then come on in and I'll get you a coffee."

"Yeah," Mel said. "Hop out."

If looks could kill, Mel would've been last week's roadkill.

"I'd stay but I've got work to do," he added. "The work of two, mind."

"Fine, I'll get out but all I'm going to do is call a taxi, and head straight to the apartment."

"Sure. You do that," Mel agreed. "You get out and I'll take your bag up to the house."

Mel hauled a hefty duffel bag from the truck, while Alexi stepped back to let Seth keep his end of the bargain. He managed to lever himself out of the cab enough to slip out and hang on to the door.

He seemed to be gauging the distance to the truck box and made his move, only to stumble and fall against the cab. His gaze fixed on a distant point, he said through gritted teeth, "Would you mind getting me my crutch from the back?" He paused. "Please."

Alexi squelched a smile and complied. He slipped his left arm from the sling to maneuver the crutch into position on the left side. Alexi watched Seth lean far too much weight on the one crutch, and instinctively reached for him.

"I can do this," he growled and swung away.

She caught him as the crutch skidded on the gravel. She took the crutch as she slipped underneath, her shoulder now his crutch, her arm slipping around his waist. She absorbed his weight, adjusting to his hops as he regained his balance.

Firm on their feet again, they stood together side by side. She could feel his warmth, his solidness, his heaviness.

He didn't say anything, and then he whispered, "Thanks."

Wrapped together, they headed for the

front porch, Mel already on his return trip to the truck. "I'll be back later to check on you," Mel said, not breaking stride.

"I won't be here," Seth said.

Mel didn't answer, just kept walking. They'd reached the front porch steps when the truck door slammed and tires crunched on gravel, in departure. Callie sat on the top step, wide-eyed behind her glasses, squeezing her squid stuffie for all it was worth.

Seth stopped and his grip tightened on her shoulder. She glanced up at him. He was staring at a spot in front of the door as if…well… as if there was actually something there to look at. Maybe he was focusing on getting inside.

"I thought we could just sit out on the deck for a bit," she offered as a way out for him. "We often have suppers out here. It's always shady and even if it rains, it stays dry."

Seth's lips flattened into a grim line. "I'll go in." Except by the time they'd swung and heaved his body up the four steps, it was Callie who hurried to pull out the nearest lawn chair for him at the deck table.

Seth collapsed into it, the plastic chair keeling to one side before righting itself. Alexi took a matching chair beside him, and Callie crawled into her lap, her dark eyes still on Seth.

Already pulling out his phone, Seth hesitated. "Hey, you," he said to Callie, his voice quiet.

She smiled and buried her face in the pink squid and gave a muffled answer. "Hey."

Seth didn't exactly smile but his face softened. Alexi grabbed her opportunity. "Listen, before you call, can we talk?"

"Has the adoption been approved?"

"No."

"Then nothing we talk about is going to change what's got to be done."

He didn't move to continue his call, though, and she plunged on before her courage flagged.

"I've missed you."

He set his phone on the table.

"I know it's unfair of me to say that. I know it complicates things. But when I saw you fall off that roof, I thought… I thought…"

"Yeah," he said softly, "I thought I was a goner, too."

"It was like—" She stopped, aware of Callie. "Like before. One moment he was there, the next gone. Forever. No goodbyes."

"I'm not going to die, Alexi."

"But you could've. And...I told you that I came here to make a new life for the kids. But I still missed Richard, I still wanted to keep the promise we'd made to Matt."

Seth shifted. "Nothing wrong with that promise, Alexi. Nothing wrong with wanting to give a kid a second chance."

"But that's my point!" Alexi struggled to say what she meant. "I wasn't giving Matt a second chance. Or my kids. You are our second chance, and I pushed you away."

Seth shook his head. "I pushed me away. For good reason."

"You did it because that's what you thought was best for the kids and me because I told you that. I was wrong. You are what's best for me and the kids."

Seth let out a grunt and hitched himself in his seat. He took hold of his crutch and thumped it against the deck. He avoided eye contact. The man clearly didn't know what to do with a compliment.

"If I stay," he said, "how will it affect the adoption?"

Alexi rested her cheek on Callie's head. She really didn't want to say this next bit. "It'll be rough. I told her that I'd let her know if you tried to contact me."

He snorted. "I'd say living under the same roof constitutes contact. Do you have to tell her?"

"Yes. Even if you leave before she comes next, I'm not going to risk Matt telling her, and then dealing with the fallout. Besides... besides the fact of the matter is, at least for me, these two months away from you has made me realize that you will be part of my life—and Matt's—at some point. Time to put all the cards on Marlene's table."

There, and she'd laid her own cards on the table, too.

"When is she coming?"

"Next Friday."

"It's Thursday now. We'll have more than a week to make a plan."

"Yes." There was really nothing more to say. It was his call to make.

He must've known that, too, because he gave his phone serious consideration. "I don't want to do something I will regret later," he whispered.

She squeezed Callie as if her own heart was getting squeezed.

"And I don't want to not do something I will regret later, either," he said.

Her whole insides tightened.

He looked at her then, his green eyes soft, as soft as they were when he opened his arms and she'd let herself be held.

"I'll stay with you."

She jumped up, sliding Callie off her lap. "Great! I'll get you a cup of coffee before you settle in."

At the door, he called to her. "When I saw you yesterday, getting out of your van, I realized—" his mouth twisted and he winced "—I realized that I…I missed you and the kids, too."

His eyes connected with hers, then skittered off to the porch deck, then just as quickly settled back on his phone.

Her heart gave a victory whoop but she resisted thanking him. "Wait there. I'll be right back."

ALEXI SCANNED HER ROOM, just off the dining room. What a mess. Hopefully, Seth would take his time—as in all morning—to finish his coffee. The room was intended as an office but it was large enough to accommodate her queen-size bed, which meant there was enough room upstairs for the kids. Callie, of course, slept with her. They'd have to take the pullout couch.

Callie popped off Alexi's leg and scrambled across the covers to bury herself among the stuffies. She looked like one herself. "Okay, Callie, we need to take these off and put them—somewhere. Seth is going to sleep here."

Callie extracted a camouflage moose from the pile. "He can have this one."

Alexi doubted the likelihood of Seth's cuddling with that during the night. "Sure," she said. She opened the closet door, gathered up an armful of stuffed animals, tossed them in and shut the door fast.

She opened the bottom dresser drawer. She needed to clear it out for his stuff. Behind her, she heard the tap-thud of the crutch. She snatched up a bunch of lingerie—back when she had special date nights—and shoved it into an upper drawer.

The tap-thuds ended at the open door. "I'm sleeping here."

She wasn't sure if he was stating a fact or confirming one, so she went with the latter. "Yes. Callie and I will use the pullout couch in the living room."

"I can sleep on the pullout."

"No. You need a room separate from the rest of us." That came out harsh so she added,

"I figure being on the same level is easier. I remember that from when I had a cast on." She hurried on, annoyed she'd mentioned an old past. "Is this drawer enough for you? Oh, wait, I should empty the top one so you don't have to bend."

She wrenched the drawer open to realize that it had her lingerie. She slammed it shut.

"I could do that later," she muttered.

"I can take care of it," Seth said.

"What? No—I—" Alexi caught sight of Seth's broad smirk. He had seen, the brat! Heat crawled into her cheeks. She yanked open the drawer below it which held her socks, leggings, scarves, belts and other non-intimates. "Or you could use this one."

"I could try to remember that," he said, drawing his voice out. He grinned and the suddenness of it left her breathless. He looked so…good. His mouth was still crooked upward when he asked, "You broke your leg?"

She grabbed hold of as much clothing stuff as she could. "Years ago. I was in my teens." She bent to the bottom drawer and dumped it all in, frantically trying to think of a different topic.

Seth leaned against the dresser. "What happened?"

She gathered up a second load. "Oh, I fell down the stairs. My foot hooked on a step." There was more to it. There was always more.

"This was in a foster home." Seth said it as if it were important he got the facts straight.

"Yes." She shed her second load into the bottom load and straightened for her third and final transfer.

"The same one you and Richard met at?"

"No. An earlier one. A couple before that one."

Seth hobbled to the dresser and propped himself against the side of it, while she stood in front. "A couple? You moved around a lot, then." Again, confirming the obvious.

Only Richard understood about her past. Maybe someday she'd tell Seth about what it was like to be someone else's job. It was why she'd wanted to adopt the kids as soon as she could.

"A fair amount." She emptied the last of her stuff and toed shut the bottom drawer. "Ready for your clothes." She reached for his duffel bag.

"Uh, no. I can handle that." He jerked forward, causing himself to teeter, hop, spin and land on the bed so heavily Callie bounced amid the stuffies and fell against Seth who accidently elbowed her in the face.

Seth grimaced. "Sorry, Callie. Sorry." Before Callie even had time to cry, Seth placed his hand on her back, his face close to hers as he inspected her cheek.

Callie froze.

Alexi held her breath. Callie didn't even permit Richard to touch her, except for the allotted time it took to cross the street or to lift her into her car seat.

Alexi sat on the bed and held out her arms to Callie. Callie scooted to her, then turned and picked up the moose and handed it to Seth. "You hold this."

Seth met Alexi's gaze, and she shrugged, trying to communicate an apology and explanation as best she could. He gave a short nod, and turned his attention to Callie's substitute.

"You made this." Again, a statement.

"Yes."

"Who'd buy a camouflage moose?"

Her back stiffened. "Boys like stuffed toys more than they're allowed to admit. Nearly half of my sales are for boys."

"Yeah. All right." He sounded dubious.

"You going to be okay with the duffel bag? I can put away your things."

"No. I don't want you to touch my underwear, any more than you want me touching yours."

Beside her, Callie giggled. Alexi started. How much of the conversation about lingerie and broken legs had her little ears and big eyes tracked? Time to get her out.

"All right, then. Let me open up some room in my closet, and Callie and I will let you make yourself at home."

At home. She'd meant it only as an expression, except that as soon as the words filled the space between her and Seth, it sounded like an invitation, to which the man she'd declared her intent to shake up her family so he could be part of it responded with, "Sure."

While she skidded her clothes to one side and freed up a few hangers by doubling up her clothes, Seth was attempting to zip open his duffel bag while balancing on his crutch. She couldn't see this ending well. At that rate, his entire day would be spent unpacking.

She paused at the door. "I know a bit about feeling like a burden. I don't want you to feel that way. Because you aren't. I wanted you here. The kids want you here. I don't mind doing things for you, okay?"

Seth gave a short nod. "Yeah. All right." Again, sounding dubious.

Alexi didn't push it. She also knew a bit about how hard it was to change.

CHAPTER SIXTEEN

A FEW YEARS back Seth had roofed for nine-teen hours straight to help a builder keep his deadline. By the time he'd finished, he was bone-tired and so light-headed he felt as if his body was about to float off across the town. Now, having finally managed to put away his clothes, he felt the same way.

He hobbled to Alexi's bed and eased himself onto it. Sit down before you fall down. Wasn't that the saying? He absolutely was not going to drop to the floor in Alexi's house. She was already putting herself out enough for him, despite her little speech about him not being a burden. Fact is, she wouldn't have said it, if she didn't somehow see that he was.

Seth leaned against the pillows. Her pillows. Her room. Alexi was everywhere. In the stuffed animals, her scent in the air, her jeans on the back of the chair, her hairbrush. Would she come in here to change into pajamas?

They'd be sharing the closet, the drawers. Like a married couple.

Had Richard used the same drawer for his socks and underwear? Had she pushed her stuff to the left in the closet because Richard had always hung his stuff on the right?

It shouldn't matter but it did. Just like it mattered that he was sleeping under the same roof his father had died on. It had taken all he had to walk up the steps his father had died on. To walk inside the house.

Every fiber of his being screamed to leave.

Except there was Alexi. Telling him that he was the best thing for her and her kids. Opening up to him about her hard upbringing. How could he walk away from that?

As if he was in any state to do that anyway. Seth closed his eyes. He'd rest for a few minutes, maybe until Callie was napping, and then he might chat with Alexi. Just her and him.

He woke to the clashing of pots and clattering silverware, punctuated by high-pitched whispers. Then, above it all, rose Matt's voice. "Shut up, you guys, or you'll wake him."

Amy matched his volume. "You can't let him sleep that long. He'll get a concussion and die! Mom, please."

He'd better get himself moving or else Alexi would have to deal with a panic attack. But how to do that? A nurse had got him up and out of his bed this morning, and Mel had commandeered a wheelchair to take him to the truck. Then Alexi had taken him the rest of the way.

"No, no," he heard Alexi say. "It's normal for people with injuries. It's the body's way of repairing. Here. You all wait here. I'll go check on him, okay?"

Seth did a hard ab crunch while simultaneously swinging his good leg onto the floor so that when she opened the door, he was more or less sitting upright. No way did he want her seeing him more helpless than he already felt.

"Oh, you're up," she said. She slipped inside and closed the door. "We're about to have supper. Would you like to join us?"

She'd changed clothes. Her top was airy and flowery, and she wore white jeans. She'd done something with her hair, too. Lifted it up and away with little squiggly bits that grazed her neck. Had he slept while she dressed right in front of him?

"You look better than usual," he said, without thinking. "I could have said that better."

"At least you noticed," she said in an extra perky voice. The corners of her mouth were pinched tight. Yep, he'd insulted her hospitality and now her appearance.

He eyed his crutch, which had fallen from where he'd left it propped against the dresser. "Bet you're wishing you hadn't invited me."

"Bet you wish I was thinking that so I'd kick you out," she retorted. She picked up the crutch and rested it beside him on the bed. As she did, he got an eyeful of the curve of her backside flattened in one spot by the rectangle of her phone. If she said he was her second chance, why did she have to carry Richard around all the time?

"Do you go anywhere without that phone?"

She touched the phone, and he realized that she knew exactly which part of her he'd had his eye on. She crossed her arms. "As a matter of fact, no. I never know when I might need to make an emergency call."

Yeah, there was that. He squeezed the padding on the top of the crutch. "I never thanked you for putting in that call. So, uh, thanks."

"You're welcome." She didn't uncross her arms, though. She seemed to be waiting for him to say something, and while he had a fair amount to say, he didn't want it to be the wrong thing.

"Uh, I'll just sort myself out and come for supper." He looked pointedly at his crutch, hoping she'd catch his meaning. No way was he going to let her watch him hitch himself up and hop around.

She shook her head. "You really hate asking for help, don't you?"

"I don't need help to get up," he said. "I just need time."

"If you need time," she said, "you should ask for help. It wouldn't take as long and therefore you'd be saving time."

"I don't need more time. I just need the opportunity to use the time I've got well. And alone." He grabbed for his other crutch, which slid from his reach and clunked to the floor.

There was a knock on the door. "Is everything okay?" Amy called.

Alexi opened the door. "Everything's more than okay. Seth will join us for supper." Amy's head appeared between Alexi's hip and the door in a covert attempt to get a visual on the house patient. Alexi cranked Amy's head a quarter-turn and began to nudge the door close. "Come on, let's check the burgers."

After they left, Seth blew out his breath. Finally, a bit of peace. He eyed the fallen crutch and the closed door. Yep, plenty of time and opportunity to think about his complete lack of common decency.

ALEXI FLIPPED THE burgers on the barbecue set up on the front porch, the meat smoking and hissing like her feelings about Seth. She'd stated she wanted him, that he was good for her and the kids, and all he could come up with was a sour, muttered thanks. She wasn't looking for a lifelong commitment. Well, maybe she was, but a little reciprocity would be nice.

Especially when she knew he was staring at her behind, which would've been flattering if he hadn't made a comment about her attachment to her phone.

She poked at the baking potatoes and veggies before peeking through the kitchen window at the oven clock. Right on schedule. Providing Seth got himself mobile soon.

"Is the table set?" she called through the screen.

"Yes," Matt said.

"Can I set the good napkins?" Amy asked.

The good napkins were the red cloth ones only brought out for Christmas and Amy's birthday. Clearly the presence of Seth was a monumental event in her life. Alexi was about to decline, when Bryn spoke up.

"We should because it's not every day you get to have supper with someone who could've died."

Alexi dipped her head, her forehead brushing the cool window screen. What was she thinking? Life snatched from the jaws of death was always a cause for celebration. "Sure, Amy. This one time only."

Behind her, she heard a vehicle. It was Mel in the Greene-on-Top company truck. "Mel's here!" she called through the window. "Set another place."

"I already did," Matt called back.

It wasn't wishful thinking on his part but a response to past performance. Mel showed up for supper more often than not.

She turned back to the barbecue as Mel approached with a grocery bag from Mac's. Alexi blew out her breath. Seriously? Only last week, she'd managed to explain to him not to load up on donuts before coming. He'd just switched his source of junk food.

"Hey, Alexi. How did your day go?"

She knew the real question he was asking. "Your brother is a real joy."

Mel snorted. "That well, eh?"

The screen door crashed open and Bryn appeared on the front deck. "Mel! What's in the bag? Did you bring something for me? Is it gluten-free?"

"Bryn!" Alexi said.

Mel grinned and climbed the stairs with the bag in hand. "I got a bunch of stuff because I didn't know what any of you liked."

He set himself and the bag down on the top stair and at once all four kids flocked to him like seagulls around overturned fries. Even Callie hovered close.

Lovely. A well-balanced supper about to be ruined by a sugar rush.

There was a bumping and rattling of the door and it opened far enough for the bottom of a crutch to appear. It then shot wide-open and there was Seth, his earlier grumpiness like rainbows and unicorns compared to his current thunderous expression.

"All right! None of you kids eat or drink any of that junk until you've had your supper. Even then, it's up to your mother."

Seth swung himself into the middle of the porch.

"Go. Wash your hands, the lot of you. Bryn, wash your face, too. And Callie's, while you're at it. Matt, fill up the cat dish."

The four kids hopped to it, playing rounds of rock, paper, scissors to see who would get the bottle of pop or the licorice later on.

Next Seth targeted his brother. "Whaddaya doing bringing junk food at suppertime?"

"It's rude to come empty-handed."

"It's ruder to insult the cooking with crap food."

"Mel, it was really sweet of you to think of the kids," Alexi interrupted. "I hope you'll still stay for supper."

"You betcha," Mel said. "I'll go wash up."

Which left her and Seth alone, if only for seconds, time he didn't waste.

"Sorry for being a jerk back there. You were only trying to help."

Instantly her own growliness melted away. "Apology accepted."

He looked down at a kitten using his crutch as a scratching post. "I know how Connie must've felt now."

Alexi snapped the tongs together in a sharp

metal bite. "You mean what it's like to be mean for no good reason?"

"To feel helpless."

"Helpless? I don't think she was feeling that when she kicked us out."

Seth adjusted his posture on the crutch. "I'm not so sure. It's not like her."

Alexi waved the tongs at him. "Don't. Don't even think about putting yourself out for her. It'll only get you in trouble."

Seth looked at her square-on. "The kind of trouble you're getting into for me?"

She didn't have to answer that because Bryn came out to say they were ready and when was supper. "Now," she said, transferring the burgers onto one plate, before passing it to Bryn who disappeared with it inside, declaring his claim on which one was his.

She shoveled the vegetables onto another plate, stacked the foil-wrapped potatoes into a bowl, switched off the barbecue and with heavy bowl and plate balanced on one side, she opened the door with her empty hand for Seth.

He was staring at the porch deck, frozen there.

"Seth?"

His head shot up. "Coming," he said gruffly.

He wouldn't look at her as he passed her into the house. What was up? Any questions were swept aside in the last-minute flurry of getting the food on the table and the kids around it. Without thinking, she loaded the first plate and handed it to Seth.

"He shouldn't get it," Bryn said. "Mel should. He's older."

When Richard was alive, that had been the tradition. The oldest first. Really it had been a way to show her love.

She looked at Seth. A small smile played at the corners of his mouth and his eyes shone on her in a warm, intimate hold. Exactly the look she'd hoped for when she'd dressed for supper.

"He can go first," Mel broke in. "I'm happy to get what I get."

Alexi shook herself loose and turned to Seth's brother. "Which in your case is a double-decker hamburger." She loaded Mel's plate and was filling up plates for Amy and Callie when she noticed that Seth hadn't touched his.

"I'm sorry, Seth," she said. "Is there something wrong?"

His eyes met hers. "Nothing at all. Just waiting until you can eat with us, too."

As one, the kids and Mel froze. That had been another tradition that had fallen by the wayside since Richard's passing.

Alexi choked up and Seth's face blurred. No! Not allowed.

"There's no need," she said.

"Daddy-R made us wait, too," Matt muttered to Seth.

"Then I guess we'd better do what he would've wanted," Seth answered with a sharp edge Alexi wasn't sure she liked. She filled the plates in record time. The instant her butt hit her chair, forks and mouths got busy.

"What's your favorite food, Seth?" Matt asked. He had claimed a position right next to Seth.

"Hamburger, roast potatoes, grilled vegetables and fruit salad."

"That's this food!" Amy crowed. "You're so lucky Mommy made it."

Seth pierced a potato, and gave Alexi another of his half-smiling looks that sent a wave of heat through her like she'd opened the fired-up barbecue. "I am."

Matt directed the question to Mel now and the conversation moved on to the merits of ketchup on noodles. This was so much like old times. The easy flow of conversation, the high-pitched excitement of the kids countered by the baritone of the adult male. Except there were two adult males. Brothers. Both with a strong drive to help others. With Mel it was easy to reciprocate. Share a meal, a conversation.

Seth was different.

Watching him as he tipped his head to listen to Matt, a bowl of her fruit salad heaped in front of him, she realized what she'd done.

Yes, she'd told him that it was because she owed him. But she'd made it seem that it was all about the kids when it was far more than that. She wanted Seth for herself.

And what did it say about a mother who'd risk the future of one of her children so she could be with a man?

As best he could with his arm in a sling, Seth rammed stuffing up the sorry end of a gorilla-gator, the creature being a special request from one of Alexi's online customers. She'd assigned him that job while she stitched fangs onto something that was mostly snake. It was his sixth day at her house, and the first time they'd had more than five minutes together.

Callie had crashed on his bed—or Alexi's—in the middle of her favorite stuffies.

The sixth day and the sixth evening of excellent, noisy suppers, the food going down a lot easier than he would've thought possible given his dad had fallen to his death from the roof he slept under.

He didn't think about his dad when the kids were on the tear. It was in the quiet moments like now on the couch, his broken leg stretched out on the coffee table, that the memories drifted in like a toxic gas, poisoning his peace with Alexi.

Seth prodded more batting down the tail with a chopstick, stealing a look at Alexi. She sat at an old table in the living room, her temporary manufacturing headquarters. Judging by the piles of cloth, yarn, cotton batting and shelving units crammed with little bright shiny objects, business was booming.

Right now she was, she'd explained, pleating the wattle of a cassowary, which involved her long fingers having to tuck, smooth and gather pink and blue cloth into folds. It also meant that her lips were puckered in concentration, inches away from a faux leather beak.

"Any of your customers heard of bunnies and teddy bears?"

Alexi's gaze didn't shift from her pleating. "Dime a dozen at all the stores. I specialize."

"In the gruesome. Child services would have a field day profiling your customers."

Alexi began to poke pins into the wattle. "They already have a field day with me."

He didn't want to bring it up but who knew when they'd get time alone again? "You got any ideas about how to handle Attila the Caseworker?"

She nailed him with the same look she gave her kids when they got lippy. "We might start with using her name."

"The easiest would be for me to clear out while she's here. Pack up my stuff and hide out in the barn."

Alexi shook her head. "She'd find out from Matt. Besides…besides I don't want to hide it."

"Some secrets are worth keeping."

"Like the one you're keeping from me?" Her voice was casual, her eyes on her work, but she might as well have fixed him to the chair with a hundred of her little pins.

"What do you mean?"

"You're with us. Then you're not. You're staring off into space. I'm wondering if you might be experiencing memory loss."

She knew. She'd gotten it wrong, but she'd been watching. "It's definitely not memory loss," he said. "The opposite, actually."

And maybe because it was a fact that had become a secret through twenty years of not telling it or that he could neither leave nor enter this house without dealing with it, he told Alexi the story of how his dad had died.

She listened, her busy hands quiet on her lap, her eyes filled with tears. When he was finished, she said, "I'm honored."

"What do you mean?"

"I mean that despite your pain you came to stay anyway. It would be like me choosing to live where I could look out the window and see where Richard had died."

Seth straightened a tooth on the gorilla-gator and waited.

Alexi stroked the wing feathers of the cassowary, in a caress that Seth wished was for whatever part of him wasn't in plaster. "I used to wonder how people could stand to build those cairns alongside the road where their child or father died. And then drive past it while going where you're going. Wouldn't it wear a person down after a while? On your way to a movie or to buy laundry detergent or the latest computer, and facing that pain?"

Alexi poked in another pin. "And then Richard died."

Would there ever be a conversation with Alexi without that man in it?

"I put up a cairn. I didn't have to drive by it every day. It's north of Calgary. Still, it's there. It has helped me to let go. Knowing it's there."

Seth watched her smile at the photo on her phone. "So you're saying you've moved on?"

"Yeah," she said softly, "I am." Still looking smiling at her phone. Saying one thing, doing another.

"Then who are you looking at right now?"

She raised her head, her eyes slightly unfocused, her mind no doubt still on the image of her husband. Then her eyes cleared and narrowed.

She turned the phone so he could see. "This," she said, "this is what I'm looking at."

It was him. Just him.

On a deck chair, his leg thick with the white cast stretched out in front of him, smiling down at a kitten nestled against his chest. He'd done that each evening, sat there petting kittens and mixing it up with the kids, while she barbecued during the chill sun of autumn. She must've taken a shot of him when he wasn't looking.

"Oh," he said and nothing more, because that picture pretty much showed him for the jerk he was.

"There's more," she said. She tapped on the screen and started a slide show—a slide show!—featuring him and the kids, shots of the kids drawing on his cast, more of him with other kittens, him and the kids and kittens, him and Mel side by side, catching up on the day's news, some he knew she'd taken, others like him with a beer staring at the deck, he didn't know.

"No Richard," she said. He heard her breath hitch. She'd made a choice she was having a hard time living with. She'd already been dealt her fair share of sadness. He didn't need to add to it. One of her fingers hovered over the photos icon.

"You still got the pictures of him, right?" She dipped her head and nodded.

"Hey," he began, praying he didn't screw this up. "I don't know about losing a spouse. I can tell you I've met someone who, if she… who, if I lost her, I couldn't forget even if I moved on to someone else. So I don't want you to get rid of his pictures. I'm only hoping for…for maybe like a folder of my own."

Alexi raised her face to his. "Thank you," she whispered. "Thank you."

She moved to the arm of the couch and tapped here and there on her phone screen before turning it to him. "Your folder. Already with fifty pics."

He began scrolling through them. "You're not in any of them. Time to change that." He did his own tapping of the screen and handed her the phone. "You do it. Us together," he said softly. "Get close."

Alexi had to get both of their faces in the selfie, and to not fall against him. She slid her arm across his shoulders and he slipped his arm behind her and along her thigh. Her cheek brushed the top of his head. "Smile," he said and they did. Big, happy ones.

He reached for his own phone. "One more." He snapped a few, deliberately messing them up, so she could stay pressed against him, until she took the phone from him and clicked a perfect one of them grinning together over a joke they didn't need to share with anyone.

She moved to pull away but his arm tightened reflexively around her. She sank back against him with a soft, contented sigh as if he was the bed she lay on at night.

He shifted in his chair to open a bit more room for her. "Let me kiss you."

She laughed, barely louder than her sigh, and then lowering herself against him, she did as he asked.

Later, as he settled himself against pillows and soft, glassy-eyed critters, he remembered that he and Alexi hadn't discussed arrangements for Marlene. Tomorrow he'd be better at—and here his palm felt warm from the memory of Alexi's curves against it—not getting sidetracked.

CHAPTER SEVENTEEN

HE DIDN'T GET the chance.

Seth was on the front porch with a second cup of morning coffee, Callie drawing what she said was a flower on his arm cast, when a pickup pulled up and a beefy woman dressed as if ready to shovel out pens got out. He pegged her as a neighbor, until he spotted her bulging briefcase.

It couldn't be.

Callie dropped her markers and ran for the porch door to be met there by Alexi coming out.

"Marlene. The caseworker," she said, confirming his unspoken fear, her jaw tense.

"I thought she wasn't due until Friday."

"Yeah, well, the only schedule she follows is her own." Alexi raised her voice. "Hello. It's Wednesday. Do we have a mix-up with the dates again?"

The caseworker was coming up the short walk, her eyes pinned on Seth like a hawk on a mouse. "Nope. My timing's impeccable, as usual."

She climbed the steps, her weight shuddering through the boards. He was wearing sweatpants and a jackshirt over a T-shirt. His hand went to his day-old stubble. He must look like a deadbeat. It didn't matter that Marlene was in a hockey jersey and hiking boots. She carried the briefcase, which she plunked down on the table.

"What happened to you?"

"I fell off a roof. Work related. Seth Greene, by the way."

"I figured that out." She turned to Alexi. "You promised you'd tell me if you two got in contact."

Alexi jutted out one hip and crossed her arms. That was her stance before she put either him or the kids in their place. "I didn't break my promise. On Friday, during our scheduled meeting, you would've have met him."

Marlene pulled out a chair across from Seth at the table and sat herself down. "Too late. I've got my birds twittering in my ear."

Seth and Alexi glanced at each other. Informants? Who? "How about I get started here, then?" She looked up at Alexi. "You still got some of that delicious lemonade?"

"You're going to interview him? Now?"

"Since we both have nothing else to do on this fine morning except sit on your porch, why not?"

Alexi turned to Seth. "You can always say no."

But they knew he couldn't. Not unless he wanted it to go down on record that he refused to cooperate.

"No worries." He turned to Marlene and said, "Shoot."

Alexi retreated into the house for the lemonade, Callie trotting behind.

Marlene pulled out a thick yellow legal pad. "You know the background on that one?"

Seth assumed she was talking about Callie. "No, actually. She seems scared of everybody except Alexi and the kids."

"Doesn't appear to be scared of you. She was out here alone with you on the deck. Only ran off when I pulled up."

As far as Seth was concerned, Callie came and went, sneaking and darting about like a curious stray cat. It was part of who she was, but if Callie's trust in him helped his cause with Matt, then he might as well play it up. "I guess I have that effect on kids."

"And what would that effect be?"

"They like me, I guess."

"Naturally, you think? Or have you experience in that area?"

He knew what she was getting at. No use ducking it. "Experience, definitely. Gained from the majority of my two hundred and fifty hours of court-ordered community service to fulfill the terms of my sentencing for drug trafficking. Hours I paid off last month, by the way."

Marlene scribbled and nodded, as if this was all news to her. After she'd written down apparently word for word what he said, Alexi reappeared with a glass of lemonade. "Thanks. You're a doll," Marlene said and then turned to Seth.

"Thanks for your explanation. I always appreciate a little honesty," she said pointedly to Alexi.

The woman Seth had kissed and cuddled the night before looked ready to launch daggers. "Will there be anything else, Marlene?" Alexi said. "Would you like me to sit in on the interview, too?"

"Naw," Marlene said. "You can hear it from the kitchen window."

Alexi gave her a tight smile, shot Seth a warning look and went inside. Moments later, the kitchen window snapped shut with a sharp click.

Marlene seemed to take no notice. She sipped from her lemonade and looked around the place at the slumped sheds, the tall overgrown grass, the cracks in the cement sidewalk. The things he could do nothing about in his present state. "This is civilized," she said.

"Why? Are the interviews usually conducted in the basement under a bare bulb?"

"That," she said, and set down her lemonade, "can be arranged. Describe your current relations with Matt."

Years ago, Seth's lawyer had cautioned that an open-ended question was an open-ended noose. "Good, I guess. We talk."

"I heard he was up on the roof when you fell off."

"Your bird lies," Seth said. "He was on the roof, without my permission, and I guided him down. His feet were on the ground when I fell off."

"I'll have to take your word for it, considering as how Alexi didn't care to inform me," Marlene said, as neutrally as she ever said anything. "If you didn't give him permission, why was he up on the roof?"

"He showed up one morning. Instead of going to school, he came searching for me."

"How did he know where to find you?"

Seth hitched himself the best he could with two gimped arms into a more comfortable position in his chair. "Alexi said he'd overheard Mel telling her where I was working. It was a few doors down from where they'd been living in town, so he knew how to get there. Alexi and I had already decided to break off…the connection we'd made when I was renovating her house…because we didn't want the adoption process held up."

"I can see how well that worked out," Marlene commented. "Why did he want to see you?"

"I can only tell you what he told me."

Marlene kept writing. "Works for me."

"He offered to give up on getting adopted, if that meant I would be part of their lives again. I told him to stick to the plan."

"Which was?"

"Get adopted."

"That it?"

Seth felt the noose jerk a little tighter. He jutted his chin toward her briefcase. "As you know," he countered, "that's more than enough."

Marlene grunted in what Seth decided was agreement, and kept writing. She flipped to a clean sheet of paper and said, "Describe your current...relations...with Alexi."

Seth's throated constricted. Probably from the tightening of Marlene's noose. How did he describe something so raw and new? He'd get it wrong, say something that would destroy his chance with Alexi and Matt's chance for a family. Best get a few things settled first. "I'm glad you brought that up, Marlene. This is the dilemma I'm having here."

Marlene paused her pen. "Go on."

"Alexi and I are trying to build a life together but we're caught up in something of a triangle. There's her, me—" he paused for dramatic effect "—and you."

Marlene rolled her eyes. "Sorry, but I don't swing that way. I appreciate the offer."

Seth chose to interpret her remark as humor and not sarcasm, and plowed on. "The main impediment to the growth of our relationship is our uncertainty of its impact on Matt's adoption process."

"My, what big words you have."

Total sarcasm. Still, she was listening. "Naturally, neither one of us wants to do anything that will alter its natural and obvious course. Neither do I want to become involved with Matt in any way that would affect the process, either."

Seth felt he was picking up steam.

"However, it seems fair that I should be part of their lives if it's determined I'm not a negative element. In fact, if it's determined I would be beneficial, then my involvement should be recognized."

"Cut to it, Seth Greene."

"I want to know what you want from me, so I know what I need to do." He felt as if he was in an interview for a job he was seriously underqualified for.

Marlene shook her head slowly. "Thought it might come to this." She set down her pen. "This is the deal. I don't tell you what you need to do. I see what you're doing, and then I make a determination if what you're doing is good for Matt or not. That's it. What's the point of me telling you what I'm looking for? Then you do it but that isn't you. I need to know who you are. And frankly, the fact that you're trying to suck up to me isn't winning you any brownie points right now."

She picked up the pen.

"So, you two romantically involved?"

Seth hadn't dealt with anyone like Marlene in his life. However, he had dealt with Connie and right now he employed her evasive tactics. "Define *romantic*."

Marlene snorted. "Yeah, you and Clinton, pretty boy. Define it however you like it. Have you looked longingly into each other's eyes, made out at the back of the theater, had sex? Whatever."

For one wild moment, Seth wanted to tell Marlene exactly how it was between Alexi and him. How her lips softened against his mouth, how good her long fingers felt massaging his scalp, how his one arm around her waist made his entire injured body come alive. He wanted to tell the world about what he'd found with Alexi.

And how stupid was that? "This is just a box for you to fill in?"

"I have one marked 'Other,' too. Now spill."

She wasn't getting anything other than the minimum. "Yes. We are romantically involved."

"Do you see a future for this relationship?"

"If you don't screw it up, then yes."

"Didn't you hear a word I just said? You act. I react. Let's move on." She flipped over a page on her legal pad as if to demonstrate. "How much of your interest in Alexi is based on her connection with Matt, and how much of it is based on her as a unique person in her own right?"

Seth blinked. Where had that come from? Seth said what he knew in his heart to be true. Knew what Alexi also knew. "I don't see the two as separate. I'm good for them all. I'm what they need. We tried doing it your way but it's only made us all unhappy. There's got to be another way."

"You haven't gone out on dates? Hired a babysitter for a few hours and gone out to a restaurant?"

Exactly what he'd wanted to do but had never broached it with Alexi. Never a good time. Which pretty much described their relationship. Seth forced himself to appear casual. "Uh, well, no. I can't say that we have. It never seemed necessary."

The social worker gave him a look that could've cut rock. "You've never dated and yet you consider yourself romantically involved? So, to be clear, you've never seen her away from the kids?"

He hadn't. He had proved her point. "I've never seen her away from the kids. Yes."

"You still consider yourself part of this family?"

Seth paused. Did he? He ate with them, played with them. Yesterday morning, he'd signed Amy's consent form for a hot lunch because Alexi was busy packing Bryn's lunch. Yes, he had become a substitute father.

A substitute Richard.

"Yeah, I suppose so," he conceded.

"How far are you willing to go to become a permanent part of this family?" she pressed.

Seth couldn't stop himself from glancing at the window. He lowered his voice. "Are you asking me if I'd marry Alexi?"

"If you want to say that, you can."

"If I were to marry her, how would that affect the adoption process?"

"If you were to marry her before the adoption was complete, I would have to factor that in. If it were to occur afterward, there's not much I can do about it."

It was as much as he suspected. "So I should wait to have a long-term relationship until the adoption is approved?"

Marlene lifted up her hands. "How often do I need to tell you I can only base my decisions on what I know. If you don't want me knowing stuff, don't tell me!"

"You and your flipping birds find out anyway!"

She flapped her notes at him. "I already had to deal with your involvement in this family because of Matt and Matt's foster mother. Now you tell me you are contemplating a long-term relationship that might involve marriage. And you ask me how this is going to affect the adoption process. I told you from the first meeting that you and Alexi were complicating things. At first it was because of her. Now it's because of you both. Short answer—the current adoption process has ground to a halt until we deal with you. Now tell me a bit about yourself."

Seth wondered if she jumped around with her questions to deliberately keep him off guard.

It was working.

He'd hoped to take the attack to her but there was no outflanking this one. He felt cornered. "What do you want to know?"

"It's not what I want but what you want to tell me."

"We could go back and forth all day."

"I've got to go back to the office to record this interview, so the less I have to write the better. Get to the point."

She was like the paparazzi, hounding him for juicy details. "What don't you know?"

"Surprise me."

"I have a brother and a sister. My dad died twenty years ago. My mother died eight months ago. I was born and raised in Spirit Lake. I took over my dad's business. I have a pretty ordinary life. I play baseball. I served on the Rotary Club as—"

"Stop. I'm bored."

"What do you want to know, then?"

"Ever been married?"

"No."

"Common-law relationship?"

"No."

"Are you gay or straight?"

"What? Are you even allowed to ask me that?"

"I can ask whatever I think will affect Matt."

"And you think that would affect Matt?"

"Why else would I ask it? You think I have some gratuitous interest in your sexual preferences?"

Seth stared. She stared back. He sighed. "I definitely prefer females."

She drew an enormous square on her legal pad and put a huge check mark in it. "There."

Seth felt torn between wringing the woman's neck and taking her out for a beer.

On it went with questions that may or may not have applied, in Seth's estimation. What experience did he have with children? What did he see as his primary role with the boy? What stresses did he expect to have with this adoption? How did he plan to address those stresses? He answered the same question in a hundred different ways and the answer was the same. After a gruelling two hours in which he felt that they might as well have been under a bare bulb in a dark basement, she declared, "Okay, then, I'm done."

"When will you make your decision about me?"

"It's a process. Got to write a report, give it to my supervisor, follow up with my supervisor. If there are more questions, and there usually are, we'll set up another meeting. Meanwhile, I might need to talk to Matt. See how he's feeling about things. But that evil is for another day."

She stood, jamming her legal pad into her

already overstuffed bag. "You want a bit of a behind-the-scenes glimpse into the working of my mind?"

Seth got a sudden uneasy feeling in his stomach. "Sure, hit me."

"Believe it or not, I'm not usually so frank with the people in my cases. No really, I'm not. But I like you, Seth. I really do. Except I don't think you realize the seriousness of this situation. This is not quite what you call ordinary circumstances. You appeared in the life of this family at exactly the wrong time."

"I don't think you can argue that they needed me. I helped them when no one else did—or could."

"Yeah. I'll send you a medal."

"I'm not—"

"Yeah, you are. You pulled a Good Samaritan act. You got a mother who died in the past year, you take over your father's business, you do everything that you ought to do. You even took a rap for your sister."

Crap, had the woman spoken to Paul? "What bird told you that?"

"I don't know. I have a whole coop of them. Point is, you have a habit of doing whatever you think is the right thing, never mind the consequences. Actually, both of you have the tendency but you have it especially bad."

"Thanks, Dr. Phil."

As usual, she ignored him. "Thing is, there's a process none of us can pretend out of existence. Do you know that you're the fourth father figure in Matt's life?"

"No... I—"

"The first, his real father, was shot, and a good thing, too. Otherwise, I might've been up on murder charges myself. The second was his grandfather who was the sweetest man alive until cancer made him the sweetest man dead, and then there was Richard, and we all know how that ended."

Something didn't make sense. "Wait," Seth said, "you're talking like you've known Matt for a long time but you only now got his case file."

Marlene snapped her briefcase shut and leaned on it. Papers crunched under her weight. Her eyes bore into his. "Why do you think Matt came to Spirit Lake?"

"Alexi said he was following his gut."

Marlene snorted. Not the loud braying kind she'd sent his way earlier but a soft huff of understanding. "Following his gut home, more like.

"I opened a case file on him six years ago when the boy was five, and I worked north of here. I handed it over to the Calgary office when he moved to his grandfather's. Imagine my surprise when it ended up back on my desk.

"I've always wondered how that boy got along, and when he came back, I wondered why here? I did some digging. It turns out that his mother's parents lived for the first five years of his life in Spirit Lake. I don't know all what happened in those years, but I bet his only good days were spent here. What I do know is that he's gone through hell and back, and then through hell again."

There was open fury in the caseworker's eyes.

"Question is whether you have the guts to bring him back out of it."

SETH EXAMINED THE quality of his guts for the rest of the day. He thought while Callie napped and Alexi sponged wallpaper off the living room walls. From the couch, he found himself caught up in the rhythm of her movements, the up-down of her hand plunging into the bucket of water and rising, water streaming, to the damp wall, her hard dab-

dab-dab, lifting away the paper to reveal the painted layer underneath, an ugly yellow like decayed leaves.

She was beautiful, yes, and everything she did was beautiful. The stretch of her arms, lift of her little finger as she wrung out the sponge... Seth shifted into a more comfortable position on the couch. If he was turned on by a woman peeling off wallpaper, this was serious.

He closed his eyes and they never opened until the noise from the kids coming home from school woke him. He never slept during the day, and now he'd done it twice in a week. He hauled himself into a sitting position just as all four kids clustered around him. Three faces wide and wondering like he was Santa, and the last and oldest, pained like he was a ghost.

Enough of that.

"About time you all got home," he said, reaching for his crutch. "We need to pick the last of the apples for your lunches tomorrow. And there's the lawn to rake. Quick, out of school clothes and let's get at her."

Relief washed Matt's face smooth, and he shot off with the rest of them. Yeah, all of this, too.

Chores, eating, homework and bedtime meant he and Alexi barely exchanged a half-dozen words until the kids had settled into bed, Callie falling fast asleep beside Seth on the couch. Alexi sat on a chair, gluing eyes onto something with feathery fur, a long corkscrew neck and floppy puppy ears.

Seth eyed Callie. He didn't exactly want to have this conversation with her right there but he didn't have much choice.

He spoke quickly and quietly. "I guess we might as well hurry up and get married."

Alexi jerked, the glue gun slipped and a plop of hot glue fell onto the faux fur. She growled in frustration and left.

Before Seth had two thoughts about what to do, she returned fast with a bottle of cooking oil. She filled a cotton ball with it and began dabbing at the glued fur.

Seth waited.

It wasn't until the light brown fur was wet and dark with oil that Alexi spoke. "I admit I don't know much about marriage proposals having only received one in my life but I'm pretty sure yours sucked."

He'd reached that conclusion himself. "I can't exactly go down on bended knee."

"You could've maybe asked for my attention, done a little introduction to the subject, considered that I was holding a dangerous object—" her long fingers rubbed and teased the damaged fiber "—I dunno, said you've loved me, maybe."

Love. Remarkable how he could do that much thinking and still get it wrong. "Honestly, I never thought much about love."

"This is a marriage of convenience, then." Alexi gave the fur a vigorous rub.

"No, marriage is never convenient."

This time the rubbing could've cleaned the fur clear off.

"What I mean to say is that marriage is a commitment," Seth rushed on, "and I'm willing to make that commitment."

"Seth!" She gave the stuffie an impatient shake and the puppy head on the spring-loaded neck swayed in contemplation. "You're the kind of man who's willing to commit himself to a criminal record on the spur of the moment. Believe me, I don't question your ability to commit. But you're doing exactly what Marlene said you do, which is what you think is the right thing and damn the consequences." By now, she had the head bobbing in fierce agreement.

Seth chose to sidestep her point. "You were listening to the interview."

The puppy head was pointed to the sliding door off the living room. "The porch is wrap-around and you two weren't the quietest."

Speaking of quiet... Seth glanced at Callie who frowned and kept on sleeping. "Then you know I was already considering marriage. It had nothing to do with the interview today," he said in a low voice.

Alexi matched his voice level. "But what made you decide to pop the question—no, wait, make the statement—tonight?"

"Because I decided to act on what I want."

"Which is what exactly?"

"To make a life with you and the kids."

"No, you marry someone to have a life with her. Not with her kids. You could have a life with the kids without marrying me."

Seth opted for silence. Whatever he said next would last forever. He wanted Alexi, more than anything in his life. But she was right. Mel was right. He found commitment easy. He didn't realize how much his intentions burdened others. How much he judged others for their inability to commit.

Alexi seemed to interpret his silence as agreement. "No, Seth. I'm not going to marry you. You want to do this for my family, but marriage is to me. Me. And I want us to feel that we belong to each other. I've had that in my life. I want it again. I thought I could have it with you. But not like this. Do you understand?"

Though he didn't trust that he could say what was in his heart, he gave it a shot. "Listen. I know I started this off badly. But I do want you, Alexi. I do. Is it so wrong that in wanting you I also want to do the right thing?"

Her hand cupped the puppy head, stilling it. She set the toy on the table. "But is it the right thing? All this could do is complicate the adoption process, and that would build up resentment between you and me. I'm not sure what you're thinking, Seth. I honestly don't know."

Seth sat back in his seat. What was he doing? He wanted to be with Alexi and her kids but—

"I'm not doing this just for myself, truth be told."

This time, Alexi waited.

"Mel told me a few weeks back that Dad planned to buy this farm. Mel did it now to set things right. I guess Dad wanted it because he thought I'd like to farm."

"Are you saying you want to marry me because your dad would've wanted you to be on the farm?"

"No. I fell off a roof, too. I fell off, wanting more. Like Dad. I lived but the wanting's still there. You said yourself that you didn't want to live with regrets. That was why you invited me to stay here. I just feel that not marrying you, not getting on with life, that's what I will regret."

Her face softened. She scooted on her wheeled chair to him, raised his good hand to her cheek. "If we got married, and we couldn't adopt Matt because of your past, would you regret marrying me?"

Hadn't he made himself clear? Then Seth felt a cold certainty, like the kind that comes with knowing a death has occurred. "I think," he said, "the question is would you?"

She rested her forehead against his hand, the hard curve of her skull pressing against his knuckles. Her head bowed, she spoke quietly, as in prayer. "I let you stay with us out of respect and gratefulness for what you've done for us, and yes, out of a hope for what we might build together down the road. It sucks that Marlene caught us. Still, I don't regret it. But yes, I feel that if we married and things fell through with Matt, then we would've let him down."

She lifted her head, her eyes wet, and returned his hand to his knee.

"I don't trust that our marriage would survive that."

Seth stared at his hand, the undamaged body part that had swung a hammer more than half his life, and little else until now. In the past week, he held hands instead, the hands of everyone in this family except for Matt who had lent his shoulder to lean on. It took all his willpower but he used his hand now to push off from the couch. He swayed a little but he got his crutch squared under him and made it to his bedroom before collapsing on the bed. He loved her.

Not that it made a difference. Love wasn't going to solve their problems.

CHAPTER EIGHTEEN

IT WAS A QUIET BREAKFAST, mostly just the clink of bowls and spoons, and Bryn's occasional gusty sighs brought on by the inescapable prospect of school. Amy was reading a book and Callie sat beside Seth, watching him with one eye, Alexi with the other, such intensity in her expression that Alexi wondered if Callie had overheard last night's conversation.

Seth sat sideways to the table to extend his leg with the cast, replacing flashlight batteries, a cup of coffee by his elbow. She'd brewed it strong enough to rev a jet but Seth didn't seem to mind. It was hard to tell with his chair turned away from where she stood at the kitchen counter, making lunches.

"Hey, Matt," Seth said. "You know how to use a hammer?"

There was a pause. "I understand the concept."

Alexi smothered a smile, knew that Seth

had to be doing the same. "How about after school we put fresh wire up around the apple trees? Ground's only going to get harder, and the deer and rabbits will strip the bark off come winter."

"Can I help? Why can't I help? I can hammer, too," Bryn piped up.

"You and I," Seth said, "will put on the wire after Matt hammers in the stakes."

Clever. Bryn agreed to anything that teamed him with an adult. Sure enough, Bryn gave a whoop. Matt said nothing, his head down.

"Matt?" Alexi said. "Sounds like something you could handle."

"Okay," he said in little more than a whisper.

What was this about? "Matt? You feeling okay?"

Matt lifted his head. "Sure, Seth Greene. I'd like to help you out."

Amy groaned and looked up from her book. "Why do you always say his full name?"

His gaze travelled past Alexi through the kitchen window. "I call Seth Greene by his full name because saying it makes him real."

Seth's grip on his coffee cup tightened. Good thing it wasn't made of paper.

Bryn opened his mouth, no doubt to challenge Matt, but Alexi cut him short. "Bryn, Amy. Time to brush your teeth and get out the door. The bus will be here in exactly eleven minutes."

Which gave her time to stuff the lunch bags into their backpacks. As she reached for Matt's, he took the lunch from her hand. "Here, Mom. I'll do it."

She resisted the urge to hug him as she handed him his lunch. She couldn't resist, however, sneaking Seth a glance. He didn't meet her eyes.

Seth jutted his chin at the pack. "How come that's so full? I thought you said you didn't have homework last night."

Guilt flushed across Matt's face. "Uh…it's my social project."

"What?" Alexi flipped open his agenda on the counter. "It says here you only had your independent reading to do."

"I know but I wanted to get ahead on it because then I don't have to work on it on the weekend. Then I could help out here more."

Once again, she resisted hugging him but signed and handed over his agenda before clocking the time. "Bryn. Amy," she called in the direction of the bathroom. "Hurry up. Wipe faces. Move it, team."

In the last-minute flurry of jackets, backpacks and hair brushing, Alexi didn't notice Matt leave.

"Matt!" It was Seth out on the front porch, holding up Matt's lunch kit. Matt jogged back, his heavy pack like a turtle shell.

Alexi joined Seth. "Here, I'll take it to him. He'll fall over before he gets back."

He handed it to her without a word, without eye contact. She met Matt, who took it, head down. Could no one look her in the eye?

"Thanks, Mom," Matt mumbled. He straightened. "Thank Seth Greene, too."

She could resist no longer. She hugged him, bulky backpack and all. It was a good call because the hug he gave back meant she could get through her day.

And from the grim look on Seth's face when she returned to the porch, she would need all the strength she could get.

"I think I've overstayed my welcome," he said. "I'll stay in town tonight, after the kids are in bed. Mel will drive me back to my place." His voice was quiet and soft—and unyielding.

She didn't want him to go, but they both

knew there was little point in him staying now. He could get around on his own, and last night had made it clear that they were at a stalemate. "You'll be okay?"

His eyes searched hers. "Yeah, I'll be okay."

Alexi wasn't sure she was going to be. She sat on a deck chair. Callie sat on the top porch step. "I want you to know—"

"Unless," Seth interrupted, "you've come to a different conclusion than you did last night, let's leave that door closed."

She hadn't, and she lowered her eyes until all that occupied her vision was the bottom tip of his right crutch on the deck. Seth was silent, his weight pressing the rubber tip against the wood. All at once, he swung the crutch forward.

She rose. "Here, I'll get the door—"

But he was already swinging it open, getting himself inside. She sat back down. When she finally came inside, Callie in tow, she figured from the closed bedroom door he was inside. She could pick out the faint sounds of a drawer opening. She remembered accidentally opening her lingerie drawer in front of Seth. His grin, her excitement at having him close to her, her awareness of how it could become so much more.

The drawer scraped shut. It would be empty now, ready to be filled with just her stuff. Tears began to clog her throat and she grabbed the silverware, clattered it and the plates together, anything to cover the sounds from the bedroom, anything to get through this moment and on to the next.

Callie padded to Seth's door and before Alexi could stop her, turned the handle and began to slip inside. Alexi called, "Callie. Come help me clean up the table. Let Seth be."

The door widened, and she heard Seth from behind the door. "Come in, Callie. You can help me, okay?"

Just like that Callie disappeared inside, having made her choice. Alexi stood in full shock. Two forks and a spoon fell from her hand to the floor. Callie was alone in a room with a man.

Did Seth realize how momentous this was? No, of course not. She had never told him. Had never told him anything about her kids, really. About how Bryn hadn't spoken for the first three years of his life, about Amy's three major surgeries, each one carrying with it the risk she'd never walk again, even the details of Matt's horrific upbringing. Seth had accepted them all as they existed now.

And she had rejected him because he'd loved her kids more than her. How much love did she expect from him? Wasn't marriage also for the purpose of creating a family? Need it always be about two people loving each other?

Yes. It is always about that. And Seth didn't love her. She left an opening as big as a barn door for him last night, and he'd dodged it with his talk of commitment.

She couldn't marry a man who didn't love her, even though… She froze, holding a plate covered in toast crumbs and bits of egg.

Even though she hadn't told Seth she loved him. She'd been so fixated on hearing about his love she'd kept her feelings hidden from him. She'd welcomed him into the house, wondering if her feelings reached to love but she'd never made a decision. Why couldn't she have made the first step?

Because loving Seth was not easy. Loving Richard was like loving a good friend. Loving Seth was like loving one of her little wonders. It required imagination.

Of that, she had plenty.

She stepped toward the bedroom door. Stopped. No point. She could declare her love right now, which would leave him with two options. Lie and say he loved her, too. Or avoid the truth, as he had last night. The result was the same: a closed door between them.

Alexi shoved her hands in her hair. She couldn't stand looking at that door one second more. She pivoted on her heel and walked to Matt's room. Time to absorb the good energy from his hug and move on.

Step one. Bed making. She straightened his sheets and shook out his quilt. The sudden billowing sent a plain ruled sheet free from his bedside table. Part of his social project, she assumed, as she retrieved it. Then she caught sight of the words, Dear Mom.

Dear Mom,
When I've run away before, I haven't told anyone. There was no one I wanted to tell. But I want you and Seth Greene to know that I am not running away because of you and him. I know if I stay, you two can't be together. That means I won't have a dad but Bryn, Amy and Callie won't have one, too.

I am the problem. I thought Seth Greene could make everything better, except if I'm here, nothing will get better. All three of my dads have ended up dead. Seth Greene nearly died. I can't take the chance I will end up getting him killed, too.

Don't worry. I will go someplace safe. I won't do anything stupid. Bryn and Amy and Callie can have whatever I left behind.

I love you, Mom. I love Seth Greene, too.

By the time she got to his signature done in handwriting, her hand was shaking so bad the letters appeared broken and blurred. She was panting, her breaths hard and labored in the still room.

No, Matt. No.

Her phone rang. She whipped it out of her pocket. The school. "Please," she whispered, "please, please, please." She brought it to her ear, holding it with both hands to steady it.

"Hello? Alexi Docker? Oh, good. Hilda at Matt's school here. We're just checking on him. He didn't turn up for class. Is he with you?"

Alexi couldn't get her mouth to work.

"Hello? Alexi?"

She couldn't say he'd run away. There'd be trouble. He'd be taken from her. She just needed to find him. She needed time. Had he even got on the bus? He must've.

Where are you, Matt?

"Hello?" The tinny voice of Hilda prodded her.

"Yes. There was a mix-up," she said. "I need to go. Thanks." She ended the call before she had to say another word, another lie.

She stood, stumbled forward. At the bedroom door, she felt light-headed and grabbed the frame. She couldn't go on. She had to go on. She had to find Matt.

Where to start?

She looked at the picture on her phone.

"Seth," she whispered and ran out of the room. "Seth!"

WITHIN THIRTY MINUTES of Seth getting the news, the facts started trickling in. Fact: Matt had boarded the bus and arrived at school. Fact: he did not enter his classroom. Fact: the school was within easy walking distance of the secondary highway that ran north and south through town. Fact: he was not sighted at Tim Hortons.

Seth fell back against the kitchen counter when he gleaned this last bit from Mel. He had hoped against hope that Matt might have walked there to find Mel.

He hadn't felt this scared since his dad died. Alexi stood beside him, her face creased with worry, having heard her husband die, Matt wander away without permission, Bryn bolt, all in little more than a year. How did she do it?

He called Greyhound. No scheduled stops that day for Spirit Lake and sorry, no kid loitering outside, either.

After the first hour, Seth called Paul at the police station. "Look, I know it's only been an hour but he has a history of running."

Alexi gasped. "His backpack," she whispered. "I bet it was filled with his stuff. That's why he made a big deal about packing his own lunch."

"He left a note," Seth relayed to Paul. "And he's got a fully loaded backpack. Listen, Paul. You have to know this kid does nothing without a purpose. This running off, he's good at it."

"I hear you."

You got a picture? Seth mouthed the request to Alexi. Alexi immediately scrolled through her phone and sent it to the email address Paul gave her.

"Got it," he said. "I'll take a car out now. He couldn't have gotten far."

After finishing with Paul, Seth turned to Alexi. "Can you text me that picture, too? I'd like a copy to show around."

Alexi did, and Seth's stomach churned at the sight of it. She'd cropped it to just show Matt, his smile wide, with a kind of aw-shucks embarrassed look, but he could see his hand on Matt's shoulder.

Seth tapped and scrolled and a few minutes later, announced, "Okay. It's up on Facebook."

Alexi clutched her hair. "No, Seth. You can't. No pictures of Matt are allowed on social media. It's part of my agreement. Plus, I don't want them to know he's missing. Especially this way."

Of course. What had he been thinking? *I thought Seth Greene could make everything better.*

And all he'd done was make it worse. His head was as messed up as his body.

"I did it," he said. "I took the picture. Delete it off your phone. And the email, too. We'll say Mel took it. But, Alexi, we need to get the word out."

She frowned. "I don't—"

"It makes no difference to me," he said. "I can't get any more in trouble with Marlene than I am now."

Alexi bit her lip. "I just don't want—want to lose it."

He stared at her. "It's a picture, Alexi. Why are you worried about a picture when you stand to lose the real thing?"

"Because pictures might be all I'll have left! And it can happen, it can." She was clutching her phone, clutching it so hard. "It already has."

Her blue eyes were wide and pleading, her entire body vibrating. He reached for her, to quiet her shaking, but she stepped back. "I can't," she said, "or I'll lose it."

He nodded. He didn't feel far different himself.

His phone pinged. Saw your FB post. Are you serious? Don't screw with me. A text from Connie, of all people.

Wasn't that rich? Yes.

Immediately she replied: Hold tight. I'll see what I can do.

Who made her chief of police? It's okay.
Paul is in a car right now.

He's got his ways. I've got mine.

His phone pinged again. A friend from the
baseball game. No sighting but she'd shared
it. Another ping. No sighting, another share.

And on it went through the morning. Seth
checking his incoming messages from the
couch. Two sightings, supposedly. He contacted Paul, who turned up with nothing. One
was a different boy; with the second, nobody
could be located.

By noon, there'd been no sighting of a kid
hitchhiking within forty miles of any road
out of Spirit Lake. He received seventy-six
comments on his post and thirty-four shares.
Seth had no idea he was so connected. He
wouldn't wish his worst enemy popularity
this way.

Seth hobbled into a very clean kitchen.
Alexi had scrubbed, sorted, mopped, wiped,
sprayed, treated the kitchen like a surgical
theater. For the first time he'd known her,
she'd set Callie up on a laptop with a movie.
Torn between her unexpected treat and her
worried mom, Callie had tugged at Alexi's

leg at the twenty-minute mark. Alexi had simply continued with her manic cleaning. Seth hadn't stopped her. He wished he could be up on a roof right now, doing something worthwhile.

She spun to him as he entered, her face bleak. "I can't just do nothing. I should've known." He couldn't tell her that it wasn't her fault because as much as it wasn't, he understood because he felt the same way.

"How about you drive to town? I'll take care of Callie." All on her own, Callie released Alexi's leg and slid her dark, soft arms around his cast and squeezed like it was a stuffie. His leg couldn't feel it but his heart sure did.

Alexi left with phone and keys and purse, hair every which way, in an old T-shirt and jeans. Just as he'd met her. Same look of naked worry.

Seth cupped Callie's fuzzy head. "Everything's okay."

A lie and a hope.

AFTER CIRCLING THE SCHOOL, Alexi edged the van down back alleys, then along random streets, twice nearly going up onto the curb from focusing on the sidewalks. She walked

along bike paths, peering into the bushes.
She got into the van and drove randomly,
whispering a prayer every time she turned
a corner.

Without intending to, she ended up at the
house. There, at the front door, was Connie
talking to…Marlene? Yes, the sneakers and
girth were distinctive. Connie was gesturing
wildly, Marlene with her fists punched into
her wide hips. What the—

Connie was Marlene's bird. Connie had
fed Marlene the information about Seth that
had demolished him in the interview, driven
a wedge between them.

Of course, she would. Hadn't Connie told
her that she wasn't fit to be a mother? And
God help her, for a while she believed it, even
when she knew better. How much easier it
would be for Marlene to believe lies about
Seth.

The vibrations that started with the words
Dear Mom had risen through the morning
with each text, spiked with the news of possible sightings, beat against her insides as
she drove into town, now exploded in pure
white rage.

Later, she couldn't remember how she'd
covered the ground between the driver's seat

and the front steps, but all at once she was there and in Connie's perfect face.

"What exactly did I ever do to you? What is it? Why have you made my life hell? I did nothing to you and you've taken away everything. A home. Seth. And now my kids?"

The woman's eyes widened as if she'd no idea what she'd done. Behind Alexi, Marlene started in. "Now, just hold your horses, Alexi—"

Alexi whirled on her. "As for you, why do you believe her lies? Don't you check the background on your so-called birds? Don't you know what she's done? How about you speak to Paul with the RCMP? I bet he could tell you a story or two. Oh, but wait, you can't because he's out there right now, trying to find Matt who ran off because he thinks he's a problem when it's you two with your lies and paperwork and processes and meanness that have driven him away from the only people in the world who love him. You hear me? Love, love, love him."

Alexi couldn't speak anymore. Already the last words had come out shaky and stuttering. All she could do was stand and shiver. The other two women were staring at her.

In a slow and quiet tone with none of her

usual brashness, Marlene spoke. "Alexi, did you say that Matt has run away?"

One look at Marlene, and Alexi knew she'd screwed up. Marlene had no idea about Matt's disappearance. But… Alexi pointed at Connie. "Didn't she tell you? Or was she too busy coming up with more lies and innuendo about her brother?"

Now Connie spoke in the same calm tone as Marlene. "Actually she just showed up a minute before you came. I was going to tell her but I first wanted her to promise that she would stay calm."

"I always stay calm," Marlene interjected. "You just don't bring me the beers fast enough. Now, what's this about Matt running off?" Her gaze switched back and forth between Alexi and Connie.

Alexi blinked. What was the deal with the two women? "This morning. After Matt left for school on the bus, I found a note in his bedroom. He said he was running away."

Marlene made a noise of anger and disgust and kicked at a flowerpot. It toppled over and out spilled dirt and plants.

"Marlene! Look what you've done." This from Connie.

"Whatever. I hate geraniums. They stink. He say why he ran?"

Alexi went eye-to-eye with Marlene. "Because he figures that if Seth is part of the family, he can't be. Now, where would he have got that idea?"

Marlene punched her fists back into her wide hips again. "I did not tell him any such thing. I told you. I told Seth. You tell me where he got the idea."

Alexi stopped, her mind sorting through the scenarios until the only possible one surfaced. "He must've overheard Seth and me talking about it. But we weren't blaming him. We weren't even talking about him, at all."

"Well, think. You two must've said something that set him off. If we can figure out what it was, then maybe we can figure out where he went."

Alexi bit her lip. She didn't want to reveal that conversation, especially to these two. It felt like such a betrayal. But if it meant finding Matt, then she had to. "Seth proposed marriage. I said no, because as you'd told him, he was doing the right thing for us. Not for himself."

"Marlene!" Connie squawked, and this time it was going eye to eye. "I told you that

Seth would do the right thing even if it wasn't for his own good. I did not say that Alexi and her kids were not for his own good."

"You didn't say that last time we talked," Alexi corrected. "Apparently, I was the problem. Or don't you remember that?"

"Yes, I did. But that was back in July. Before I saw Seth get all quiet and depressed because he couldn't see you and then he falls off the roof and you stick your neck out for him. In other words, I changed my mind and Marlene knew that because we talked not three days ago at some stupid interview she had me do about Seth." She fixed on Marlene, fists on her hips, a slimmer mirror image of Marlene. "Am I right or am I right?"

Now Alexi and Connie were glaring at Marlene, who ignored the question entirely. "You got Matt's note on you?" she said to Alexi.

Alexi pulled the note from her front pocket. It was already soft from the sweat in her hands and repeated foldings.

Marlene took it from her. "All right, then. Let's get inside and I'll read through his files. Again. See if this boy left us some clues. And when we find him, it's time he got set straight on how love works."

ALEXI LEFT MARLENE to do her thing, though every fiber of her being ached to study the files herself. She didn't trust Marlene to care enough. But it did give her an idea.

She parked at a curb and called her old caseworker, Brenda. Since the cat was out of the bag regarding Matt's disappearance, Alexi left an explicit voice mail requesting her to work with Marlene to come up with any background info that could help them.

She hadn't driven five blocks, her attention switching back and forth from one sidewalk to the other for any trace of Matt, when Brenda called back.

"Matt left you?"

Alexi expected censure but all she heard was concern and almost disbelief. "Yes. He left a note. He said that he was running away to give me and the kids a better life."

"What made him think running away would do that?"

How could she explain how something simple became complicated so fast. "He met a man…" She fumbled. "I…met the same man. I couldn't adopt Matt and also have this man in our lives."

"Who said so?"

"I suspected it, and our new caseworker as much as confirmed it."

"You mentioned Marlene is your new caseworker. Is this Marlene—" She strung out a long unpronounceable name that mirrored what Alexi had seen on the paperwork.

Alexi's confirmation elicited a loud sigh from Brenda. "Thank God. I was hoping you'd be assigned to her. She's in your corner, believe me."

Definitely in Matt's corner, but hers? "Uh, it doesn't feel that way. Feels the opposite, actually."

"Oh, she's a softie once you get to know her. Listen, I better go here. Please keep me posted."

Marlene a softie? To kittens and kids, yes, but with Seth and Alexi, she was an attack dog.

There was nothing to do but drive around, which she did. She texted Seth a couple of times. Nothing to report, other than someone thought they'd seen Matt eating at a picnic table by the lake. By the time Paul arrived, whoever it was had moved on.

As the end of the school day approached, Alexi felt her body grow leaden at the thought of telling Bryn and Amy about Matt. She couldn't bear their questions and their worry, not with parents and children flowing around her, carrying on as if nothing was wrong. Maybe she could let them ride the bus and she'd meet them at home.

But if Bryn and Amy didn't see their brother on the school bus, they'd panic, and she was not about to have a school bus driver inform her kids that Matt was not riding the bus because no one knew where he was.

The principal must have had the same thought because Alexi got a text when she arrived to say that Bryn and Amy were waiting in her office. The kids were on an oversize couch cozied up with the school's boss, a petite woman with gray hair and a gray suit, who was twisting purple pipe cleaners into an octopus. On another day, Alexi would've been thrilled at the picture the three of them made.

But today, it was enough to muster a faint smile.

Ms. Lever didn't press it, either. "Let me know if there's anything I can do for you or your family."

The kids started in as soon as Alexi ushered them out of the principal's office.

"Ms. Lever said Matt was away from

school, and that you know more than her," Amy said. "Where is he?"

Alexi trotted out the only answer she'd been able to come up with. "He's on a field trip and will be home later."

That, of course, triggered its own flood of questions which she brought to a grinding halt with, "Kids, I have had one hell of a day. Enough."

She never cursed. Even now, it felt more like a truth than a curse, and they must've sensed that because they immediately fell silent. Even their greeting of Seth was subdued.

It was Callie who destroyed the peace. Telling her first ever story, she wailed, "Matt ran away and Mommy can't find him anywhere!"

CHAPTER NINETEEN

BRYN AND AMY stared at Alexi, their eyes flooding, exactly like when she'd broken the news about Richard. She dropped to her knees in front of them.

"No, it's not like that," she said. "He'll come back."

Sobs broke from Amy. "No, he won't. When he runs away, he doesn't come back. He told me that."

Bryn began pacing. Alexi's breath caught, afraid of what was coming next. "Why did he leave?" Bryn demanded. "We weren't mean. I shared with him. He didn't even say good-bye." With a furious shrugging, he slid his backpack off and began tearing at his jacket. Alexi reached for him, but Bryn wrenched away from her and bolted for the front door.

Seth blocked the entrance, a solid, immovable obstacle. That didn't stop Bryn from flinging his jacket on the floor and starting to peel off his shirt. "Bryn," Seth said, "you know the rules. Hang up your jacket. Take your clothes off in your room."

"But I'm mad," Bryn said, "and when I'm mad, I take my clothes off wherever I'm mad. That's the rule."

"You're also sad. Where do you take your clothes off when you're sad?"

"I don't take my clothes off when I'm sad," Bryn snapped, and then when he realized what had happened, he scowled at Seth.

Alexi held her breath.

Seth leaned against the door frame, as though the conversation was about Matt on a sleepover.

Still on her knees, Alexi felt her own coiled tension loosen. "This is the truth. Matt is not here. People are looking for him. He will be found. Until then, you both have homework and chores. No different from any other day."

Bryn studied his jacket and no one moved, except for Amy whose quiet sobs shuddered through her. Then, in a huff, Bryn scooped up his jacket, hung it on the peg and went, as he usually did, into his room to change. Amy, swiping at her tears, followed.

Feeling like an old woman, Alexi slowly stood. "Thank you, Seth."

He shifted on his crutch and reached for his jackshirt. "It's what I'm here for."

His words dug into her, rooted there, unalienable and true. He was here with her because he did not want to be anywhere else. She'd released him from any commitment to her, and yet still he remained. Matt wasn't even here. Seth could leave with his phone and still help Matt from his own apartment, but he stayed under the roof that caused his father's death because of her.

He was here for her.

Last night, she'd doubted him, challenged and rejected him.

He was struggling to get the better of his two arms through the sleeve. She moved to his side. "Here," she said, "let me help you."

He did. When she could've stepped back, her hand lingered against the soft front of his shirt. "I couldn't get through this without you," she whispered.

Seth shifted, a slight move away from her touch. "Yeah, you could. You already did once."

Yes, with Richard, and it had nearly broken her. Seth pushed open the door. "Tell the kids I'm outside."

MARLENE CALLED DURING SUPPER, her timing as impeccable as always. "I called some of my people, Alexi. Matt hasn't given us a lot to go on. You know what he took, by chance?"

Deciding what Matt had actually taken and what was just misplaced had been a guessing game, but Alexi had come to a few conclusions. "He probably left with clothes, I don't know how many or what of. I do know he left with a green baseball cap with the name of Seth's business—Greene-on-Top. His hoodie. Gray. No lettering. And—" Alexi drew a deep, steadying breath "—pictures. One of him with Richard. Another of him with me and the kids."

"Huh. None of him and Seth?"

"Those are still on my phone." Another example of her involvement with Seth but at this point, so what?

"Huh," she said again. "He said he never wrote a note before, and nothing in his file says he did, either. He ever write one to you before? Like the odd time he bolted?"

"No."

"That's what I thought. I've got a theory. Tell me what you think."

Marlene asking for an opinion? Was this her being a softie? "Twice before when he ran away, he just ran," Marlene said. "No note. He didn't take anything, either. Except for money, and a good coat and pair of shoes. This time, it's different."

"What do you mean?"

"I don't think he's running, so much as he's wandering."

"Which means what?"

"I don't think he's gone too far. I think he's waiting to be found."

"But where? So many people in town have their eyes peeled. Where? Where?" Alexi stopped, knowing she was getting high-pitched, knowing Marlene would not appreciate histrionics.

Marlene's reply was unusually mild, like a manager with a frustrated customer. "It's only a matter of time, you'll see."

But time was taking its own sweet time. As the evening dragged on, Alexi thought she would shatter from the worry and desperation. Mel came over, apparently just to be with them because he didn't eat, didn't talk business. He sat there like in a waiting room.

Bedtime was the worst for Bryn and Amy. Normally she and the four kids roosted on Matt's bed for story time, before they all drifted to their various beds. Tonight, neither

Bryn nor Amy wanted a story on any bed. Callie refused to come upstairs at all, huddling next to Seth on the couch as he scrolled through Facebook.

"Why doesn't he just call us?" Bryn demanded. "He doesn't have to tell us where he is. The least he could do is call us so we don't have to worry."

"Yeah, this is really rude of him," Amy said.

"At least with Dad," Bryn continued, "we knew he was dead."

"Bryn! Don't even say that!" Amy reprimanded him.

"All I'm saying is that I don't know. I don't know if he's okay so I don't have to care, or if he's dead and then I get to cry. Because I feel like crying and I should only do that if he's dead. If I do it now that means I think he's dead, and I don't want to think that." Bryn took a long, shaky breath.

Alexi took one herself, and told him what she'd been telling herself every minute since the morning. "He's alive. And he's well. We all know Matt. Have faith."

She ended up snuggling with each of them, and as she started down the stairs, she could hear them whispering together across the hall. Their bedtime conversations were a ritual that Matt had introduced right after Richard had passed. One more way he'd bound the family together.

What would happen to them all if—

No. Don't go there.

Callie was slumped in sleep against Seth, and she didn't stir as Alexi transferred her to Seth's bed.

Seth glanced up from his phone when Alexi returned. "Leave her there tonight. I'm sleeping out here."

Which meant that she would be sleeping in his bed, too. No, her bed. His and her bed. Alexi took up her current project and glued on an eyeball only to discover that she put on one that was too big. She applied the second one the same size only to discover that it was a different color. She tossed the stuffie aside and stood. She wouldn't make her deadline and she didn't care.

Seth jutted his chin at the discarded stuffie. "Here. I'll do it." He levered himself up and hobbled over to the table, sitting in her seat. He reached for the glue gun.

"No. I'll do it. I just—"

He hooked the toy, a gecko mostly, on the end of his crutch and flipped it into his lap.

"It needs eyes, I take it?" He picked up a pair from her eye collection. "How about these?"

"They're red and too small. I'm looking for ones with some green, and the pupil has to be a vertical slit." Seth began sorting, his large, tanned hands nimble among the small pieces, while Alexi reapplied herself to removing the eyes. He was distracting her, and she let him.

Later, Alexi laid her head on the pillow, expecting Callie to jerk awake at the nighttime disturbance. Instead, she burrowed into her squid stuffie, fitted to her small front, the tentacles hooked over her torso and legs, and slept on. Arms empty and folded neatly on her chest, Alexi stared at the ceiling. Immediately questions buzzed to life. Was Matt someplace safe? Was he warm? Had he eaten something? Why had no one found him if he was close?

Moonlight, pale and bright, cut between the slats on the bedroom window, casting the room in an eerie glow. There was just enough light to make Alexi feel that she should be neither asleep nor awake. She certainly felt as though she were in some kind of altered state.

Was Seth asleep? Part of her yearned to check, just to talk as she'd done with Richard but she'd closed that door when she refused his marriage proposal, albeit his clumsy, flat-footed proposal.

Now Matt was missing, and Seth was still here even though he'd no reason to be. Which meant one thing: she, not Seth, would've destroyed their marriage because she couldn't cope with loss.

She had driven Matt away. She'd made him feel that everything was a choice, and that every choice involved a loss. That was the message he'd heard last night. He'd heard her doubts and fears, her what-ifs and what-abouts.

Well, no more.

She forced herself to stand, walk to the door, open it and cross to the couch. The light on the end table was on but Seth was asleep, his good hand holding his phone to his chest.

She should wake him. No point saying a word, otherwise. She shook him, and his eyes drifted open.

Courage failing her, she glanced away and saw the gecko toy they'd worked on. To it, she whispered, "Seth, no matter what happens with Matt, whether we find him, whether—whatever happens, I want you to know I love you. I love you. And…and if your proposal is still open, I'd…I'd like to accept it."

Silence.

She stole a look at Seth. His eyes were closed. He must've fallen right back to sleep. She didn't know whether she felt exasperated or relieved.

No need to choose. Both.

And determined. Because, she decided as she walked softly back to her room, if she said it once, she could say it again.

BY MIDAFTERNOON OF the next day, Matt was still missing, and Seth was borderline crazy. Even though it was Friday, Alexi had let Bryn and Amy stay home, giving her a desperately needed distraction but driving him to distraction.

It frustrated him to no end that he couldn't help her or the kids other than stay out of their way while they did chores, which was why he'd parked himself out on the porch, putting himself on an endless loop of checking messages, watching social media shares pile up, noting Retweets. The hunt for Matt had gone viral.

His phone sang out. Mel. Probably wanting another update but there was always a chance he had news.

Nope, just another update.

Mel replied with the same thing he'd said when he'd first heard the news. "The boy'll show up."

"You know," Seth said, "I figure that with the shares, and how many people would've told other people, the reach has to be in the thousands by now."

Mel made a disgusted noise. "Well, of course. You've spent the last two years solid helping out people in this town. You don't think that they'd tap a button for you when you ask? Especially when you aren't even asking for yourself. You have a whole town behind you. You're the only one doesn't know that."

A whole town behind him and no Matt to show for it. His gut was sore with worry and frustration. It didn't help to be so close to Alexi and not able to do anything for her. She looked as if she hadn't slept a wink last night. He'd fallen into a dead sleep until three in the morning, then had checked messages again and again until the kids woke, even though he knew the police would be in touch if there was any real news. Good or bad.

An unknown number came up on his phone. At any other time, he'd let it go to voice mail. Not today. It was Melanie Lever, the school principal. "I have a friend. He's the station manager at Centre. Do you know it?"

It was the local station in the region for weather and news. Greene-on-Top had run a modest advertising campaign with it four years ago, and their jobs shot, well, through the roof.

"I spoke with Paul," Melanie continued, "and they're setting up a time for a news conference. Do you think Alexi could make a statement?"

Seth frowned. "Why are you asking me?"

There was the slightest pause on the other end. "Usually, in these situations, there is someone close to the family who vets the calls. From your involvement on Facebook and from what Paul told me, I understood you were that person. Am I correct?"

Someone close to the family. That was who everyone assumed him to be. He straightened. "Yes, you're correct."

Seth got the details and swung himself inside. Alexi was curled on the couch, all three kids settled around her, watching *Finding Nemo*. He'd never seen it, not having had a single kid in his life up until now. On the screen, a father clown fish was calling out frantically to what Seth assumed was Nemo, who was being taken away in a boat.

Silent tears streamed down Alexi's face, and the kids were uneasily shifting their focus between the show and their mom. One by one, tears broke from Callie, then Amy, finally Bryn. One by one, Bryn, then Amy and finally Callie looked up at him with deep, pleading eyes. Alexi didn't look at him, her head bowed, her arms tight around the three kids she had.

Seth swung away, phone in hand. Time for someone close to the family to do something real.

SETH STOOD IN the bright arc of lights and cameras, his speech on the stand in front of him. Paul had spoken just before him, and he was introduced as a friend of the family. One person after another had reviewed his speech, chiseled it down to just a minute. He was told that no more than seconds would run on the show, but that the entire segment would be uploaded to the station website, released through the RCMP social media and from there go viral to be relayed not only through people they knew but among strangers who couldn't stand the thought of a lost kid.

He cleared his throat, and stared at the words. "Matt. I hope you're well," he began. He remembered the camera and looked up. The white glare of the camera light stabbed his eyes and when he looked back at his sheet, he saw nothing.

Later, he realized that it could've been re-shot. Right then, all he knew was that he was about to fail the family he considered his yet again. Black spots jiggled in his vision. He raised his head and focused on where he thought the camera should be.

"Matt." He couldn't for the life of him remember what he was supposed to say. He plunged on. "My brother and sister, we lost our dad, and I since figured out that we each felt responsible, even though it was an accident. But we never told each other that, otherwise we could've set the other straight. Matt, taking the blame for things you didn't do doesn't make it better. Doing the wrong thing for the right reasons is still the wrong thing.

"I know you run when you think you're done. But you have a mom, and sisters and a brother, and…you have me. Together, we're six, plenty to fill a house."

Where was he going with all this? He needed to finish this. The spots were floating away, objects refocusing. He spotted Mel off to the side. No, by his side. Mel beside him and a whole town behind him.

Seth stared into the camera. "It's your choice, Matt. If you can keep away, then it's probably for the best. For you, anyway. Just let us know—or somebody know—that you're okay, so we can let you go, too. But if you're like me and find it too hard to stay away from your mom and your family, then come back to us. Okay?"

Seth suddenly felt out of words, out of breath. Mel stepped closer. "Come on," he said, "I'll take you home."

They both knew where that was.

CHAPTER TWENTY

IF MATT HADN'T FOUND Cruel Connie so interesting, she wouldn't have caught him at her house. He'd meant to hitchhike out of town as soon as leaving the school bus but his feet had taken him down Spirit Lake's back alleys, along her walking trails until he came out at the lake.

Mom had taken him and the others to the lake only three times for a couple of hours. They'd all wanted to stay longer but something more important always needed doing. "Next summer," she'd promised, "we'll spend the entire day there. All of us and all of your friends. We'll have a party."

Matt believed her. Only Seth Greene wouldn't be there, so it wouldn't feel like much of a party. Matt found himself building a castle in the cold sand, squatting to observe the seagulls, walking the red gravel path along the shore. He'd done all this before when he was much younger. He couldn't

remember who he was with—if anybody—
or how he'd gotten there, but he remembered
the sand and the water and the feeling that
he was right where he belonged.

He might've stayed all day, except that two
women stopped him and asked him why he
wasn't in school, and he'd shrugged and kept
walking. Faster.

His feet slowed him again at the far east
end where the boats were moored. At this
point he could turn away from the lake, cross
two streets and cut back four blocks to a restaurant where he could hide in the back of
a pickup with an out-of-town logo. He decided to do that in a bit, after wading in the
frigid waters. It was good until once again he
caught the looks from a mom with toddlers.
Time to move on. Except he hadn't turned in
the direction of the restaurant but walked on
until he was well around the lake, beyond the
million-dollar lakeside homes and along the
narrow shoreline thick with rocks and trees.

He stopped at an open space to have his
sandwich. Two bites into it, he heard people
on the narrow path and hid in the bushes as
a teenage boy and girl appeared. Her gig-
gles, his murmurs and their deepening noises
drove Matt to yell, *Gross!*

The boy had returned with, *Perv!* Thankfully, he hadn't come after Matt and the two had moved on. He emerged from the bushes in time to see a seagull dip down and take the entire sandwich from where he'd left it on a rock.

Matt broke then. Yet one more thing stripped from him, one thing meant for him and taken away. He cried, slowly and softly, an endless trickle of defeat.

Fact was, he didn't know what to do. If the plan was to live without a dad, then there was no longer any need for a plan. He might as well turn himself over to Marlene and take his chances. He stood, cold and cramped, and headed back to town. The sun was setting when he reached the outskirts, darkness coming faster now that it was October. Chill needled through his jacket and into his flesh. He scanned the parking lot of the restaurant. Two cars and the truck of a local plumber. Two he couldn't get into and a third that wouldn't be leaving town. Maybe he should sleep the night somewhere in town, and then try again early tomorrow.

He knew of the perfect hideout—the backyard shed at Seth Greene's old house.

In the rush to move out to the farm, his

mom had left a roll of bubble wrap she used for shipping her stuffed toys, the fancy ones with fake jewels and sequins and prosthetic limbs. She refused to retrieve it, she said, if it meant running into *her*. That was as nasty as his mom spoke of Seth Greene's sister. The kids, except for Callie who was silent on the subject, secretly called her Cruel Connie. The point was, she wouldn't come to the shed. She was probably working and wouldn't be home all night.

Sure enough, the house lights were off and the wrap was exactly where it was supposed to be. He woke later, cocooned in the warm, noisy wrap, his stomach squeaking from hunger. It hadn't been that empty in years, and all because of a seagull. Maybe, if Cruel Connie was still at the bar, he could sneak into the house, grab some food and go. He still had a key, so technically it wasn't break and enter.

The house was dark as he snuck up the back stairs of the deck, but through the back door window, he'd seen that there was a single overhead stove light on, and in the weak glow, he spotted a person stretched out on the island, an odd-looking one, both stiff and limp at the same time. Connie in a halter top and shorts held a book in one hand and was bending over, kissing the weird person on the mouth.

Matt turned and ran. He heard the back door open and her shout and he almost reached the back fence when she clamped him on the back of his shirt and dragged him back into the house. She didn't let go of him as she reached for her phone.

His gaze slid to the person on the island who had not moved when they entered. Now he knew why. It was a human doll. Which made things really weird. "No, no. Please, don't. Please."

Her thumb paused. "Give me one good reason why not. Screw that. Give me any reason."

"Because if I do, Seth Greene will die."

She still didn't let go of him, if anything her grip had tightened. She leaned right into his face. She had the same green eyes as Seth Greene. "All you did was give me a reason I should call the police. And believe me, I really don't want to be calling them." She gave him a shake. "What are you talking about?"

Maybe it was because her eyes were like Seth Greene's or because Matt was standing in the kitchen of the place where he was robbed of a chance for a new start, but he said, "All the dads I've ever had died. That's three. Three. Seth Greene is not going to be the fourth."

She gave him a look, the kind hairdressers did when they were figuring out what to do with him. Sort of at him but around him, too. Connie set down her phone but held on to him. "Unless you actually shot them or knifed them or poisoned them or drove over them or whatever, you're not responsible. It's called bad luck."

"But that's my point. I'm cursed. And this time, if it happens, it will be my fault because I wanted him to be part of our lives. And then he was. And then he left. And then I wanted him back. And then he was. And then he fell off the roof and nearly died. Next time, he will."

Connie pointed to the stool by the island, right close to the human doll. "Sit there."

She circled around until she was standing over the doll again.

"You're not going to kiss it again, are you?"

She made a disgusted noise. "I wasn't kissing Annie. I was doing CPR." She waved a large, soft-covered manual at him.

"Oh. Very interesting."

"You know I'm going to have to call your mom, right?"

"I'll just run away."

"Can't if you're tied to a chair locked in the basement."

"You can't. That's abuse."

"What you're doing is a crime called public mischief." She leaned on the doll's chest and gave it such a savage pump it flinched.

Running away was a crime? It couldn't be. He called her bluff. "You're lying."

"It's when you provide false information or behave in a way that make the police investigate when there's no reason."

She said it so quickly that Matt knew she had to be right. She pinned him with Seth's eyes. "I'm not making it up. I was charged with it once. Ask your Seth Greene."

"I'm a kid. They can't charge a kid."

"That kind of crap follows you through life, one way or another."

Yes, he did know that. And he knew that his mom would be worrying, despite leaving her a note. "I just need to come up with a plan."

"A plan. For what? To save Seth's life? Or your own?"

He shook his head. Annie stared up at him

with her lifeless gaze. "I just need to figure things out."

"Okay. Here's the deal. When's your bedtime?"

"Eight thirty on school days, nine thirty weekends. Why?"

"You got until seven thirty tomorrow, which at two in the morning here, is actually today, to come up with your plan. At that point, you got a choice. Either I drive you home to Alexi's or I call Marlene and she picks you up and she takes you."

"You can't keep me here."

"No, because I will have your word, right?"

"Why should I trust you when you were so mean to me and my mom?"

"I had my reasons, and don't ask me what they were because I can't tell you."

"Did you kill someone and needed some place to bury the body?"

The green eyes narrowed. "Not yet."

But he was no longer scared of her. She was a bit like Seth because she didn't take long to answer him, and kind of like his mom because she was pretty.

"Why are you learning CPR? Did you find someone you couldn't resuscitate and now you're learning so that when it happens again, you'll know what to do?"

She gave him a look as if he were either a freak or God. "Yeah," she said. "Something like that."

"So you did kill someone."

"No," she said. "I didn't. Remember, it's not me going around thinking that I strike people dead. It's you."

She slung Annie over her shoulder. "Me and her are going to bed. You can sleep on the couch. There's a blanket on it. Watch for the nails in the floor. You know where the bathroom is."

He settled down in the covers. He could hear her moving around, hear her come out of the bathroom, the quiet snick of the light turning off.

He was comfortable and warm, and he should've been able to go to sleep. But it was no use. He raised himself onto his elbow and called out, "Connie?"

There was a moment of quiet, then an irritable and groggy, "What?"

"Good night."

"Yeah, good night."

He settled back down, and sleep came easy. He'd slept straight through to nine when

Connie shook him awake to demand an answer. He could only tell her that he wanted home and he wanted Seth Greene.

"As if I don't have enough problems," she told the wall above his head.

"You stay here," she said to him. "Inside."

And he had. She'd left and returned with the video of Seth while he was making a peanut butter sandwich for lunch.

MATT WATCHED SETH GREENE'S statement on Connie's phone, and it took all he had not to call his mom and go back home.

Connie plunked down beside him on the couch and handed him a can of ginger ale. "If that doesn't prove you're in the wrong place, you are one seriously screwed-up kid."

Matt snapped open the can and drank. "I know I don't belong here. I just don't know how to get where I want to be."

"Kid, that's a life issue," Connie said. She crossed her legs, just like he'd done, and because the couch was the short kind, their knees almost touched. She had a tattoo just above her knee. There was also a tattoo of a long vine that twisted up the side of her leg and disappeared under the cutoffs. It made Connie even more interesting.

She nudged him. "Hey, I've got a plan to catch you Seth Greene."

After she told him, he couldn't call her Cruel Connie anymore.

THIS WAS LIKE a scene from a procedural drama, Seth thought. Matt was on the top ridgeline of their old place, Connie's house. Alone. The police and fire department were spread out below but so far none had ascended.

Matt had threatened to jump off if they did.

Seth doubted he'd carry through, but the kid did cut a dramatic figure with the last hour of sunlight spilling around him.

Beside Seth, Alexi was made of wood, eyes fixed on Matt. Seth murmured, "He's okay. I taught him how to sit properly on a roof, and he's doing it. There's no wind. And the guys at the fire department are here, too."

Her focus didn't shift. "But why is he even up there?"

Seth would like to think that the release of his statement that afternoon had done the trick but…he looked over at Connie. She stood by herself, biting her lip, arms banded tight over her chest, appearing to all the world like someone distraught about a lost boy stranded on her roof.

He didn't want to leave Alexi right now, but he hadn't grown up in a family of roofers without knowing how to scale up his own roof. Connie must've felt his eyes on her because like a guilty kid she dragged her gaze to his. He tilted his head toward the old wooden rain barrel pushed under the eaves trough.

Her expression became blank, feigned innocence. She gave a one-shoulder shrug and a faint grin. Exactly what he'd expected.

Then she did something unexpected. She came across the front lawn to him, to him and Alexi and the kids who sat in a huddle at their feet. Seth straightened as best he could on the crutch. Alexi must've noticed because she tore her gaze from Matt to latch on to Connie.

Alexi's hands curled into fists and Seth brought himself tight against her side. "Easy," he muttered. Thankfully, Connie stopped well outside of their reach.

"Full confession. I caught him lurking outside the house at two in the morning last night. I brought him in and he made me swear I wouldn't contact anyone."

She'd known all this day and not told anyone? "Why didn't you tell someone? Do you know how worried we were?"

A truck pulled up. Ben. Connie's mouth twisted and she spoke faster. "Yeah, I knew. I told him that, too. But I decided that if it would stop him from running, then I could deal with you bawling me out one more time."

Alexi looked up at Matt, small and solid above them all. "Thank you, Connie," she whispered. "Thank you."

"Uh, yeah, no worries," Connie said, taking note of Ben approaching from the side. "Anyway, I'll see you later."

If her intent was to get away from Ben, it didn't work because as soon as she moved away, he checked his stride and followed her. Seth might have said something but who was he to talk about wanting someone even when it wasn't for the best? At least, Ben would only hurt himself. Seth wanted Alexi, even when it would hurt her and four children. Had it stopped him? Heck, no. He'd even justified it, saying that he was best for them. Yet, here a boy had climbed on top of a roof, in no small part because he could not stay away.

"I love you."

What had Alexi just said? Her deep blue eyes were on him.

"Right now before anything happens, I want you to know that no matter how this turns out, my feelings won't change. Because you were never the problem."

She loved him. Matt was alive. Everything else was a matter of time. Like life itself.

He pulled her tighter to him, bent his mouth to her ear and—

A loud truck pulled up.

"Marlene," Alexi said, relief and bitterness rolled into one. "Come to take our boy."

ALEXI COULD SEE no other reason for Marlene showing up. She knew what Matt was up to. He thought he could talk reason into Marlene, but the caseworker's hands were tied. Her only choice was to investigate.

Then as Marlene opened her door, another vehicle pulled in behind her. A van with Centre News emblazoned on the side. Of course, they'd follow up on Seth's appeal. Out came a man with a camera and a young woman with a microphone.

Paul and another police officer quickly stepped over to them. "He'd better be telling him that none of this is to be filmed," Alexi said fiercely to Seth.

"Human tragedy turned into something

to enjoy with popcorn," Marlene said as she came up to them, fat briefcase bouncing off her leg. "Media gets involved, and suddenly the whole process is out of our hands. I've seen solid cases cave like a house of cards because of media pressuring departments to make decisions they otherwise wouldn't."

She made a loud clicking noise. "Yep. A real shame if that were to happen."

Marlene, who'd always cut to the truth, was saying something entirely different. Marlene strode forward and yelled up to Matt.

"Here I am, just like you wanted."

Matt waved, said nothing.

Marlene dropped her briefcase with a thud. "So, what do you want?"

"I want to go home."

Alexi's heart stopped.

"You were at home," Marlene said. Her shadow on the lawn stretched clear across to Alexi's feet. "It was you that ran off."

"I didn't want to."

"Did someone make you go?"

"No."

"Did you feel safe there?"

"Yes."

"Did you want to be there?"

"Yes."

Marlene raised her hands. "Then, get off the roof and go home."

"I can't. Because if I do, then you'll take my dad away from me."

"Your dad? Who's your dad?"

"Seth Greene."

Alexi felt Seth's arm wrap around her shoulder, felt his entire body tense. Marlene pointed her thumb at Seth. "What? You saying this man is your dad?"

Alexi banded her arm tight around Seth's waist, as tight as when she'd helped him the day he'd come to the farm.

"Yes," said Matt. "He's Dad."

Alexi understood what Matt was declaring. Seth was not Daddy like his biological father nor Daddy-R like Richard. Seth was Dad. Alexi and Seth. Mom and Dad.

Seth pulled Alexi close to him. He'd picked up on it, too.

"Yes," Alexi said, loud enough for Marlene to hear, for Matt to hear, for the whole neighborhood and world to hear. "This man is his dad."

Marlene shifted her focus to Seth. "You agree?"

His hold on her tightened. "I do."

Marlene turned back to Matt. "Then who am I to stand in the way?"

Matt still didn't move. "Promise?"

Marlene snorted. "On behalf of whomever I represent, I promise. Now get down before I climb up there myself, and let me tell you I don't know if that roof is strong enough for the both of us."

In the circle of Alexi's arm, Seth shifted but it was Mel who said it. "Yes," he called, "it is."

Marlene didn't have to carry through on her threat because Matt began his descent under the supervision of the fire department. The whole exchange between Marlene and Matt felt staged. Alexi caught Marlene and Connie exchanging a quick, secretive glance. Her two enemies colluding for her benefit. Or Matt's. Or Seth's. For them all.

She tightened her arm around Seth's waist, and his around her shoulders did the same as it had when he'd been about to whisper what she had hoped were the three words she'd said to him.

But he was looking straight ahead at Matt, at everybody else except her. She swallowed against the rise of tears.

"I love you, Alexi Docker." Seth's words

were loud, loud enough for everyone to hear. Matt's foot on the ladder froze in midair. His head came up. "I love you and your kids, and the second Matt's feet hit the ground, we will be together and stay together."

He looked at her then, and there was no holding back the tears. Thankfulness welled inside her but she didn't say that. Instead she said what she'd always meant. "Your love fixes me every day of my life."

Out of the corner of her eye, she spotted Matt, on the ground, half running to them. Just as he reached them, Bryn stepped up and slapped him upside the head.

"That," Bryn said, "was for scaring Mom."

Then Bryn hugged his brother, and soon they were all hugging, arms wide and tight. Bound together, stretched together, loving and loved.

* * * * *

If you enjoyed this debut Heartwarming story by M. K. Stelmack, watch for Connie's story in June 2018. Available at Harlequin.com or wherever Harlequin ebooks are sold.

Get 2 Free Books,
Plus 2 Free Gifts—
just for trying the Reader Service!

YES! Please send me 2 FREE Love Inspired® Romance novels and my 2 FREE mystery gifts (gifts are worth about $10 retail). After receiving them, if I don't wish to receive any more books, I can return the shipping statement marked "cancel." If I don't cancel, I will receive 6 brand-new novels every month and be billed just $5.24 for the regular-print edition or $5.74 each for the larger-print edition in the U.S., or $5.74 each for the regular-print edition or $6.24 each for the larger-print edition in Canada. That's a saving of at least 13% off the cover price. It's quite a bargain! Shipping and handling is just 50¢ per book in the U.S. and 75¢ per book in Canada.* I understand that accepting the 2 free books and gifts places me under no obligation to buy anything. I can always return a shipment and cancel at any time. The free books and gifts are mine to keep no matter what I decide.

Please check one:
- ☐ Love Inspired Romance Regular-Print
  (105/305 IDN GMWU)
- ☐ Love Inspired Romance Larger-Print
  (122/322 IDN GMWU)

Name	(PLEASE PRINT)	
Address		Apt. #
City	State/Province	Zip/Postal Code

Signature (if under 18, a parent or guardian must sign)

Mail to the **Reader Service:**
IN U.S.A.: P.O. Box 1341, Buffalo, NY 14240-8531
IN CANADA: P.O. Box 603, Fort Erie, Ontario L2A 5X3

Want to try two free books from another line?
Call 1-800-873-8635 today or visit www.ReaderService.com.

*Terms and prices subject to change without notice. Prices do not include applicable taxes. Sales tax applicable in N.Y. Canadian residents will be charged applicable taxes. Offer not valid in Quebec. This offer is limited to one order per household. Books received may not be as shown. Not valid for current subscribers to Love Inspired Romance books. All orders subject to approval. Credit or debit balances in a customer's account(s) may be offset by any other outstanding balance owed by or to the customer. Please allow 4 to 6 weeks for delivery. Offer available while quantities last.

Your Privacy—The Reader Service is committed to protecting your privacy. Our Privacy Policy is available online at www.ReaderService.com or upon request from the Reader Service.

We make a portion of our mailing list available to reputable third parties that offer products we believe may interest you. If you prefer that we not exchange your name with third parties, or if you wish to clarify or modify your communication preferences, please visit us at www.ReaderService.com/consumerschoice or write to us at Reader Service Preference Service, P.O. Box 9062, Buffalo, NY 14240-9062. Include your complete name and address.

LI17R3

Get 2 Free Books,

Plus 2 Free Gifts— just for trying the Reader Service!

HOME *on the* RANCH

HRCBPA18

Get 2 Free Books,
Plus 2 Free Gifts -
just for trying the *Reader Service!*

Get 2 Free Books,

Plus 2 Free Gifts—

just for trying the Reader Service!

Get 2 Free Books,
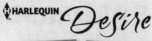

Plus 2 Free Gifts—

just for trying the Reader Service!